Dear Paramount Pictures

*To John & David—*
*"The hottest couple in town."*

# Dear Paramount Pictures

## Stories by Iqbal Pittalwala

*With best wishes,*
*Iqbal Pittalwala*
*2-19-03*

SOUTHERN METHODIST UNIVERSITY PRESS

Requests for permission to reproduce material from this work should be sent to:
  Rights and Permissions
  Southern Methodist University Press
  PO Box 750415
  Dallas, Texas 75275-0415

Some of the stories in this collection previously appeared, in slightly different form, in the following publications: "The Change" in the *Seattle Review*; "Lost in the U.S.A." in *Blue Mesa Review*; "Great Guruji" in *Confrontation*; "A Change of Lights" in *Wascana Review*; and "House of Cards" as "Outsiders" in *Trikone Magazine*.

Jacket photograph: "India. Bombay. 1966. Mother and child at car window" © Steve McCurry/Magnum Photos

Jacket design: Tom Dawson and David Timmons
Text design: David Timmons

*Library of Congress Cataloging-in-Publication Data*

Pittalwala, Iqbal, 1962–
    Dear Paramount Pictures : stories / by Iqbal Pittalwala.— 1st ed.
        p.    cm.
    Contents: Dear Paramount Pictures — The change — Lost in the U.S.A. — Great guruji — Kulsum, Nazia, and Ismail — Bombay talkies — A change of lights — Ramadan — Trivedi Park — Mango season — House of cards.
    ISBN 0-87074-475-5 (alk. paper)
        1. India—Social life and customs—Fiction. 2. South Asians—United States—Fiction. 3. South Asian Americans—Fiction. I. Title.

PS3616.I88 D43 2002
813'.6—dc21                                                          2002075822

Printed in the United States of America on acid-free paper

    10    9    8    7    6    5    4    3    2    1

*For Mom*

# Acknowledgments

THE ENCOURAGEMENT I received from many good friends at the State University of New York at Stony Brook, the University of Iowa, the University of New Hampshire, and the University of California, Irvine, made this collection possible. I wish especially to acknowledge the advice and instruction of Adele Glimm, John Yount, and Sultan Hameed; their unwavering faith in me kept this project going. I am indebted, too, to Jamila Bookwala and Kanchan Mhatre for their support and for enriching my life. Mrs. Bookwala was often subjected to reading and listening to early drafts of most of these stories. Her suggestions, always constructive, gave the stories better shape.

A special expression of appreciation goes out to the staff of SMU Press. Kathryn Lang's sharp editorial eye vastly improved the stories in this collection, her skill, insight, and patience making all the difference.

# Contents

DEAR PARAMOUNT PICTURES     1

THE CHANGE     13

LOST IN THE U.S.A.     19

GREAT GURUJI     41

KULSUM, NAZIA, AND ISMAIL     57

BOMBAY TALKIES     79

A CHANGE OF LIGHTS     91

RAMADAN     103

TRIVEDI PARK     133

MANGO SEASON     149

HOUSE OF CARDS     167

# Dear Paramount Pictures

**SIRS, I WRITE THIS LETTER** because the information I wish to share with you on Mr. James Dean, the film actor, will be of interest not only to you, I believe, but to all moviegoers in America. Mr. Dean is alive and well, and is living at present in India. You are intrigued, I'm sure, and it would be best, therefore, if I introduce myself right away. My name is Chandralekha Sengupta, I lived in your country with my husband from 1954 to 1956, and I even have one publication in an American literary magazine. While my husband, then on a two-year sabbatical from the University of Bombay, taught Advanced Heat Transfer and Thermodynamics 1 and 2, and I don't know what else at Indiana University, Bloomington, I used my time in the faculty home assigned to us by writing plays, a long-standing interest of mine since my childhood days.

I wrote seven plays in Bloomington (five mysteries, one tragedy and one comedy) and am proud to mention here, if I may, that one of them, a two-act suspenseful play entitled "Reshma, Saviour of Mother India" appeared in the winter 1956 issue (Vol. 1, No. 2) of *The Unknown Artiste,* a little magazine based in Payson, Arizona, that, to my surprise and annoyance, apparently ceased publication soon after. This news came to my attention when the sequel to "Reshma, Saviour of Mother India," which I wrote upon our return to Bombay, came back to me from Arizona one rainy afternoon in 1957, unopened, via surface mail, stamped "Forwarding Address Unknown." Sirs, photocopies of both plays are available. If you are interested in reading them, I would be delighted to mail them to you.

As you will have noticed from the return address, I currently reside in Bombay (you may have seen the poorer, neglected sections of the city in the movie *Salaam Bombay!* which, I understand from popular film magazines here, was rather successful in New York and Los Angeles and other large cities in America). Since my husband's demise nearly eight years ago, I have been dividing my time between Nasik, where my son, an architect, lives, and Bombay, where I spend five to six months each year with my daughter Vimla, her husband Jawahar, and their son Sunil. Jawahar, it may interest you, sirs, also spent two years in America in the late 1970s when he was a graduate student in electrical engineering at Columbia University (New York City). Today, he is Vice President of Larsen & Toubro Pvt. Ltd., a reputable engineering firm near Powai Lake in the northeastern quadrant of Bombay.

Bombay, as you may already know, is the Hollywood of India. In fact, the local film glossies refer to the city as "Bollywood." But what many Americans are not aware of, I am certain, is that Bombay produces some two hundred films a year, merely 30 percent of the Indian film industry's total annual output! Of course, "quantity is no match for quality," as the familiar adage goes, but a handful of our actors, like Om Puri and Shabana Azmi, are deserving, in my opinion, of many, many Oscars.

Last month, my grandson Sunil who, I'm proud to mention, is a second-year student in mechanical engineering at the prestigious Indian Institute of Technology at Kanpur, was home to spend his month-long winter holidays. Each time he returns home at the end of a semester, he seems taller than before. Perhaps it only appears to me that way because he comes back so thin. So whenever he's in Bombay for the holidays, I make sure that I am at Vimla's, too, and I see to it that he gets to eat whatever he wants: *parathas* and *puris*, *malai kofta*, *saag paneer*, *navratan curry*, *aloo muttar* and, of course, *rasmalai*, his favourite.

Lest I digress, I should mention right away that one Sunday afternoon last month, while we were seated at the dining table, and Laxmi, Vimla's young and incompetent maidservant, was heaping our plates with rice (scattering grains all over the table, too, I might add), Sunil announced that a friend would be visiting him for a day. The friend was someone from his institute in Kanpur, which, I neglected to mention, is a city about 1100 km northeast of Bombay. He would stay overnight with us, Sunil said. He was on his way to attend somebody's wedding in Poona, some 150 km southeast of here. My daughter Vimla said that was nice and asked who the friend was. Sunil's eyes were on the steaming rice on his plate. He said the friend was a Muslim boy. Naturally, we were surprised and I understood his hesitation in breaking the news to us. You must understand that neither Vimla nor Jawahar have many Muslim friends and, although we have nothing against Muslim people, we mingle mostly with strict vegetarian Hindus like ourselves. I was sure Sunil was trying to shock us on purpose (he often does), or was challenging us in some peculiar and novel way since, as you may have heard, we recently experienced ugly riots between Hindus and Muslims in Bombay in which several hundreds of people were killed and thousands more were forced to flee the city. Jawahar didn't go to work for three days, I remember, for we'd learned from friends that motorcars were being stoned or overturned and, in some sensitive areas, set ablaze with the passengers still inside.

At the table, Jawahar, my son-in-law, asked Sunil the friend's name to ease the tension in the room, but alas his gruff tone only heightened it instead. Sunil had his eyes fixed on his plate. "Nuruddin Ali Ahmed," he told his father. "A very good friend." None of us spoke for a while and the only sounds to be heard were those of our eating. I saw Jawahar and Vimla exchange glances. It seemed imperative that someone speak, so I said, "How nice. Your friend is also our friend." Some moments later, I asked Sunil if he and the friend stayed in the same hostel at the institute. He nodded solemnly and continued to play with the rice grains on his plate with his fingers. He said Nuruddin Ali Ahmed's room was two rooms down the hallway from his. Vimla reached out to stir the dal; she stirred vigorously, knocking the ladle hard against the bowl, and, as I'd feared, she spilled some dal on the tablecloth, whereupon Sunil raised his eyes from his plate, leaned forward, and in an agitated tone said, "For this small-minded family in this prejudiced, riotous city, my having a Muslim friend is difficult to accept. Isn't that right, Mummy?"

The rest of the meal was eaten in an uncomfortable silence. Sunil is at that rebellious age, glorified so often in Hindi movies nowadays. At the table, I could tell from Vimla's pressed lips that she was containing her anger. When Sunil rose from the table later, I asked him when he expected the guest to arrive. He said, "Today. His train will be stopping at VT Station in half an hour. I should get going to receive him," which left hardly any time for Laxmi to tidy up the guest room. Of course, I asked Sunil why he hadn't told us sooner. "You know how it is around here," he mumbled, hurrying from the room to wash his hands. I quickly summoned scatter-brained Laxmi and broke the news to her. She only grinned and nodded, as she does in response to anything I say. (Last week, she answered me back while we were plucking roses in the garden. I informed her, without raising my voice, that in her previous life she was a braying donkey. To my chagrin, she threw back her head with laughter, clapped her hands quite close to my ears, and yelled that she agreed. Then she proceeded to bray like a donkey and laugh at me. Later I overheard her telling Ramlal, the driver, that I have a screw loose. Sirs, respectful servant-girls are so hard to find in Bombay these days.)

Nuruddin Ali Ahmed arrived late that afternoon with Sunil who, despite my pleas, had sped away on his motorcycle to VT Station soon after lunch. I had called for Ramlal, the driver, and asked him to take the Ambassador out of the garage but when Sunil gets an idea into his head it's no use arguing. "You don't love me," he'll say. Or he'll whisper in my ear, "I won't come home for the holidays again," and eventually have his way. Later, when we heard him and his friend enter the house, Jawahar, Vimla, and I halted our conversation in the living room and rose to our feet. Jawahar called out to the boys to join us. When they came into the room, I was struck by how different our guest looked from how I had imagined him. I was expecting someone in a close-fitting, knitted prayer cap and perhaps an untidy beard, someone with betel-juice staining gold-capped teeth, with fire smoldering behind narrow, unblinking eyes. But the boy standing before us was clean-shaven and shy, and startlingly handsome (like Dev Anand, a popular film star of 1960s and 1970s Hindi cinema and grand marshal of countless India Independence Day parades in your country). Our guest's thick hair was brushed back carefully to form a small pompadour (just like Dev Anand's), and sparkles danced in his large, dark eyes. He was light in complexion, rather like a Kashmiri, and when he smiled, deep dimples appeared on his cheeks.

"Everybody, this is my best buddy Nur," Sunil said, thumping the boy's back a few times. Nur put down the suitcase he was carrying and joined his hands to greet us in the traditional Hindu way instead of stooping a little and touching his forehead with his right hand as I've seen Muslim people do in Hindi movies I watch each afternoon on Vimla's large-screen TV. "The train was delayed at Igatpuri," Nur told us. Nur wore faded blue jeans (like all the young actors do in Hindi movies these days) and a light jacket over a white T-shirt even though it was not particularly cold that day. Sunil introduced us one by one to Nur and even included bird-brained Laxmi in the round, for she burst into the living room that moment to answer the doorbell, late as usual. She's often late in doing most things, especially when it comes to responding to the doorbell. I've pointed this out to Vimla and Jawahar a thousand times, but each time they bat their eyelids at me and nod their heads or they say, "Yes, yes, Maji," and do nothing about it. So I was the only one to scowl at Laxmi when she merrily skipped into the room that evening. She saw me, covered her teeth with her hand, and giggled. I shook my finger at her to issue a warning. When I looked away I found that Jawahar, having stepped forward, was shaking Nur's hand.

The moment my eyes fell on the boy again, I was seized with the feeling I had met him before. I searched my mind but came up with nothing. He was working his feet out of his shoes when I asked him if he had visited Bombay recently. In a gentle and respectful tone he said this was his first visit to Bombay and, for that matter, to western India. I wondered if he had relatives in Bombay, and as though he'd read my mind, he said his father and brother lived in Hauz Khas, Delhi, and that he knew no one besides Sunil in Bombay. He smiled at me. His eyebrows arched upward and his eyes nearly disappeared. That's when I felt even more certain I had met him before.

I informed Sunil I would escort Nur to the guest room. As Nur and I walked toward the guest room in back of the bungalow, I probed him with questions. He responded with a good measure of politeness in his voice. I learned that his parents were divorced, that he was the younger of two brothers, that his father was a business-man in New Delhi. I was interested in learning more about his mother, for, as you may be aware, divorces are uncommon in India. I asked him point-blank, "How does your mummy manage on her own? What does she do for a living, if I may ask?" He remained quiet for some time. But then he said she was a stage actress in Delhi. I said nothing, hoping he'd go on. After a period of silence he said she had had a small role in *Mister Hero,* the highly recommended Dev Anand classic of the 1960s.

When we arrived at the guest room, I showed Nur where the towels and blankets were. As I was about to leave, he approached the window, held the grill, and stared at the garden outside. "I've been jealous of her freedom all my life," he said, his voice so soft I thought he was speaking to himself. He said no more, so I quietly departed from the room, leaving him standing by the window.

In the living room, I found no one. I proceeded into the kitchen to supervise Laxmi. Hardly had five minutes elapsed when I heard the boys preparing to leave the house. I pushed Laxmi away from the kitchen window and saw them mount Sunil's motorcycle. Nur sat in front. The boys had already drawn up an itinerary of their own. Nur had the engine going so loudly I had to clap my hands to get Sunil's attention. "We'll be eating out," he yelled. Before I could protest, they bore down the driveway, Sunil's arms wrapped around Nur's waist. Later in my room, I wondered for a long time about the well-mannered, soft-spoken guest, scarcely older than Sunil who, I neglected to mention before, is nineteen. In the evening, while keeping an eye on nitwit Laxmi chopping onions in the kitchen, I wondered how someone who claimed not to have met me before, could nevertheless seem so familiar.

That night I had difficulty sleeping. I tried to read *Star & Style,* my favourite magazine about the glamorous lives and intimate secrets of our movie stars, but I could not concentrate. I kept thinking about Nur and closed my eyes and pressed my forehead, hoping to provoke some memory of him. It was no use. In exasperation, I flung the magazine against the bedside lamp and left the room. I went out on the verandah and sat on the cushion-swing, propelling it gently with my feet. I could hardly wait for the boys to return. I felt anxious even though the night air was cool and calm and the fragrance of Queen of the Night flowers hung everywhere. I tried to draw up a list of people who reminded me of our guest but I had to give up soon because, besides Dev Anand, whom I rate as the most handsome man in Indian cinema, I could think of no other name. When I heard the roar of Sunil's motorcycle in the distance, it was approaching midnight and, before the headlight could fall on the bungalow's gates, I left the swing and slipped into the darkness of the house.

I saw Nur again at eight o'clock the next morning. I had to remind myself not to stare at him. He had risen early, showered, was all packed and set to leave. The feeling of having met him before had swelled in me through the night and seemed to have assumed a discernible shape in my mind. Sirs, my eyes settled on Nur every few seconds. He was seated at the dining table, wearing the white T-shirt and jeans he'd worn the previous day. His red jacket lay folded on his suitcase in the corner. Seconds later, Sunil ambled in, sleepy-eyed and still in his pajamas, the hems of which, I regret to mention, were sweeping the floor. He slumped into a chair and struggled to keep his eyes open. "Laxmi, breakfast!" he mumbled and swallowed a yawn. Nur said he would have only a cup of tea. I told him he had to eat something before he left for the railway station, but he shook his head.

Sunil assured him he'd get him to VT Station on time for the Poona-bound train. Vimla entered the dining room (in her nightgown!) and Sunil sat bolt upright and good mornings were exchanged. (I am embarrassed to mention, sirs, that Vimla was up early not because we had a guest in the house but because her weekly card party, scheduled for later that morning, was in Colaba, south Bombay, an hour-long drive from the bungalow.) She took the seat next to mine and called for breakfast. Laxmi rasped in her screechy voice that everything was on its way.

The boys talked between themselves, breaking into peals of laughter now and again. Of course, I could not understand their words, what with the trendy phrases and westernized accents our youngsters use nowadays. Incidentally, may I express here my dissatisfaction also with the dialogue delivery of many of your Hollywood stars? Sirs, they are impossible to understand at times. Two weeks ago, Ramlal rented a movie entitled *Cliffhanger* for me from the video store and it took me more than three hours to see it on account of my having to rewind the tape each time Mr. Sylvester Stallone, the film's hero, spoke. I hope Paramount Pictures will use its influence to urge all Hollywood stars to enunciate more clearly in the future. I sometimes fear that your actors have become role models for speaking among Indian boys here, for it's becoming harder and harder for me to make out anything Sunil and his friends say. And then Sunil complains that we don't pay him enough attention! At the table that morning, Vimla, too, wasn't paying the boys' conversation any attention, and I feared Nur would mistake our silence for rudeness. This worried me so much that when Vimla asked me why Ramlal had not returned with the Ambassador after dropping Jawahar at Larsen & Toubro, I said, "He must be caught in a traffic jam," without really affording her query serious attention. Vimla insinuated, as always, that Ramlal was up to no good, and unfolded the *Times of India* lying on Jawahar's chair. Rattling the sheets, she flicked through the paper in search of something to read. I considered leaving the table to check on Laxmi in the kitchen but then Nur's eyes met mine. I could tell he was aware that he was intriguing me. To our good fortune, Sunil paused while speaking to him and, before he could continue, I asked Nur what he intended to do after he received his Bachelor of Technology degree in mechanical engineering.

"I will go to America," he said.

Sunil said Nur aspired to be an actor in America. This didn't surprise me, for Nur's few words about his mother were still on my mind. "He plans to buy a Corvette when he makes it big," Sunil went on, "and drive the American girls wild!"

Poor Nur looked like he had eaten hot chilies. Embarrassed, he peered into his teacup. Sunil patted him on the shoulder and said it was all right, that both Vimla and I were "cool" with talk like that. Vimla folded the *Times,* set it aside, and said it was interesting that an engineer wished to pursue an acting career.

"Do what you must while you can," Sunil told her, leaning forward and tapping the table with his knuckles. "Live fast, even if you must die young."

Vimla sighed and sat back in her chair. She turned to me and asked if, like her, I thought it was too early in the day for Sunil's nonsense. Naturally, I said nothing in response and motioned for her to spread marmalade on my toast.

Sirs, I was about to ask Nur which schools he intended to apply to, hoping to convince him to send an application to Indiana University, when Sunil told him that I, his grandmother, had lived in the United States in the 1950s.

"My grandfather taught for two years in Indiana," Sunil continued, just as Laxmi stormed in to place before him a bowl of cereal and sliced bananas and a plate with a dollop of mango jam and buttered slices of toast. "They didn't take my mother with them," Sunil went on with a snigger. "Left her behind with relatives. Poor Mummy. She never forgave my grandfather."

There was an awkward silence as there always is when Sunil says unnecessary and provocative things. I didn't know what to say, what to think, so I began to spread jam on Sunil's toast. To break the silence, I mentioned to Nur that I often thought about Indiana and the friends I made there, and that I longed to visit them all again some day. He nodded slowly but I could tell that he, like Vimla and Sunil, wasn't listening to me. There was more silence.

Mercifully, the Ambassador sounded its horn outside. Vimla rose to leave the table and stopped. That's when we all saw Nur clenching and unclenching his fingers. He said to no one in particular that Sunil was lucky to have people who cared about him. We kept silent and held our eyes on him. "To feel unloved is the worst thing in the world," he said, sliding his finger along the table's edge and keeping his eyes lowered.

Sirs, we were as perplexed as you might be now, and even Vimla, still standing by the table, was fully attentive for once. We waited for Nur to continue but he said no more.

"Why did you say that?" I said, wanting to rush over to his side and touch his arm.

He smiled, turned serious momentarily, and then, without warning, he threw back his head, Dev Anand-like, and guffawed. "I was just joking," he said. Not a word did he speak at the table thereafter.

Half an hour later, Vimla left for Colaba in the car. Soon after, Nur and Sunil left for VT Station on the motorcycle. I waved to them from the verandah. When I could no longer see the boys down the road, I sat on the swing, resting my head against its iron chains. It was bright outside. The roses and sunflowers were in full bloom; the marble tiles of the verandah were ablaze with sunlight. I shut my eyes. At once, my mind returned to Nur. I thought: How wonderful it is that a stranger can walk into your life and leave an indelible impression on your heart. Destiny had brought him to our door, but why?

Later that day, I was saying my prayers in the pooja-room when it all came together and crystallized in my mind. I went to the living room and collapsed into the sofa. The walls appeared to be receding from me and the ceiling seemed farther away than it really was. Sirs, I could hardly breathe. I remembered my days at Indiana University in the mid-1950s and how one day in 1955, perhaps in late September or early October, when I was working on the final act of *And Where Exactly Were You When Sister Meera Drowned?*, everyone in the country fell silent or spoke of only one thing in hushed, melancholy tones: the actor James Dean had died.

Sirs, it is my sincere belief that Nuruddin Ali Ahmed is a reincarnation of Mr. Dean. I have absolutely no doubts about it. As a firm believer in reincarnation, I submit Nur to you as evidence of life after death. Reincarnation, as you know, is a fundamental belief in Hinduism. Here now is the proof. I will confess that, under my husband's influence, I wrote such beliefs off as nonsense when I was younger, during the two years I spent in your country for instance, but age, wisdom, Laxmi the incorrigible donkey, and now Nur have shown me the truth. Fortunately, Vimla returned early from her card party in Colaba that day. I shouted for her as soon as I heard her enter the house. She rushed into the living room with her hands over her chest. I took her arms in mine and shook them till all her bangles jingled. Then I cried out my discovery. To my dismay, she patted my shoulder, and said I needed rest. I told her to go away. When Sunil strode into the house later, I reached for his elbow and broke the news to him, too. "James who?" he said, not having heard of Mr. Dean. He yawned and said yes, of course I was correct. He gave me a light embrace. Then, he sauntered into the kitchen and searched the refrigerator for something to eat, abandoning his dear grandmother in the living room.

That very afternoon, I ordered Ramlal to drive me to the British Council Library. I asked the librarian, a young and pleasant woman, to help me locate books on Mr. Dean. To my surprise, she asked me to spell the surname; she, too, had not heard of the man. At first, I was annoyed by her ignorance but later I wondered if I was being reasonable. Why would she know of an American actor from her grandparents' generation, or of his untimely death in an automobile accident in California that, as I recall, sent aftershocks around the world for years and years thereafter? Sirs, it turned out that the library had no books on the actor and, resignedly, I returned to the car and instructed Ramlal to drive me back to the bungalow.

But now, after a string of sleepless nights and nearly a month since I encountered Mr. Dean's reincarnation, I feel compelled to write to you about the matter. Jawahar and Vimla tell me I am wasting my time writing long letters to people all over the world about my insights and discoveries. They tell me my letter to you, like the others, will either not be opened or, if I am lucky, opened, scanned, and promptly discarded amid peals of laughter. I do not agree. I told them you would investigate the matter right away, that a studio as prestigious as yours would give it the serious attention it deserves. After all, the essence of a man from the West has found life in the East, in a strife-torn country no less, crossing lines of race, culture, language, and religion. What can be more wonderful, I ask you, sirs?

I hope you will not mind when I inform you that I intend to write similar letters later this week to Warner Brothers and Metro-Goldwyn-Mayer only because I do not know, and am unable to determine here, which studio produced the films of Mr. Dean. I will be leaving for my son's house in Nasik in ten days' time but I assure you that your reply will reach me faster if it is mailed to Bombay. Vimla has already agreed to read your letter to me over the telephone or, if the phones are out of order, have Ramlal drive it over to Nasik as soon as it is received.

I must conclude this letter now, for Ramlal has started the Ambassador and Jawahar is set to leave for the office. He surprised me this morning when he asked to read this letter about which, he said, Vimla talked to him at length. As I'd hoped, he has agreed to mail this one, too, for me. I need hardly add that I enjoyed writing to you and now I patiently await your reply. Please also note in your letter, sirs, if you wish to have copies of "Reshma, Saviour of Mother India" and "Reshma's Revenge from Exile in Kathmandu" (the sequel). "Take care," I will add here, the quintessentially American phrase my dear husband learned to say to his colleagues and students in Bloomington, and thank you so very kindly for your attention.

# The Change

**SIXTY-FIVE-YEAR-OLD AMINA** stood at a bus stop one afternoon, a few yards from her home in Khar, a northern suburb of Bombay. She had on her finest clothes for she was on her way to attend the marriage ceremony of a neighbor's grandson. She was in a joyful mood not only because she loved weddings and hadn't been invited to one in years, but also because she had only that morning received a postcard from her son Rafiq in the United States. She pulled it out from her purse now and reread his words with a smile. She wished Rafiq would write more than the few lines he mailed her biannually. After all, didn't she spend hours elaborating on every incident when she wrote to him each fortnight?

Amina pressed the postcard lightly to her heart and then put it safely back in her purse. For the third time at the bus stop she counted the items on her person: her wristwatch, her four bangles, her necklace, her purse, and the gift for the newlywed couple. She was glad she had had little difficulty selecting the wedding present—four fancy glasses, which the salesman had assured her were not the type used to serve alcoholic drinks. The smell or even the mention of liquor sent chills down Amina's spine, for it had been alcohol that had robbed her of the best years of her life when a drunk motorist killed her husband in a road accident four decades ago. Thereafter, she had raised their child single-handedly, and with no small difficulty, by tutoring algebra and geometry each evening at home to dull children of ambitious parents. Now, as she peered down the road for signs of a bus, she shook the gift box gently beside her left ear. She felt relieved to hear not a sound, and sense not a movement in the box.

When a bus did arrive, Amina counted her personal items one more time before boarding. Once in the bus, she felt fortunate to find an aisle seat. She glanced at the person next to her. A boy in his early teens. About the same age as her grandson in America, she thought. When would Rafiq and Maxine, his American wife, come down to Bombay with their son so that she could finally set her eyes on him and embrace him? Why was it that something always had to come up each time? She had seen Maxine just once, nearly fifteen years ago, when she and Rafiq had flown in to visit her and India like tourists, soon after their unannounced wedding in the States. How quickly they had left! "Something has come up," they told her without looking her in the face.

Again, Amina cast her eyes on the boy sitting next to her. She was a little hurt that he hadn't acknowledged her presence beside him. He had his ear resting against a small transistor radio which gave a live commentary on a cricket match being played in the city. Amina smiled as she recalled the days when her Rafiq did the same. How she would scold him for that, and how she would guide him to his textbooks instead, her fingers twisting his ear. But what else could she have done? Unlike his friends, Rafiq had no father to set him up on his legs. And in any case, hadn't the disciplining paid off eventually? She liked to think that had she not been strict with him, he would never have excelled enough to win a scholarship to attend an American school.

Amina lifted her gold embroidered sari a few inches to keep it from grazing the dirty bus floor. She had to be careful, for it was the only fine one she had. She looked around, noticed the others in the bus studying her attire with raised eyebrows, and felt instantly overdressed. Everyone seemed simple; all were dressed plainly, and most were returning home from work, weary and spent. Amina now wished she had carried the jewelry in her purse instead of wearing it. It was inappropriate to display gold in a bus, she concluded. But she had only wanted to look her best, she thought, calming herself. There was nothing wrong with that, was there? Yet now, all eyes were focused on her. Maybe she should have taken a taxi. But how could she afford one? She could barely make ends meet with her small income, and prices in the city had escalated so alarmingly she had had to purchase the wedding gift by using her savings. As soon as she noted that some of the passengers had stopped looking at her, she decided to take off her jewelry. She had just reached behind her neck to remove her necklace when the bus conductor came up to her, clicking his ticket puncher a few inches from her face.

"Bhulabhai Desai Road," Amina informed him. "One ticket."

"One rupee, twenty paise," said the conductor as he looked Amina over, pausing on her sparkling earrings and necklace. Amina, painfully aware of his stares, opened her purse and extracted a five-rupee bill.

"Give proper change!" the conductor said, noisily chewing betel-leaves.

"I don't have change on me, I'm afraid. I can—"

"I see. Brothers and sisters, we've got one of those rich types on our bus, it seems to me," the conductor announced at the top of his voice. Heads turned swiftly in his direction. The conductor bent down toward Amina and said, "Have you not taken a bus before? Don't you know you ought to carry exact change nowadays? Even a four-year-old child is aware of the shortage of coins in the city. What do you take this bus to be? One of your banks?" There followed much laughter from all around.

"I'm sorry," Amina began. "Why don't you take this five-rupee note and give me the balance later?"

"Give me the balance later," the conductor mocked. Then facing his attentive audience in the bus, he said, "Bloody rich swines have nothing smaller than five rupees nowadays. Corrupt leeches sucking on the blood of us poor."

"Listen, Conductor sahib! You can't talk about me like—"

"Who says I'm talking about you? Sit quietly or I'll stop the bus and have you get off." Then turning to an amused young man, he added, "First of all, no proper change. And acting tough on top of that."

Amina felt cold, turned shades paler, and began to shrink in her seat. The conductor snatched the bill from her unsteady hand and trudged away, mumbling invectives under his breath. Everyone in the bus continued to look in Amina's direction. The boy next to her had even stopped listening to his radio. Amina was surprised to find not one person who sympathized with her. Instead, she noticed that some people wore looks of indifference, others resentment. Encouraged by the conductor's behavior, someone said, "Serves her right." A woman up ahead laughed and announced to her companion,

"We've had the British Raj in our country for two centuries. Could someone tell them they forgot to take with them this Indian Raj they left behind?" There was more laughter and some applause.

Amina decided she would write a long letter to Rafiq that night. She'd describe every moment of this horrible incident. Maybe that would make him send her an airplane ticket. Bhulabhai Desai Road. When would it come, she wondered. For the rest of the journey, she sat motionless and silent. Her mouth felt dry and she fought to hold back her tears. She felt small, yet very conspicuous. Feeling more uncomfortable by the minute, she noted that before alighting, passengers threw a certain look in her direction, as if it were she who personified the daily hardships they battled in the city. Her jewelry, which Amina had borrowed in the first place from a friend, hung on her like massive rocks, and soon Amina found that their weight gave her a headache.

Suddenly, she missed her husband, something she hadn't in years. Next, she longed for her son's support and company. She wished he were beside her now to protect her from everyone watching her in this bus. She wished he had never left for the States, wished she had let him listen to all those cricket commentaries. What had the disciplining done for her? Today she was alone with hardly a soul interested in her well-being. O Rafiq! Amina cried in her mind. Please let me live with you. Come back to India or take me with you to America. I promise I will never be in the way. I'll try to be more fashionable and interesting so that Maxine won't be embarrassed or bored like she was in India.

Amina shut her eyes and tried to relax. Becoming hysterical never helped. She reminded herself she was about to attend a festive function, and that she ought to keep her spirits from sinking. She had so wanted to attend this wedding and had spent weeks in anticipation of the fun she would have and the people she would meet. She couldn't let a rude conductor and the impudent attitude of her fellow passengers ruin what she had been waiting for. With difficulty, Amina fought to restore her hopes. She looked out the window and noted with relief that Bhulabhai Desai Road wasn't too far.

When her stop was a few minutes away, Amina rose to leave. As she walked up the aisle toward the conductor, who stood guarding the rear exit, a cigarette dangling from his mouth, Amina sensed the hard stares and heard the soft whispering of the passengers behind her.

"Can I have the rest of my money, Conductor sahib?"

"What money?"

"Why, the five rupees you took from me earlier. What about the balance?"

"Five rupees? Nonsense. I don't remember you giving me five rupees."

Amina turned around with the hope that someone would back her claim. To her dismay, heads began to look down or turn away. She faced the conductor again.

"Don't you remember I had no change, and I gave you five rupees instead?"

The conductor stubbed out his cigarette with his shoe. "Are you accusing me?" he said. "Are you? I can stop the bus and have you get off."

"But . . . I don't understand."

"Listen, woman. Go back to your seat or get off my bus if you want. I have no time for this." He spat betel-juice out of the bus.

Amina could take no more. "Listen, you thief!" she cried. "You have insulted me enough. I demand the rest of my money back."

"Is that right? So I am the thief now, is it? Listen to me carefully, rich woman. Everyone here is a witness to your slanderous remarks. Don't think you're going to get away with them. I'm stopping the bus right now."

With a tug on the rope running along the bus's wall, the conductor signaled the driver to halt. The bus screeched to a stop, throwing Amina nearly off balance.

"Get out," the conductor said.

Amina stepped off the bus, ashamed and enraged. What had she done? It wasn't her fault she was dressed well for a wedding and could afford no better way of transport. What had happened to courtesy, to the polite and civilized ways of yesteryear? Things had been so different when she was a young girl. Well, at least she was on Bhulabhai Desai Road, she thought, consoling herself. She looked around. Out of habit, she began to count her precious items and realized to her horror she was one short.

"The gift! The gift is still in the bus. Stop!" Amina screamed at the departing bus and waved her arms in the air. "Stop the bus. Please!"

The bus that had moved a short distance, came to a second halt. The squeal of brakes was followed by raucous laughter. Before Amina could catch up with the bus, it started to move, but not before a box flew out and hurtled toward her feet with a crash. Amina picked up her gift. In the distance, her watery eyes saw the entrance to the wedding hall. Voices and *shehnai* music reached her ears. Amina raised the gift box to her ear. She gave it a gentle shake. With a defeated sigh she let it fall to the ground again. For from the box this time came a million tinkling sounds.

# Lost in the U.S.A.

**WHEN SHE USED TO VISIT HER SON** in the States with her late husband, it was different. But now, without the husband and with her son Ravi at the office all day, Pramila could think of nothing to do in the small suburban house with its square piece of lawn in front, a similar but more unkempt patch in back, and a pair of reserved and dead-silent neighbors on either side. After all, how much television could one watch alone each day, particularly when one barely understood a dozen words of the language, not to mention the strange accent? Pramila reached for the remote control and switched the set off, sucking in her breath through her teeth. She was frustrated not only at comprehending almost nothing of the talk show, but also at her own compulsive switching the set on from time to time anyway, as if she herself had become like the talk show guests who, to Pramila's confusion, today appeared as men in the first half hour and as women in the second half, and who by the hour's end were weeping along with a few from the studio's audience.

Distancing herself from the television, Pramila found herself before the telephone. She thought of lifting the receiver, but changed her mind. Ravi would be annoyed at her calling the office as she did almost every single day. And if he were away from his desk, she'd be faced with the challenge of speaking with his secretary. Despite the few English words Ravi had taught her over the years, Pramila would get tongue-tied, embarrassed, and would slip the receiver back into its cradle. Guilt would descend on her then. The disadvantage of being uneducated, Pramila thought. And in her case, it was worse—she was illiterate as well. She couldn't read; she had never written a word. Even numbers often confused her. Ravi's fancy telephone, for example, was nothing like the one they owned in India with its simple rotary dial and punched-out numbers you could count back on your fingers. This one was like a compact computer with so many little colored buttons projecting from its face, that the first time she used it, Pramila feared the telephone would splash red light around the walls and wail out some sort of siren to scold her for having used it the incorrect way. But fortunately for her, one day Ravi programmed the telephone to make it simpler to use. With a red marker-pen he circled the button that speed-dialed his office.

Pramila approached the living room window and peered out. Amazing! Not one person on the road in front of her. In India, this could never happen. She began playing the game she had devised for herself this visit: count the cars that drive past in a whole minute. The record high to date was four. A blue bus roared past that moment. Blue buses were to be equated with two cars for their size. They went by the house every half hour, Pramila noted. Ravi had told her they were probably public buses but she had shaken her head and argued he was mistaken for, really, how could *public* buses be so empty? He had thrown back his head and laughed, she remembered.

Pramila narrowed her eyes and turned to the sky. A few fleecy clouds rolled by lazily. Between two trees a bird stood like a watchful sentry on a telephone wire, its feathers ruffled by the wind. Pramila took a deep breath. How sad, she thought, that Ravi insisted she remain indoors when everything outside was insisting it was a marvelous summer day to take a long stroll with a neighbor, or to visit someone's house for a cup of tea, or to sit later on the concrete "sunset-view" benches before the Arabian Sea as she would surely have done on such a day in Bombay. There, it would take her less than ten minutes to walk to the local market, for instance, where she would inspect the new saris the stores draped one after the other like sails. Here, on the other hand, Ravi had to *drive* for twice as long to the huge mall at one end of town.

On the occasions they had gone to the mall during the month she had spent in America already, Pramila had enjoyed herself. Although everything back in Bombay was close by, here, when you reached it, there was no need to look elsewhere. There was such a variety of items on display under one roof, and in such abundance, that the first time Ravi had played guide there to Pramila and his father six or seven years ago—drawing their attention to this store and that as if he were personally responsible for their success—she had pressed her fingers to her lips throughout the tour in amazement. Pramila thought of the mall now. Trips there were the only occasions she got to see people—the American people—of whom Ravi said such wonderful things at home and during his telephone calls to Bombay.

But as she turned away from the window now, brow furrowed, shoulders drooping, feet heavy, Pramila decided this would be her last trip to the United States. She'd rather stay behind in their tiny flat in India. At least there she'd be busy doing something: answering the doorbell, or chatting with Mrs. Dinshaw two floors downstairs, or bargaining furiously with some stubborn fruit seller squatting by his basket outside her door. Vacations here in America were too dull for her. How could Ravi like this place? How could he have spent nine years here? There was nothing to do at all! Cooking, no matter how painstakingly she went about it, rarely took her more than an hour. The rest of the day then yawned before her and nothing in the house changed until Ravi came home at seven in the evenings.

Today, she would tell Ravi she was tired of taking her vacations here. Fifty-eight, she would say, is a delicate age for a woman to embark on long journeys. Journeys that required her to travel with complete strangers for one thing. Everyone on board the airplane clicked their tongues at her in sympathy, she would exaggerate. They steered her by her arm in the aisle. Pramila sighed as she imagined the effect her words would have on Ravi. He would laugh, come up to her and hug her, and then, as happened each time, she would hug him back and tell him she would come to see him no matter what. Come even if she had to climb the Himalayas and swim across the Ganges. He always laughed more heartily when she said that. "*Meri ach-chhee Ma,*" he would say, and kiss her on the forehead. My good mother.

But this time she would remain firm and insist it was his turn now. When was the last time he was in Bombay anyway? Three years ago for his father's cremation. But America is my home, he would surely say, and she would tell him again that was ridiculous.

And ridiculous it is, for how can this place with all these different-looking people locked forever inside their homes with their strange way of speaking and strange social customs (and just as strange TV shows) be home? Home was where someone or other was always dropping by, where the laughter of children rose from building compounds, where hawkers sang out their wares from the streets, where buses and trains were packed with people conversing, where the language spoken was one everyone understood. Home, she would tell Ravi, was where a few buildings away the Sharmas lived, and just down the road the Vakils lived, and where the chatty vegetable-lady Tulsi and the old bread-man Rahim Chacha made daily deliveries door-to-door, and where just a short walk away bustled the marketplace of course.

Pramila found herself by the window now. She leaned out and took a deep breath. A pleasant fragrance reached her from the flower bed below. She shut her eyes. Oh, it was a gorgeous day! She opened her eyes and her pulse revved when she saw, standing on the pavement before the house, a young woman and a little boy holding hands. They had their backs to her; their eyes were set on the road. Pramila decided she would invite them in for a cup of tea. So what if she didn't know their names? Ravi always said the American people were friendly, "with faces that break easily into smiles." Yes, she would call out to the woman and her son. They would be delighted, of course, and would come in, sit beside her on the couch and ask her everything there was to tell about India. She would ask them everything she wanted to know about America. They'd become good fast friends. After she returned to Bombay, they would keep in touch with each other, and when she came back here—after Ravi made, say, at least two trips home—this lady and her son would be thrilled to see her as well. Pramila sighed. If she could speak English, she would invite them in this instant, she thought. If she could write a few lines, even a few words, she'd keep up a steady correspondence with them. But of course she was thinking nonsense, and recognizing this, she brought her chin down on her arms folded awkwardly across the windowsill and continued to look out.

The woman outside bent down to adjust the boy's cap. When she straightened up, they both took a step forward. They looked left and held hands even tighter now. A blue bus appeared, slowed down, and stopped before them. Its doors swung open with a *whoosh*. Pramila heard the woman say, "Mall." She could not hear the driver's reply, but the bus was on its way there evidently, for the woman helped the little boy climb the steps and boarded the bus after him. The doors snapped shut, making that sucking sound again, and the bus shifted out of view, leaving everything as vacant, quiet, and still as before.

Pramila wished she could go to the mall. Why couldn't Ravi come home early sometimes for her sake? Couldn't he drive her, take her to the mall, rush back to his office, and then spend as much time as he wanted with all those files and manuals he brought home each evening? He could then pick her up from the mall whenever he wished. Pramila decided she would call his office and ask him if he would do at least this one thing for his mother. She strode over to the telephone and grabbed the receiver. She pressed the circled button on the top right corner and, almost instantly, heard the phone in Ravi's office ring. What's for dinner, he would ask her. Like his father he always thought of food. He'd ask her how her day had gone. Good, good, he'd absently say to her. Then he'd ask what she'd seen on television. She would describe the shows, make up quite a bit about them at times. Of course, he'd tell her he was coming home early today or that he'd been about to telephone her. Oh yes, oh yes, she would say, hand-waving his words away.

The ringing at the other end stopped. "Ravi!" Pramila was about to cry when his secretary's dulcet voice jingled from the earpiece. Pramila gasped and slammed the receiver back into its cradle. That poor woman, she thought and covered her mouth. How awful that she, Pramila, was doing this to her. She's probably complained about the mysterious caller to everyone in the office. Pramila hoped Ravi hadn't guessed. She found herself before the couch and slumped onto it. She sighed. She traced the design on her sari with her finger. She imagined it repatterning itself—stars now, triangles next. She had seen the neighbors' car in their driveway from the window. Who were they? Their home was so silent. Didn't they like to talk to one another? Didn't they argue about anything at all? Maybe she should just invite herself into their house. In Bombay, everyone did this. And people are people after all. The same everywhere. They would find a way to communicate with each other. But who knows what the rules of etiquette are in America. She had better consult Ravi about this, Pramila thought, and reached for the remote control with a sigh. She poked at the orange power button harder than ever. *Hai Bhagwan!* It was far too boring in the house. She wanted to be where people were around her. Not little buttons circled off in bright colors.

A talk show was in progress. Pramila recognized it at once—the show of the white-haired man with eyeglasses. Pramila saw him each afternoon on TV. She had decided he was a nice man. An honest, religious, and good-hearted man. A man who loved his family. She had also made up a little family for him. His wife worked in a huge office in a building as tall as Bombay's Hotel Oberoi Towers and was a secretary for somebody like Ravi. She loved to cook for the white-haired man. *Samosas* and extra-spicy *murg makhani* were his weakness. They had three wonderful children: two girls—Meenakshi and Deepa—and a boy—Sunil. Sunil was the youngest and the white-haired man's favorite. Meenakshi and Deepa were the mother's darlings, of course. Pramila had a feeling that after dinner the white-haired man told the family about the guests on his show and how they had dressed. She could see them doubling over with laughter each time. That was happening on the screen now. Everybody was laughing.

Pramila punched the ▲ button on the remote control. The channel switched and now a movie was in progress. A bearded man in leather clothes sat on a horse. He was wearing a broad-rimmed hat; his sunburnt face was tilted up to the sky. Bald brown hills rolled away behind him. A woman, wearing a frilly white gown and a lacy white hat, was clutching the man's boot, refusing to let go. The man sat unaffected as though he were sculpted from rock, his square jaw protruding, his fingers squeezing the reins. To Pramila's surprise, he rolled off the horse, hit the muddy ground with a thud and lay sprawled, face down, by the woman's feet. An arrow stood at attention from his back. Pramila switched back to the talk show, to the friendly white-haired man. Two of his guests were holding hands now, sniffing into their handkerchiefs. A toothpaste commercial came on. Pramila switched the set off, but unsatisfied, she unplugged it from the wall. That, she hoped, would make a difference. But a difference to what, she asked herself and plugged it back in.

She should have called out to the lady and her son. She could have clapped her hands and they'd have turned around and waved to her. Now they were in the mall with all the happy people there, sifting through new clothes, trying on all the fancy shoes and sandals in shoe shops and examining rings and necklaces in jewelry stores. If she had offered them tea, they would have taken the next bus and asked her to come with them. How nice it would have been. They'd have taken the bus together and would have returned together as well. Pramila clenched her fist at having missed the opportunity to go somewhere, do something. Ravi would have been proud of her venturing out, of her not depending on him for once. Went all by myself, she could proudly have said.

When the wall clock chimed four times, Pramila thought of the blue bus to the mall and how another would soon drive past the house, sucking in the few people left on the streets. She paced the floor, shuttling between the window and the television, her thumbnail caught between her teeth. She could easily take the bus to the mall herself, couldn't she? There were two jars of coins beside the laundry bag in Ravi's room: one, she had noticed, was full of small copper coins, the other had bigger and heavier ones like those in India. She would scoop out a handful from the second jar, grab her purse, and wait by the road. When the bus arrived, she would say, "Mall," and climb the steps. What could be difficult about that? "Mall," Pramila said, satisfied with the sound of it. She wriggled her feet into her slippers. She grabbed the duplicate key to the house that lay beside the telephone. Just in case, Ravi had said. Surely, he'd meant for occasions like this. "Mall," Pramila repeated, using a different inflection in her voice. How amazed he'd be when she told him about her trip. She took a quick look around the house. "Mall," she said again, now with feverish excitement. Then, satisfied everything indoors looked just fine, she stepped into the bright afternoon sun and shut the front door gently after her.

• • •

When the blue bus arrived, Pramila greeted the driver with the word she had been rehearsing diligently, but it came out more like "mole."

"Whatzat?" the driver said. Pramila repeated the word. "Oh mall. This ain't the bus, Ma'am," he said. He read his wristwatch.

"That one should be here in half an hour."

How courteous of the driver, Pramila thought as she climbed into the bus. He had taken the trouble to tell her when the bus would reach the mall. Now Bombay drivers did no such thing. She fetched a handful of coins from her purse and began dropping them one after another into the coin drop beside the driver.

"Ma'am, this bus ain't going to the mall."

The coin drop beeped and swallowed the coins one by one. Pramila looked into the driver's eyes and smiled.

"O-*kay*," the driver sang and shut the doors.

Pramila walked along the aisle, her heart pounding, her arms trembling. She was on her own now, traveling to the mall by herself. She took a look around and lowered herself quickly into a seat, sliding all the way in toward the window. The bus was cool—oh air-conditioned!—and nearly empty. There was a woman sitting across the aisle from her, two rows behind. She had lifted her face when Pramila entered, but now she was reading a magazine that she held close to her glasses. Some rows behind her, a young boy, chewing gum, had spread himself across an entire seat, his shoulders smack against the window. Pramila took a long look at him. He was wearing his cap backwards; a pair of small wheels seemed to drop from it. They were speakers, Pramila realized as faint music reached her ears. The boy's head bobbed up and down, his fingers drummed the air. Pramila knew there was a man with a suit and a hat some seats behind. She could not see him now. He hadn't looked up from his newspaper when she had taken her seat.

Pramila peered out the window. A mailbox sailed past. She recognized it from her occasional walks. Now the bus should drive across railtracks, she thought, and to her excitement it did. Everything was so soundless, Pramila observed, like an underwater scene in some movie. This was most unlike a bus ride in Bombay—no scrambling for seats, not a standee in the aisle, not even a bus-conductor on board. She studied the houses drifting by. Now and then she spotted people inside. She wondered if there were any mothers like her: bored and lonely, lost in a world of complicated telephones and fancy remote controls. She would like to meet one of them. They would have much in common; they'd become good friends and embrace each other. In the driveway of one house, Pramila saw a young couple unloading a huge box from the trunk of a car. A little girl with ribboned ponytails stood by and watched the couple intently. From the way her elbows were winged out it seemed as if she were ordering the couple around. Pramila smiled and kept the girl in sight for a while longer.

One day Ravi would give her such a lovely granddaughter too. Deepika, she'd name her and take her away to India. Deepika is Indian, she'd inform Ravi. Deepika belonged to India. Ravi would then *have* to follow with his wife, wouldn't he? But what if his wife was not Indian, was someone like the American woman from his office who'd come to dinner two weeks ago? Deepika would not be fully Indian then. Oh what fantastic ideas you have, Ravi had told her when she'd probed him about the guest. She's just a good friend, he'd said, his booming laughter resounding in the house. Secretly, Pramila had felt relieved. The woman was nice, no doubt, but communicating with her had been such a strain.

The bus turned into a narrower winding road. After a span of dark leafy trees on either side, houses reappeared. These were larger, Pramila observed. Certainly larger than Ravi's. The lawns were better nursed, the hedges more fashionably groomed, the driveways were longer as well. From the corner of her eye, Pramila saw the woman with the magazine rise from her seat. Then the man with the hat suddenly filled her view. He approached the driver and spoke to him. The driver replied. They both laughed. The bus slowed down to a stop. The doors flipped open. "Good-bye," the man said and alighted. "Thank you," the woman said and waved. Hardly had the bus moved a few blocks down the road when the boy with the music came forward to take the seat beside the front doors. He swung his head from side to side even faster with the music now, his lips silently mouthing the words. His eyes met Pramila's. She smiled. He looked away. Seconds later, he jumped to his feet and now all of him swayed back and forth. The bus veered to the side of the road. The boy skipped down the steps. When the doors burst open, he sprang out and was off, his head continuing its graceful bounce, his hands dug deep into his pockets.

As the bus swerved to the left and shifted gears, Pramila's heart thumped harder and faster. This bus was not going to the mall! She looked around her. Everyone had gotten off. At least one other person, surely that singing boy for one, ought to have been going to the mall. No, this bus was not headed there, had never intended to. The mall wasn't this far away from Ravi's house! And these lovely homes on either side of the road—she would certainly have remembered pointing them out to Ravi on their drives to the mall. Pramila shut her eyes and tried to calm herself. The bus is taking a longer route there, she told herself. That happens in some parts of Bombay too. That was it, of course. Didn't Bus 221 take a circuitous route from Khar to Bandra, skirting the Arabian Sea? Buses do that all the time. All over the world. Pramila opened her eyes and found the bus climbing a gentle hill. The houses had grown bigger and prettier, the distances between them longer and woodier. A fountain spouted in one garden. A statue stood in the middle of another. Tall gates began appearing before lawns. Homes—immense stone and stucco mansions now—were tucked in far too deep to be seen fully from the road. *Hai Bhagwan,* this was the wrong bus. Where was it going? Outside, there wasn't a person about.

Pramila's frantic glances found the driver in his rearview mirror. He had lied to her. Was he going to park the bus somewhere and rob her now? She had nothing, she would confess. Only a house key and loose change to take the bus back from the mall. That is all I have in my purse, she'd say and show him. You can take the purse, she would tell him. Indian leather, she would say and he'd snatch it from her. Such things did happen, Pramila knew. Mrs. Sharma had told her she'd been robbed by a taxi driver in Hong Kong. He'd fled with her gold bangles, she'd said. Quickly, Pramila drew her sari over her bangles. She had better get off the bus before the driver saw them, get off while there were houses still around. With her purse slapped against her heart to muffle its beating, Pramila lumbered up to the driver.

"Mall," she said.

The driver started. "I thought I . . . Now wait a minute. I told you this ain't the bus going there."

He looked at Pramila directly for a second and then in the mirror. His forehead creased, his eyes went narrower. He threw up his hands in the air. He gestured roughly toward the bus steps and shifted in his seat.

"Ma'am, when you came up those steps I told you this ain't the bus."

Pramila hid her bangles from view. "Mall," she said again, her voice quivering so much she had to repeat the word. The driver shook his head and brought the bus to a halt. When it came to a complete stop, he idled the engine for a while. Then he pointed at a lane up ahead.

"Do you see that street? Make a left there. It will take you to Dogwood Street. Now Dogwood's parallel to this street and is also one-way but in the opposite direction. Wait there for the S-23 or the S-24 going to Brannon Square. Ask the driver for a transfer. Then get off at the intersection of Dogwood and Waterfield Street and wait for the S-17. That will take you to the mall."

He drew the automatic doors open. Pramila made sure she didn't look at them. She smiled and blinked at the driver. He shrugged and threw open his palms. Pramila stepped down from the bus onto the pavement below. She turned around. Driverji, there is no one on your bus, she said in her mind. Couldn't you drive me to the mall? Pramila imagined he would if she asked him politely.

"Mall," she said. "Go . . . pleej?"

The driver turned to the road before him. He gripped the steering wheel. The doors closed with the *whoosh* sound. The bus groaned and inched forward. As it coughed dark bursts of smoke, Pramila's heart sank. Her body shook. She held her breath as she watched the bus steer away from the pavement and begin its climb uphill. She stepped into the spot where the bus had stood just as a furious roar from the bus filled the air. Everything was growling at *her*, Pramila imagined. But then all sounds subsided and the world fell into a solemn silence as she saw the blue bus, her only link to Ravi's house, sink little by little over the hill.

• • •

"Yes?"

The woman at the door was young, in her twenties or early thirties; Pramila couldn't tell easily with American women. Her face was long, her mouth small; her hair fell in rich coppery waves about her face. A few strands flopped over her brow, fallout from a minor hair explosion on the top of her head. A tiara was what Pramila first thought it was—a maharani's gold tiara. Small earrings dangled from the woman's earlobes; her long neck and slender arms were bare.

"Can I help you?"

Pramila had been on her feet for about three-quarters of an hour, walking back on the road the bus had taken. The tall iron gates and the deep driveways of the houses had seemed intimidating, hostile, and even eerie. Dogs had bounded toward her across undulating lawns, barking ferociously, angered, Pramila believed, because of the gates. Keeping herself erect, she had walked hurriedly, watching from the corner of her eyes the dogs rise on their hind legs. She tried not to look at their teeth, tried not to hear the crash of their bodies against the gates. She imagined the gates of one of the houses drawing open for a car. She could see the dogs fighting with each other to get out first. She saw them flying for her throat one by one. Pramila shuffled her feet as fast as she could. She held her purse close to her, not daring to look behind her shoulder. Finally, to her relief, the houses lining the road grew smaller, friendlier, closer to each other. Exhausted, she approached the first house that looked safe.

"Are you all right?" the woman at the door now said.

Pramila reached for her left knee and massaged it vigorously. She wanted to sit for a while. Her throat, moreover, was dry and she longed for a cup of tea. The woman, however, had not yet invited her in for tea. In Bombay, they'd have been merrily chatting by now, exchanging recipes and gossip.

"Bus," she said, her finger pointing to the road, her arm shaking. "Bus," she repeated, her voice smothered to a whisper. Somewhere in her mind, Ravi appeared. He was circling her, hammering numbers on a giant calculator with a hooked finger. His cheeks were trembling, his brow was inflamed with rage.

"Uh-huh," the woman said. "What about it?"

"Driver. Bus," Pramila said. She felt her eyes moisten, her heart knocking hard in her chest.

The woman wrinkled her brow and seemed to be working her mind to understand the words. "I'm sorry," she said finally. "I don't follow you." She blinked her eyes. "You want to take the bus, is that it?"

"Ravi," Pramila now said, struggling to hold back the tears gathered in her eyes. "Ravi Malhotra."

"Pardon me?"

The woman's fingers curled tighter around the doorknob. She shook her head. The hair resting on her shoulders rose lightly with the wind. She proceeded next to shut the door.

"One mi-nut," Pramila cried, stepping forward and raising her index finger to illustrate her point. Her voice was frayed with worry. She could feel her chin quivering. Her heart had swelled, was nudging her ribs out determinedly. "Pleej. I . . . bus . . . mall."

The woman shrugged. "No really, I'm sorry. I can't seem to . . ." She shook her head. "I'm terribly sorry. I wish I knew which bus could take you to the mall. I've no idea. To be frank, I don't think there's one that goes there from here. Wait. Hang on a sec." She leaned back and cupped the side of her mouth. "Dan! Da-an!"

Somewhere in the house, the wooden floor groaned to the leisurely pace of footsteps. A tall man emerged from the shadows, newspaper in hand, glasses slipped halfway down his nose. He took up a position beside the woman and held her waist in his arm. They made such a handsome couple, Pramila thought. Like those on American TV commercials. One day, Ravi would be just as happily married, she imagined, her worries dissipating for a moment. She could see him and his wife standing like this before her, too. She studied the man's face; there was something about him she liked. His hair was abundantly and prematurely silver like that of the white-haired man of afternoon television. A similar air of kindness hung about this man, too. He was younger of course, a few years older than Ravi. Maybe this is what Ravi would've been like had he been born in America. And like Ravi, this man, Pramila decided, would understand her now. Like him, he was an intelligent man. He spoke many languages, had, in fact, traveled to India several times. Came every winter and took up the topmost room in Bombay's Hotel Oberoi Towers to gaze fondly at the Arabian Sea.

"Yes?" the man said, looking Pramila quickly over, his eyes resting on her slippers poking out from below her sari.

"I think she wants to take the bus to the mall," the woman said. "Is there a bus that goes there from here? Doesn't speak English very well."

"Ravi," Pramila said, keeping her eyes fixed on the man. "Ravi Malhotra."

" 'Revvy.' She said it again." The woman stooped low and looked harder at Pramila. "Is that your name? Is Revvy your name?"

"Yes," Pramila said. "Bus. Mall. Ravi Malhotra."

"She's lost," the man said. "Are you lost?"

"Last? No. Bus go, go, going. Up, down, *idhar, udhar*. Mall no."

"Yeah, she's lost," the man said.

He took off his glasses and held its stem in the corner of his mouth. His eyes were grayish-blue. Like the white-haired man's, Pramila noted. But this man's eyes were kinder, bigger. He was a very good man, Pramila told herself. He helped people get to their homes. He helped them get to the mall. In fact, he often escorted them there to keep them company, to make friends with them. At the mall, he often advised people on what to buy, on where the best deals could be got. He drove people home if they were lonely or stranded.

"I hope she doesn't expect us to drive her to the mall," the woman whispered.

"She's hopelessly lost," the man said. "That's for sure. She's probably from India or Pakistan. We may not have to drive her anywhere if we offer her the telephone."

Pramila stepped forward and shook her fist with excitement. "India. Phone. Ravi Malhotra," she cried, her voice abandoning all fear for once, her eyes swung wide open.

"Why would she repeat her name like that?" the woman said.

"Maybe that's not her name," the man offered. He bent down until his face was level with Pramila's. "Would you like to use the telephone?"

Pramila shook her head and pointed at the road where she'd seen another blue bus approach her during her flight from the fortresslike homes. She had been about to flag it down when, recalling the other bus, she'd let it pass. It would have driven toward the dogs, too, and taken her who knows where else from there. Now she stepped away from the couple and waved her hand in the direction the buses had gone. She made roaring sounds of an engine with her mouth, rolled her fists around each other like a spinning wheel at the same time. Then with one finger pointing at the road, she enacted the movement of a snake with the other arm. The road had curved, she remembered, and then had come that slope, hadn't it?

With both hands, Pramila sculpted a little hill in the air. Then scissoring her fingers to indicate she had walked the distance to their house, she returned to stand before the couple with a smile.

"What was that all about?" the woman said. The man shrugged.

Pramila lowered her gaze from their bewildered faces to the doormat before their feet. Her heart tightened. It was hopeless, she thought, rubbing her eyes. She should have remained on the bus. Its route was a big circle probably. That was why it passed Ravi's house again and again. Warmer tears flooded her eyes. Perhaps that was what the driver had been telling her. "Return to your seat," he'd probably said but she had stood there by him. She'd have been home by now. Back after a good tour of the town. Instead, here she was, miming her words, trying to make sense of what the man and woman were saying.

"Ma'am, would you like to come inside and make a call?"

The couple moved aside and Pramila could see a dining table nestled deep inside. A ceiling lamp, dropping from a chain, hung directly over it. "Yes," she said, her face breaking into a smile, her large eyes sparkling. Hastily, she wiped her feet on the doormat.

She strode into the house with an air of familiarity. The wooden floor, she noticed, was polished and bare except for a small carpet on which a circular coffee table stood. On one side of the table, a plush sofa was set against a wall that bore two oil paintings. A pair of stern-looking armchairs assumed positions on the other side of the table. Stationed in a corner was a floor lamp, watching shyly from the shadows of a wide bookshelf. Plants were everywhere, some close to the ceiling, their brass pots suspended in chains. The plants on the floor poured their leaves out furiously, filling up the four corners of the room. Taking a good look inside her first American home, Pramila settled herself on the sofa.

"*Chai*," she considered saying to the woman, who was leaning against the bookshelf, hands folded, her hair covering a cheek. "Tea." Pramila eyed the picture frames on the square side table next to the sofa. The largest one displayed the couple in their wedding clothes. She leaned closer to the picture. She had a feeling the man and woman were newlywed.

"The phone," the woman said, motioning Pramila toward the telephone across the room.

Pramila rose. There was to be no *chai*. She would have it at home, she decided. She had no strength to act out anything now, she thought, approaching the telephone. Thank goodness, it was quite like the one Ravi owned. She picked up the receiver. What would she do if he was not in the office but home already, early for once to surprise her? She didn't know the home number, didn't have it in her purse either. Her eyes fell on the telephone's top right corner. Her brows gathered. It occurred to her only now that this phone wouldn't be programmed to dial Ravi's office, that it would bear no buttons circled off in red.

"Let me try," the man said. He took the receiver from her and looked at his wife. She was still propped against the bookshelf, her chin sunk into her fist, her hair concealing much of her face.

"Ravi," Pramila said. "Ravi Malhotra."

"Okay," the man said. He punched a number and spoke in an urgent tone. No, no, no, Pramila heard him say. Yes, yes, yes, after that. Finally, he grew silent and pursed his lips. The woman approached him, raking her hair back with her fingers.

"Well?" she said.

The man shook his head and put the receiver down. A faraway look settled over his eyes. "I guess I was right," he said. "Revvy Milotra is not a name." He stroked his jaw. "The operator said there's no one in the county by that name."

• • •

With her arm slicing through the gap between the couple from time to time, Pramila gave directions from the rear seat in the car. They had been driving for about fifteen minutes when, suddenly, she shook the man by his shoulder. "Bad, bad road," she cried and pointed back at the intersection they had passed. The man pulled the car over to the side of the road. The woman set the air conditioner on high and clutched her brow.

"I can't believe we're doing this," she said, shaking her head. "This is ridiculous. We can't keep stopping like this until she makes up her mind. It's clear she has no clue where she lives, Dan. The house could be on any goddam street, in any goddam direction, in any goddam city!"

"Keep it down, honey," the man said. He turned the air conditioner back on low. "You have a better idea?"

"Have you been listening to anything I've said all along? Let's drive her to the mall or let's call the cops."

The man shook his head. "Nah," he said. "She's scared. She'll be lost in the mall. She's in no condition to talk to the cops."

"That's not *our* problem!"

The man swung the car around at the next U-turn, drove back, and took the road Pramila had suggested. Minutes later, however, Pramila was edged forward in her seat again.

"Bad road," she declared. She pointed excitedly to the road they had left. "Good road."

"Dan, please drive me home. I've had enough of this."

The tires squealed as the man brought the car to a stop by the pavement. He turned around to face Pramila. His cheeks were flushed; an eyebrow twitched.

"Look," he said, holding up his finger as though to warn her. "You've got to help me here."

"Mall," Pramila said, feeling her throat constrict with fear.

"No, we're not going to any mall. We're taking you home. Now I realize you don't know your street, but you agreed it was fifteen or twenty minutes away and that you would spot it when you saw it. Did you not agree on that?"

"Right. Like she understood you!" the woman said. "She'd have nodded yes even if you'd said three days."

"Bus," Pramila said. "Ravi."

"Shit," the woman said and folded her arms. "I say let's waste no more time and hand her over to the cops."

The man turned the car around and soon they were back on the previous road. Pramila looked out the window, her wide eyes close to the glass, her hands framing her face like fences. She couldn't recognize anything. All the houses were suddenly so similar. What would she do if Ravi's house did not come by? Or if it had flown past already? She would have to spend the night at the couple's home. She would cook dinner for them in return, perhaps press the woman's forehead to cool her down.

"Do you see anything?" the man asked. "Do you see your house?"

"Turn the fucking car around for Chrissakes!" the woman said. "The cops handle cases like this every day."

The man stopped the car by the pavement again. Someone, walking briskly outside, slowed down and looked at them. The man sighed and stroked back his hair. "She doesn't speak our language, honey. She's harmless—"

"That's not the point!"

"—and frightened."

The woman rubbed her brow with the back of her hand. "You know," she said, sitting up straight, "I've noticed that lately you don't listen to me."

"Honey, please," the man said. "Not now."

"You think my suggestions are stupid. You know damn well that the cops will take her home somehow, you know they'll contact her consulate or something, or maybe a person from her country, and yet you choose not to listen to me. Frankly, I don't know what the hell's going on."

The man thought hard for a moment, sweeping his finger along the dashboard to shovel off the dust. "I guess we've done what we could," he said with a shrug and restarted the engine. "The cops it is."

"Bus!" Pramila cried louder than before and pointed at a blue bus that roared past the car that moment. "Bus Ravi going." The bus stopped a block ahead. Someone got off and crossed the road. The bus proceeded, spewing out a cloud of smoke that veiled it momentarily from view.

The man sat up. "Do you think she's been asking us to follow a bus?" he said. "She could be saying that that will lead us to her house. What do you think?"

"What does it matter what I think."

"We've come this far. How about giving this a shot?"

"Oh, sure," the woman said. "I've always wanted to follow every bus in town." She stared out the window and shook her head.

The car reentered traffic and began tailing the bus closely. It stopped whenever the bus did, turned wherever it turned. Pramila stared out the window and concentrated. The car was moving too fast for her. Everything outside seemed like wilderness. Far too many trees were cutting her view. To her relief, the car slowed down minutes later. It bumped and shook. Pramila's forehead knocked against the windowpane. She craned her neck to look down at the road. Her spirits lifted. They'd passed a railway crossing. Shiny tracks had drifted past beneath the car. Her fingers groped for the door handle. She drew herself closer to the window and pressed her forehead to the glass. A mailbox should appear soon, she thought. When it did, she shot her hand between the couple and waved it up and down as if she were patting the air. The car slowed down. The bus sped away.

When she saw the house at last, she gripped the man's arm. She pointed out the brick house and the car pulled into the empty driveway. "We did it!" the man cried, drumming the steering wheel like a jubilant boy. The woman threw back her head on the seat. "Super," she said and blew the rest of her breath out.

Pramila stepped out of the car. She was relieved to see Ravi's car was not yet in the driveway; no explanations would therefore be necessary. Swiftly, she approached the man's window. He rolled down the glass. "Good-bye," he said. "Come," Pramila said and tugged gently at his elbow. To her disappointment, he shook his head. "*Chai?*" Pramila now said, making a gesture of drinking from a teacup. "No, thanks. It's late," the man said. He raised his wristwatch just as the woman switched on the radio inside. The car began to back down the driveway. The man waved. Pramila rushed to take his hand in hers. "It was no trouble," he said, responding to the gratitude in her eyes. Pramila followed the car down the driveway, her heart racing, her chest filling with the pain of abandonment again.

"One mi-nut," she cried just as the car was about to enter the road. She spun around and ran toward the house. "One mi-nut," she called again from the steps. After a minor struggle with the door lock, she darted in only to emerge in seconds, a picture frame in one hand, a notepad in the other. If her new friends would jot down their address, she would ask Mrs. Vakil to write letters for her. Pramila shuffled down the steps. She stopped in her path. The car was gone. An emptiness in the driveway gaped back at her as if something had been hurriedly carved out of there. Pramila sighed. She hadn't told them her name. Now she'd never know theirs. With only a sketchy idea of where they lived, she wondered if she'd ever see them again, these nice people who had come to her rescue . . .

She turned back to ascend the front steps, Ravi's graduation picture pressed hard against her chest. She had had her first exciting day in America, she thought. There would now be much to tell Mrs. Sharma and Mrs. Vakil back in Bombay. The American people are just like us, she would say. Outside they're different to look at, but inside they're like us—some nice, some helpful, some not so nice, not so helpful. They live in beautiful homes with many plants and picture frames inside, and watchdogs, statues, and fountains outside. The roads are confusing, the buses run nearly empty, she'd say.

Pramila entered the house and stepped out of her slippers. Her eyes moistened. She smeared the tears away with the sleeves of her blouse. She would come to America for her vacations again, she decided as she mounted Ravi's picture frame back on the wall. It was she who had isolated herself, made her trips boring until today. But now she had the antidote to her problem: blue buses. Tomorrow she would take one again. She would not be frightened. On seeing people out in their gardens, she'd get off, stride up to them and take their hands in hers. "Pramila Malhotra," she'd say proudly and make friends with them.

The wall clock chimed seven as she stepped into the kitchen. Ravi would be home any second now. He'd lunge in, his arms cradling thick books. He would fling them on the carpet, stretch himself out on the couch and flick on the television. "Food," he'd roar and unfasten his necktie. "Almost ready," she'd call back in reply. Then sooner or later, he would come sniffing in, his shoes still on, and she'd have to scold him again. "O-ho, Ma, in America the kitchen is not a sacred room," he'd protest with a laugh and inspect the contents of the pots one by one. "So what did you do today?" he'd ask, expecting to hear what she said day after day, but now she would wheel him around and seize his arms. "Oh Ravi, so *much* happened today!" she would say and tell him everything. How surprised he'd be, how concerned he'd become for her sake. Like a dutiful son he'd raise his voice and bar her from leaving the house alone again. "This is not India!" he'd add and charge into the living room to confiscate the spare key.

Pramila stirred a pot absently, hurriedly. She would say she had watched television all day, she now decided, just as she heard Ravi driving his key into the front door. She tried to look busy. She ran the water in the sink, pulled jars of spices down from the cabinet above. Quickly, she shifted things here and there on the counter. In any case, why risk telling him anything when there was every chance he'd not believe her anyway? Pramila wet her hands under the tap. She thought hard. Why tell Ravi anything at all? She knew exactly what he'd do. He'd put his arm around her shoulders and what else?—draw her toward him after she'd spoken. "*Meri achchhee Ma*," he'd say, and roll back his head, and the house would ring with his laughter.

# Great Guruji

**DEEPA, MY STUPID SISTER,** came to see me this morning. I don't know who to be more angry with—her or Arjun, the new servant boy Guruji has employed. Arjun let Deepa into the house even though I warned him only yesterday that I don't want to see her face ever again. When Guruji comes home, I will tell him about Arjun's disobedience. Arjun needs to be beaten. Fired actually. He never listens to me. He's slow in doing the work in the house. He's slow in the head, too, I think. Deepa told me Father is sick. Last month, of course, she lied that Mother was dying. Whose turn will it be next month? Deepa's, I suppose. As if I care about any of them now.

*Come home, Sangeeta. Come back to us. Father has forgiven you.*

Forgiven me for what, I'd like to know. For having found a great man like Guruji to teach me how to sing? For his having charged me not one rupee for my music lessons with him, for his taking good care of me, for doing more for me than they all could ever do? Just how many times need I tell Deepa I will never leave Guruji for anything in the world? And even if I should do such an unthinkable thing, what has given her the idea I will want to return to them, of all people? Deepa seems to have forgotten that day not even five months ago when Father, in one of his fits of rage, told me it would have to be Guruji or them. "Get out then and don't show your dirty face to us," he said when I made my choice. Words that still ring in my ears.

It is time for lunch, but I have no appetite. Since morning, I have been shuttling from room to room. Now my feet hurt. My back, too, hurts. I don't think I can lift myself from Guruji's bed. Were Deepa or Arjun to walk in this instant, I wouldn't have the strength to kick them out. What really annoys me is Deepa returned this morning in spite of my telling her only yesterday that Guruji and I are giving a concert this evening at Shanmukhananda Hall. She knows it is my first performance in public.

*Don't do that. Please don't do that. Father and Mother don't approve. Come back with me, Sangeeta. Before it's too late.*

What can be wrong with her? Too late for what, I want to know. I told Deepa today her visits are of no use. I simply will not go back home. Father may storm into Guruji's house again if he wants, and, like last time, drag me into the streets by my hair if he wishes. It will be useless. He will never win me over. Yes, he can heave me into his house, kick me in, but when he, Mother and Deepa are fast asleep, I will steal away as before and set out for Guruji's mansion. When they discover I have left them, they will be furious, I know, but do they know how furious *I* am with them? It is good and bad fate. That's how I console myself nowadays. On the one hand, I am blessed with a person like Guruji who has tremendous faith in me and has taken pains to train me for the song we will be singing together this evening, and on the other, I am cursed with this family that is pitted against me, set on ruining my career, jealous and unwilling to accept my impending success. Blood is thicker than water, they say. How that makes me laugh.

*But it is not right. Living in the house of a man nearly three times your age! People are talking, Sangeeta. They are whispering all kinds of things.*

So let them. I don't care. In love there are no ages. No rights. No wrongs. The whole world loves and respects Guruji (not counting three stubborn people in Bombay). How anyone can harbor ill feelings toward Guruji is beyond me. Father, Mother, and Deepa treat him like dirt only because he is a playback singer for Hindi film songs. What is wrong with that, I want to know. "No one in our family has sung in public," Mother once said. "Ours is a fine and respectable home. You are young and naive. You don't know what movie people are like. You don't know what goes on in the movie business. Your father wants you to be a surgeon or gynecologist. So stop singing love songs and study hard like Deepa. You are meant for much higher things." But what can be higher than singing with India's most famous singer, my dearest know-it-all mother? For your kind information, Guruji is not limited to only film songs. He has had fine training from Ustad Jamaluddin Khan in classical singing too. If his film songs become more popular, what can he do? Last year, Guruji gave sellout performances in London. Next year he may even take me with him depending on my progress, he said. That is why I am bent on doing well this evening at Shanmukhananda Hall. I have put in countless hours practicing the song. And Arjun, that fool, had to spoil everything by leading Deepa straight into Guruji's bedroom. "Madam, your big sister-ji is come to see you." Oof! I could have killed him.

I am nervous about this evening, about singing on stage before a sea of Guruji's fans. Guruji said if everything goes well, he will insist that I be the leading female playback singer in the next movie contract he signs. Imagine that. *Leading* playback singer. Not just any singer but a leading one. Did you hear that, Deepa?

*But Sangeeta, what else will he say? God knows how many women he makes such promises to. Think for a minute, then pack your things. Come home with me today.*

That's the kind of person my sister is. Nasty, suspicious, and ill-wishing. She doesn't know how many girls are dying to sing duets with Guruji, to see his name and theirs printed side by side on music albums. As if he is Lord Krishna, they are drawn to him by his music and flock around him like tittering *gopis* after his shows. And to think Guruji has chosen me to be his Radha, to be the one and only *gopi* he wants always by his side. "You make me feel young," he told me one night. "Since the day you came into my life, my songs have borne more meaning. My shows, too, have been super, mega hits. You have brought me luck. Don't leave me, my lucky charm." "Guruji, what a thing to say!" I said, and fell into his arms. "Leave you? What a thing to say." And today, as if to repay me for the luck I bring him, Guruji is giving me a chance on stage.

The song must go perfectly tonight. I have practiced it many times but I don't feel confident yet. That line in the third verse that goes "Phir lautenge hum sath-sath isi jahan," which follows Guruji's line, still gives me trouble. I fear I'll begin it off-key again. When I'm alone, the words flow beautifully, at the right key. But when I am singing with Guruji, my throat turns dry as we near that line. Guruji is well aware of this, and has helped me twice with the song these past three weeks.

"Relax your body and mind," Guruji said one morning. "Surrender to the music. Allow the words easy entry into your heart. Offer no resistance. Let my words reach in and fetch yours for you."

Like his millions of fans, I grew up listening to Guruji's songs on All India Radio. I bought his every album and listened to his songs on the gramophone all day. Father and Mother poked fun at me, at my adoration for Guruji. When we had visitors, they would lead them to my room to show them the albums and the newspaper and magazine clippings I had collected over the years. They would point at Guruji's photographs I had pinned on the walls. When I was younger, they would even ask me to sing his songs for the guests. How they would cheer and clap when I was done. Yet, when I declared last year I wanted Guruji to train my voice, God only knows what happened to all three of them. Mother said she was throwing all the albums away and I am certain she would have had I not first smuggled them out to my friends. One Sunday morning, I awoke to find Deepa in my room. She was humming a tune while standing on a footstool and ripping Guruji's pictures from the walls. That witch! I screamed and reached for her throat. I clutched her hair and bit her arm. She boxed me on the shoulder and scratched my neck and face. Father came howling into the room, waving the newspaper in the air. He tore us sisters apart and threw me on the bed.

"Stop this nonsense!" he roared at me. "What curse has befallen my home. I told Deepa to take that rubbish down. You are no longer a child."

"You people cannot stop me," I said, crying. "You cannot separate two people destined to be one." I covered my face and thought of Guruji. I pictured him suffering the way I was. I saw him waiting for me, far away, on a snow-clad mountain, his arms stretched skyward. I heard him calling my name and listening to the fading echoes in the valley below. I rose to my feet. I walked up to Father and folded my hands. "He is like Rama to me," I informed him. "Like Sita, I will follow him wherever he goes."

Father slapped me. I held my cheek and repeated my words. He slapped me again. "We are like Nala and Damayanti," I said as tears rolled down my cheeks. He slapped me some more. "We are like Satyavan and Savitri," I shrieked and he hit me again. We would have gone on and on like this had Mother not thrown herself between us.

"When I told you all these years that this one has problems, you wouldn't listen to me," Father yelled at her as he unbuckled his belt. Mother threw herself at his feet, weeping, and clung to his hand. He kicked her aside, flung the belt at my face, and stormed out of the room. I think *he* is the one who has problems, not I. And now Deepa has the nerve to ask me to come home because he is supposedly unwell. I know what they are up to. I don't believe them. They are cunning liars. All three of them.

I first saw Guruji on television many years ago. He and an interviewer were seated on the steps of a large house in Delhi. They were sipping tea, laughing and talking about something I couldn't understand. A blue shawl with a pink floral border lay slung over Guruji's shoulder. In the last five minutes of the programme, he sang a song with singer Chandrika, his wife, now long deceased. Guruji's hair fell furiously over his brow. With his hand, he kept sweeping the strands away. His hair has thinned considerably since then, and what remains now is long and gray. Every morning he lets me comb back the strands. I plaster them to his scalp, letting the curly ends gather over the nape of his neck.

Lately, Guruji has gained weight, especially around the waist. I've teased him about it, telling him that he's getting much too heavy for me, but he only laughs and becomes more playful. "On a man of my position and age, it is a healthy sign of success," he'll say and tickle me in the waist. "But Guruji, you were as successful two years ago, only not so heavy!" I always tell him, but he only chuckles more heartily, pinches my cheek, and crushes me in his arms. During such moments, I feel as though I have lived with him not for five months, but all my life. I feel certain then that we knew each other in our previous lives, that we were husband and wife in each.

For as long as I live, I will remember the day two years ago when I first saw Guruji in person. He was on stage in our college hall, performing for the Diwali programme. I missed all my classes that day. I stood in line for three hours and was the first to run into the hall. Every minute was worth the wait. The way Guruji sang! His words lifted my heart, his voice brought tears to my eyes. I felt as though he and I were the only people in the hall, as though he were singing his sad songs only for me. He wore a white silk *churidar-kurta* that glowed in the shower of light that was cast on him. Guruji swayed his head from side to side, especially between verses, his broad brow creasing with emotion, his fingers clenched hard. His gestures—fingertips touching one second, his hands bursting open like lotuses the next—have become popular all over India (except, of course, in one madhouse in the city). At one point that evening, Guruji's eyes met mine, a moment I will treasure forever. In that one instant, I felt his pain, understood all the longings about which he sang. I fully realized I was born to be with him, and the longer I delayed our union, the greater the injustice would be to us both. It was then, too, I heard a voice in my head. It said Guruji and I were two halves that must become whole. There would be hardships, it warned. But be brave, fulfill your duty, it said. When the voice grew louder I could bear it no more and decided to speak to Guruji about it after the show.

A disorderly crowd of students gathered backstage for Guruji's autograph after the concert. I was pushed to the fringes but that voice in my head said I, unlike the others, had a mission. So ignoring everyone's complaints, I elbowed my way to the innermost circle of Guruji's fans. What a splendid sight lay before my eyes. Guruji was seated on a leather armchair, his silk clothes shimmering, his legs crossed, his maroon leather slippers showing fine, gold embroidery. His many diamond rings sparkled when he signed his name. Each time Guruji returned someone's autograph book, a hush settled over us all. When he smiled, dimples appeared on his cheeks and the gold caps in his teeth caught the light in the room.

His bodyguards and assistants kept pushing us back. Of course, we protested but they barked at us saying Guruji was tired and needed his rest. I could hear the voice in my head, though, telling me I should stay. So I refused to leave and stood transfixed, feeling the force, the *shakti,* that in all her female might had brought us together. I understood in a moment why the *gopis* would desert their husbands and parents to be with Lord Krishna. I understood, too, why Sita followed Lord Rama on foot during his fourteen years of exile. When Guruji's dark eyes locked on mine, my heart leaped. He was also under the sway of the *shakti,* I realized. He was beginning to see we had been separated for long, we were intended to be one, that we were meant to travel through life's path hand in hand from then on. At last he signaled to his assistants, one of whom rushed to his side. With his eyes still on me, Guruji whispered into the assistant's ear. The assistant came up to me and said Guruji wished to speak to me. The crowd cleared and I stepped forward, my heart pounding in my chest. Everyone's eyes were fixed on me. I could see the students nudging one another. I could hear them asking the assistants why I wasn't being driven away. I approached Guruji and fell to my knees. I looked into his eyes. I joined my hands in reverence. His head eclipsed the light on the wall behind him. A soft, golden halo seemed to surround his face.

"You are?" he said.

"I am your Sita, your Radha, your Damayanti," I said without taking my eyes off him. "For eighteen years I have waited for this day. I wish to be your disciple. Teach me. Please be my guru. My life will bear meaning only if you do. Accept me as your pupil, Guruji."

He stared hard at me, gathering his brows. When he looked away, I lowered my head. He placed his hand on it. Then he drew my hands apart and lifted my chin. He held me by the tips of my fingers. He moved his thumbs around my palms in small circles. He leaned gently to one side and another assistant stooped at once to listen to him. Guruji whispered a long message to the man. The man whispered back. I realized they were discussing the *shakti,* about how there was nothing even Guruji could do to stop the *shakti*'s advance. When the assistant moved away, Guruji held my arms and, together, we rose to our feet.

"I will teach you," he said. My body trembled. My vision blurred. "My assistants will tell you more."

I could contain my tears no more. "Guruji!" I cried. "I have no money to pay you for lessons at this time."

He remained silent. "Money is not important to me," he said finally, addressing everyone in the room. "One day it is here, one day it is not. Devotion is the better payment."

He moved away before I could thank him. At once two men hurried toward me, one bearing a large, leather-bound book in his hands. While the other asked me questions, the man with the book wrote my answers. I felt light, suspended in midair. My heart soared, my ears hummed, and I shut my eyes to let the tears run down my cheeks and *kameez*. *Shakti* had brought us together. When I opened my eyes, the assistants and most of the students were gone. I stood there alone, moving my hands around my neck and my breasts, enjoying what became the happiest minutes of my life.

•  •  •

That rascal Arjun did it again. One would think after my scolding this morning, he'd have some sense. But what enters one ear leaves the other. I'm still shaking with rage. First, we have only about an hour left before we set out for Shanmukhananda Hall; second, with each passing minute I'm becoming more nervous about my debut tonight; and third, Guruji has not returned home although he promised to sing the song with me once before the show. And now, to add to these difficulties, Arjun barged into Guruji's bedroom without knocking, wearing a silly smile on his face.

"Mummy-ji is come now," he said, scratching his head. "Weeping outside."

I held my hands over my ears and screamed as loudly and for as long as I could. When I heard him chuckle, I grabbed the flower vase from Guruji's bedside table and hurled it toward his face. It would have exploded against his teeth but the clever rogue plucked it out of the air with one hand at the very last moment. He grinned at me like a circus clown and put the vase on the floor.

"What did I tell you about those liars?" I shouted. "Don't laugh, Arjun. Answer me. Does anything I say enter your head? Did I not tell you this morning they are all dead for me? Did I or didn't I say that? Stop smirking. Speak!"

"But," he said, veiling his smile with his hands, "this is mummy-ji. You say no to big sister-ji."

I stepped up to him (nearly tripping over this brand new sari I'm wearing to the concert) and slapped his dirty face for answering me back like that. One would think he would have left the room in shame, but instead the rascal simply stood there. He narrowed his eyes and his pupils became like two pinpoints of fire. He clenched his jaws and snorted like an animal. At first, I thought he was going to cry and beg for forgiveness. But to my surprise, he took his hand off his cheek and spat one wicked name after another at me. "Mental case," he said. "Cheap, two-paise whore," he called me too. Now I can hardly wait for Guruji to return and take his belt to him for those remarks. Maybe kick him out of the house. What does Arjun think? Does he think we can't find servants to fill his place? Imagine standing before me with his fists on his hips and his chest thrust out. Imagine saying all that nonsense to me. He said the monsoon frogs sound better than I do when I sing. He said whenever I practice in Guruji's bedroom, Guruji's musicians in the music lounge downstairs wrinkle their brows and press their palms against their ears. I was hurt and outraged by his deceitful words. How could he say that to me just hours before my concert? I raised my hand to claw out his eye but the crafty devil caught my wrist and flicked my arm aside. That is his most serious crime. For touching me, I'll have Guruji belt him ten more lashes.

He's gone from the room now—thank goodness—and I hope Mother has gone home too. I wonder what stories *she* had for me. Tonight, I suppose Father will come with his own share of lies. Crazy lot of people. They don't understand that a singer's first performance can make or break her. I'm quite tense as it is. It feels as though my stomach has been carved out. I feel faint and dizzy and want to bury my face in Guruji's pillow when I picture the crowds. And now, because of Arjun's insults, I can't bring myself to practice the song. I keep imagining Manu, Suresh Babu and Varma-ji rolling back their eyes and scrambling for ear plugs downstairs.

I can hear them tuning their instruments. Manu's tabla has been going *dha din din dha* all day. Guruji decided last week that Manu will play the tabla instead of Pankaj-ji, who has gone to his village in Karnataka for two months. It is a lucky break for Manu. Only fourteen years old and he's Guruji's percussionist today. Suresh Babu will be playing the guitar as usual. Varma-ji will take charge of the new electronic keyboard Guruji ordered from London. As for this harmonium sitting silently beside me? Guruji will play it himself. Just as the fans will want him to do.

Guruji has been called "Gem of the Music World" and "India's Heartbeat" and such things in popular film magazines over the years. Today, of course, he is best known as the "Golden Voice of India." "With the harmonium, the Golden Voice is at his best," *Stardust* magazine noted last week. Yet now the harmonium, like me, is patiently awaiting its master. I had Arjun bring it up from downstairs for one last rehearsal, but now there isn't enough time to sing even one verse of the song. We have less than a half hour before we leave for Shanmukhananda Hall and Guruji will have a thousand things on his mind. I must do well for him today. I will let his words reach in and draw mine out. Especially that troublesome line in the third verse.

Perhaps Guruji is at Shanmukhananda Hall, checking the stage lights and the sound equipment himself. He is picky about these things. In Poona last month he could not sing well because the lights were too bright. He entertained no requests from the audience that evening and ended the concert forty-five minutes sooner than planned. And what about that time in Madurai when a microphone squealed halfway through his most popular song? He turned crimson with rage, I remember. He sang the rest of the number with his fist pounding his brow, the harmonium sitting idly before the mike. When the squealing continued, he sprang to his feet and left the stage with Pankaj-ji, Suresh Babu, and Varma-ji in tow. Backstage, there were many apologies and tears and pleas from the organizers. Two young gentlemen even held Guruji's feet. But he listened to nobody and asked me to summon the Mercedes. He drank, smoked, and paced up and down the house for hours that night. His mood remained foul for days.

· · ·

We are only an hour into the concert but it feels like ten. The show started late as usual. When Guruji appeared on stage, however, the audience gave him a standing ovation and quickly forgave him the delay. Guruji is now singing his seventh song. Arjun and I are seated on stage, too, but in the dark shadows of Shanmukhananda Hall's thick, velvet curtains. Arjun has said not a word to me since afternoon. I have not bothered to talk to him and don't intend to unless he gets down on his knees, clasps his hands, and says he is sorry. I will ignore his vicious words of today. They are just words after all. Spoken by a bumpkin, for one thing. They will not harm my performance tonight, he should know. My song, the concluding piece of the show, will go off very well. Guruji told me he would introduce me as his dedicated and diligent student, as India's new voice. Then he would look at me and raise his hand.

That's when I have to walk up to him and seat myself by his side, remembering to keep a respectful distance between us. Then, only after the applause has subsided, must I greet the audience with joined hands.

What a resplendent picture Guruji and the others make on stage tonight! Guruji has worn his white *churidar-kurta* and looks like a thorough *nawab*. He sits cross-legged on a mattress strewn with roses and lilies. It is lined on three sides with fine poplin bolsters. While he sings, Guruji pumps the harmonium's bellows with his left hand. Meanwhile, the fingers of his right hand twist and dance over the keys. I am glad I brought all his rings with me, not to mention his gold chain that swings now like a thick rope from his neck. From time to time, Guruji throws up both hands, shakes his head in appreciation of the song's lyrics, and we all share his joy by shouting "Wah, wah!" in unison.

Manu, seated beside Guruji, has drawn much applause tonight. It is a wonder how his hands never seem to tire of thrumming the tabla. He sits with his back firm and erect, his fingers striking the tabla like a set of little drumsticks. Now they've become a complete blur and even Guruji is watching him play. Suresh Babu, also seated on the mattress, is strumming his guitar, while Varma-ji, rocking from side to side, is bent over the keyboard behind them all.

From the applause Guruji has been receiving after each song, it is clear that tomorrow's newspapers will be full of praise for the show. Though I can see only a dark corner of the hall from where I sit, I can feel the love for Guruji swelling in everyone's heart. Already there were two requests from the audience this evening and once, someone asked Guruji to repeat a song he'd just sung. "You are treating me like your CD," Guruji called back and everyone laughed with him.

Shanmukhananda Hall is resounding with applause now. Guruji has concluded the seventh song. How humbly he thanks the audience. How calmly he reaches for his glass of water. The applause is growing louder. I can tell people are rising to their feet, row after row.

"Brothers and sisters," Guruji is saying, motioning for everyone to be seated, "we come now to the final song of the evening . . ."

Final song.

It has come. My moment is here at last. I hear the crowd moan. Guruji is paying no attention to the protests because he knows I have waited too long. Sangeeta, here's your chance. Do it for Guru-ji. Show the world how well you sing. There is nothing to fear. "Laut aaye hain hum dono yahan" . . . no! . . . "Phir lautenge aap aur hum isi jahan." That line. How does it go? It doesn't matter right now. It'll come to me in the course of the song. But now my hands have turned moist with sweat. And my brow feels hot. And my heart is beating too fast. It is true: I never do anything right. Deepa always does. All I am good for is rubbing the family's good name in the dirt, Father will say again.

"This song is very special to me," Guruji is saying, "and comes from a recently released film."

There is no going back from here. Suresh Babu is tuning the gui-tar. Varma-ji is playing a light tune. Guruji is dabbing his brow with his kerchief. He's reaching for the glass of water again. Rise, Sangeeta. Let go of the chair. Don't you see? Guruji has turned to look your way.

• • •

Guruji is fast asleep in his bed, snoring small puffs into my hair. These concerts tire him. Two minutes ago, he was talking to me and now he is asleep. After a while, I will take his arm away from my waist and leave his side. Sleep will not come easily tonight. It is quiet outside. I can hear the city's buses rumbling far away. The window shows a clear dark sky. The moon lies alone in the corner. It is a thin crescent tonight, floating like a silver boat in a sea of stars. Once Guruji has fallen deeper into sleep, I will step outside for a walk on the lawns.

I am glad I tore up Deepa's letter. First I crumpled it but that didn't seem enough. So I ripped it into smaller and smaller pieces and flung them out the window. The envelope came sliding under the door of my room minutes after we returned from the show. Guruji had asked me to come to his room and I was preparing to leave when I saw it. I hurried to open the door. When I looked out, I saw Arjun tiptoeing down the staircase, his hand sliding along the balustrade. I called his name. He stopped and turned around. He stared at the car-pet, wringing his hands. I couldn't think of what to say. I assumed it was his own note of apology I held in my hand.

"Never mind. Go," I said, and shut the door.

*Father had a severe heart attack this evening,* the note began in Deepa's wretched handwriting. I skipped to the last line, which said, *Mother and I hope you will come home at least now.* I am ashamed of Deepa. I never thought she would go to such lengths. Imagine making up heart attack stories like this. Tomorrow she'll go further and send a note with Arjun that says Mother threw herself before an express train or that she herself has decided to drink rat poison. Crazy lot of people. "When I told you this girl has problems, you wouldn't listen to me," Father had said. Well, my dear father. Guess which girl has problems now.

Today my feelings of love for Guruji have doubled. When I entered his room, he was seated on the bed, talking on the telephone and yawning between sentences. He was discussing dates and venues for the next concert. Guruji motioned me to sit on the bed, but I remained standing. When he put down the receiver, he said, "You look ill. What is the matter?" I shook my head. He came up to me and held my chin. "Tell me. What is it? You are upset about tonight? Because of the song?"

I shook my head again. He held me close to him and led me to the bed.

"Then what is it, my little flower?" he said. "Tell me."

I covered my face. I broke down. I told him everything—Deepa's visits, Mother's visit, how they were torturing me daily with their trips and messages, how they weren't allowing me to concentrate on my singing. Guruji embraced me. I clung to him. "Oh my sweet one, why didn't you tell me sooner?" he said. I burst into more tears. I told him about Arjun and repeated all the names he called me.

Guruji clicked his tongue. "I will scold him first thing tomorrow," he said.

"You must beat him," I said.

"All right," he said, patting my back. "I will give him a sound beating, too. Happy?"

Later, after Guruji made two phone calls to his agents, he said he had indeed noted a change in my mood over the past few days. He said he suspected Deepa and the others were harassing me but decided it was a private matter and that his intervening would be unwise and wrong. "It is because you were so upset," he said, "I chose another song at the very last second to end the programme tonight. Forgive me."

I put my fingers to his lips. "Forgive *you*, Guruji? Please don't speak words that don't sound good coming from you."

"We will sing our song at the next concert," he said. "We will begin the show with you." He lifted my chin and kissed me many times. "Your father, mother, brothers, and sisters must realize that you are already a fine singer. They are ignorant and bitter people. They have no love for art. Don't waste your time thinking about them."

When Guruji said this, more tears flooded my eyes. I thought, there *is* somebody in the world after all who cares about me and my career. There is someone who wants me to have the best debut a budding singer could have. I felt bad that on our drive home from the concert I did not speak to Guruji. I stared out the window instead because I thought he considered me unprepared and had delayed my debut on purpose today. But being the observant man he is, he knew I was upset with Deepa and Mother, and he was simply sparing me further stress. My feelings for Guruji have now grown so strong that when he lay down on his bed, I quickly knelt on the floor and pressed his legs.

"You will have your big break in the next show," I heard him say. "Three weeks from today. Now stop what you are doing and lie down beside me, my good luck charm." I did as he asked. He drew me close to him. His silver curls fell on my cheek. "The next show will begin with our duet," he whispered into my ear. "I promise."

I began to laugh with happiness and rolled away from Guruji. I wanted to rise from the bed and run out of the house and into the starry night. I wanted to wake up the world by crying out Guruji's words.

"Guruji, where will the next concert take place?" I said, but there was no reply. "Guruji?" I said, and turned to him. He was fast asleep.

There is so much I want to ask about the next show. Where will it take place, I wonder. Singapore perhaps? London? New York? What would the capacity of the hall be? How much would the tickets cost? How many interviews must I give after the concert and to whom? Oh Guruji! I have fallen deeply in love with you and you have fallen asleep.

Just imagine: in Guruji's next show I will make my entrance on the stage and sit cross-legged beside him before all the rows of people applauding in the hall. Guruji will introduce me to his fans. They will clap louder to encourage me. I will adjust the microphone and tap it once or twice. Then before we begin our duet, I will make the announcement over the microphone that I have fallen in love with Guruji, that I am truly his loyal Radha, his loving Damayanti. The concert hall will burst with applause and Guruji, speechless with joy, will kiss my forehead and embrace me on stage.

*Our* duet, Guruji called it. *Our* song. I will sing it to myself on the lawns all through the night. In three weeks, he said. I can hardly wait. How wonderful it will be to have the lights trained on me at last. Manu will go *dhak din na, tak dhin na* on the tabla and Suresh Babu will pluck the guitar strings and Varma-ji will do wonders with his keyboard. Guruji will begin our song by playing the opening segment on the harmonium. The fans will go mad with joy. I will remain calm and professional, however. I will offer no resistance. Words will pour out from the depths of my heart. Two verses of our duet will pass. The third one will come and sail by, and in the end, all the people in the hall will be on their feet, clapping and cheering. "Wah! Wah!" they will cry and shower me with petals. "Sangeeta-ji, once more, once more," they will shout. Guruji will look at me, tears of joy pooled in his eyes. He will point me out proudly to the audience with both hands, or maybe with only one hand, for the other would surely be held over his heart. The applause will grow more thunderous, each round encouraging the next. Arjun, of course, will be drying his eyes with the stage curtains, regretful of his crimes. People will rush toward the stage with their autograph books and my heart will want to burst. But like Guruji, I will contain my excitement and join my palms together the way he does at the end of each show. While cameras flash away like Diwali fireworks and reporters shout one question after another at me, I will pretend not to see them, pretend not to hear their cries. Instead, I will bow gracefully. Bow first before all the fans who will be screaming and whistling and struggling to come closer to me, and then bow before Guruji—my Krishna, my Nala—the great man himself.

# Kulsum, Nazia, and Ismail

**LESS THAN TWENTY MINUTES** remained for the train from Lucknow to reach Bombay's VT station, the journey's long-awaited end. Passengers in Kulsum's compartment were bustling about, packing their things, hurling fiery orders at one another, the excitement in their voices risen to fever pitch. Children navigated themselves dexterously among the adults, as if working their way through a shifting maze, and raced each other from window to window to see the city growing furiously outside. The men in the compartment hauled down bags and trunks from the racks above; the women tidied their hair and arranged their clothes. Kulsum, traveling alone, didn't care about her appearance. She sat as she had all day, huddled in the corner, rocking gently to the throb and roll of the train. She rested her cheek on her fist, her head on one of the bars across the window. She was sitting in the direction the train was headed in the hope that would prepare her, somehow, for the new challenges piled ahead. Dusty air, warm from the day, rushed in to fill her clothes, to rake through her hair. Flying grit forced her to close her eyes from time to time. She shut them now and a tear ran into her fist. On opening her eyes, she saw, by the railway tracks, two shirtless boys waving good-bye.

She didn't have much luggage—only a small Samsonite suitcase lodged under her seat—and noted now (as she had each of the nine days she'd been away) that there wasn't much she was going back to. Ismail, her husband of—how many was it?—eight years, had telegrammed that he would meet her at VT Station, it being Sunday, the one day in the week his hardware store was closed. "Is that all that is written?" she'd asked the postman in Lucknow. He'd nodded and handed back the telegram. "If you don't believe, ask someone else to read," he said, frowning, pocketing her tip and setting off on his rounds. Ismail's offer had caused her no pleasure, no relief. If anything, it made her uneasy. She hoped he'd forget to receive her, that something would come up, that somehow the train could be delayed. She hoped there'd be no one she'd recognize at the station, that no one would call out her name. Now, as the toothless old man next to her rose from his seat, Kulsum wondered why she had bothered to leave Lucknow the previous day, what had made her leave her brother's house at all.

"Do you have a suitcase, lady?" the old man inquired as he pulled down his own suitcase from the rack. Kulsum continued to stare out the window. The man repeated himself and waited for her reply. She shook her head. Sighing, the man turned to someone in the compartment. "Throughout the journey she wept," he announced, running his fingers down his cheeks to demonstrate. "Didn't talk. Hardly moved. Ate nothing. Something has happened, maybe."

"Maybe," a woman replied. "Will you help me with my bag?"

The old man grunted. He set his suitcase by his seat and tottered away. Seeing him leave, Kulsum felt relieved. He asked annoying questions. Several times she'd sensed him staring hard at her. The engine released a shrill whistle and soon a railway crossing flew by. A boy came to stand by Kulsum's window. He stood on his toes, looked out, and turned away. The sky, Kulsum noted, was darkening quickly. A near-full moon, at times concealed, at times exposed between crammed buildings, hovered serenely in the distance. Kulsum shifted her gaze to the vacated seat before her. Who had just sat there? she wondered, and found to her surprise she couldn't remember. She returned her attention to the city roaring outside. A colorful shopping district had burst into view. Slender street lamps and loud movie billboards loomed over throngs of people scurrying like ants. Rows of open-fronted shops swung past Kulsum. The glow from their lights spilled into the train.

She was returning from Lucknow today to mark an anniversary; Ismail had broken the news to her after the Friday prayers exactly a month ago. They were seated on their balcony, she remembered. They were drinking tea, enjoying the breeze, watching families stroll on the street two stories below. She wore the pink cotton sari he often said he admired. He wore the brown *kurta* she'd bought him for Ramadan Eid. A drizzle had just commenced. Open umbrellas bobbed outside. She'd never forget how he sprang from the cane chair next to hers, his cup chattering in the saucer in his hand. Embarrassed, he put the cup down on the low table separating their chairs. He clasped his hands, as if in preparation for a plea. When he pressed them against his lips, she suspected something important, something difficult, was going to be said. She took a sip of tea. It tasted stronger than usual that evening. A bitter aftertaste lingered in her mouth.

"There is something I'm going to tell you," Ismail said, gazing at his teacup, then momentarily at her, his eyes narrowing finally on something down the street. He ran his fingers through his neatly trimmed beard. The coconut trees behind him rustled and swayed and, for one alarming instant, Kulsum thought of reaching for his arms and holding them against her breasts, for it seemed as though it were he who listed precariously from side to side. "You know I want children," he continued, not meeting her eyes, still stroking his beard. "My own. My life will mean nothing otherwise." His words, spoken poetically in Urdu, didn't startle her—she was, indeed, anticipating something like them—for she'd known for weeks, no! months, that something important was on his mind. She nodded understandingly, encouragingly. "What about *my* life?" she considered saying but sipped more tea instead. Didn't he think she wanted a child? She marveled at how steady her cup was in spite of what was to follow, the gold-rimmed saucer so stable in her hand.

"Kulsum," Ismail said and that was when she met his eyes. When had he last called her name? At forty-two he looked more handsome than ever, she thought: attentive dark eyes, hard angular features, short hair flickering like flames in the wind. "You see," he said softly, and noting no moisture in her eyes, not even a quiver on her face, but instead stoicism, an unforeseen composure, he folded his hands and went on. "You see, I have decided, after much thought, to take a second wife."

Two children clambered over the seat opposite Kulsum. A train was speeding on the adjacent tracks in the opposite direction, its engine hooting sharply. The children hung on to the window grill and peered out, taking delight in the thunderous gunfire the trains seemed to be exchanging. When the other train passed and the clangor ceased, they bounded away from the window, yelling somebody's name.

"Daughter, are you all right? Are you hungry? You have somewhere to go?"

The old man had returned to claim his seat and brought with him a fresh supply of questions. As before, he waited for her answer, refusing to sit unless she spoke.

Kulsum remained quiet for a while. Then she said, "Yes," surprising him with her voice, unrecognizable to even her ears. "Yes," she had said on the balcony that evening, too, for Ismail's words made sense to her. How else could he have an heir, someone to impart his life with meaning? Polygamy was practiced in many Muslim homes. Her great-granduncle in Lucknow had supported two families for much of his life. Her good friend Farida was betrothed to a married man several years ago. Kulsum had never feared her home would become like Farida's one day. But she should have, she thought. "Yes, I should have," she said, confusing the old man, who, now seated, had not said a word.

What were people saying about her today? That she was inadequate? That Ismail didn't love her anymore? Kulsum covered her ears. Now it seemed shortsighted of her to have kept the surgery a secret. "Just returned from Lucknow," she'd informed everyone five years ago but had lain instead in a small hospital in the city outskirts under a Dr. Solkar's care. Four weeks before her admission there, Dr. Solkar, a short, portly, and staid gynecologist, had unrolled charts before her in her office—outlines of women's bodies with detailed drawings overlaying areas where Kulsum felt ashamed to look. "Yes," she'd said then, too, nodding, cracking her knuckles, wondering when the session would end. She pretended to be able to read, to understand Dr. Solkar's medical phrases, to know exactly what the sketches on the glossy charts meant. She guessed the charts were linked to her erratic bleeding over the months. She realized the diagrams were leading to something grave.

"Uterine carcinoma," Dr. Solkar finally said, replacing the charts in a cylindrical tube with care. "Hysterectomy is advised. Excessive hemorrhaging in your case."

Kulsum smiled. When Dr. Solkar didn't go on, she leaned forward, gathering her brows.

"Sister, you cannot have children," Dr. Solkar explained matter-of-factly, in simple words at last, and then she understood what the pictures had said, what the day's session was about, what the impending operation entailed. She remembered she felt nothing at first and that she clamped her mouth and crinkled her face to force out tears, for that had seemed the appropriate thing to do. Ismail was summoned from the adjoining room. He barged in and stood behind her. She realized as soon as she saw his face he'd known all along, that he and Dr. Solkar had arranged to break the news to her this way. She turned away from him. She folded her arms. He placed his hand on her shoulder but she pushed it away.

The wedding would be over. It was to take place last Tuesday. The other woman would be in the house. Everything would be new, different, rearranged. Kulsum wiped away a tear. There would be a room in her home she could not enter now, there would be a part of Ismail she would never know. And when children would follow— surely, a whole string of them—how much weaker would her say in the house become? Kulsum clenched her fists. Her chest burned with rage.

"There is no need to go," Ismail had said when she was leaving for Lucknow nine days ago. She was at the door, the Samsonite in her hand, her taxi, hailed from the balcony, honking in the street. "You are needed here," he said. "Don't go like this. Stay." Sighing, she held back her tears and left the flat. He followed her down one flight of stairs, pulling at her hand. "Let me come with you to VT," he said. She tried to work her arm out of his. "At least eat something before you go." She shook her head. "Tell me when you will return."

She had given no thought to returning but conceded then she would eventually come back. Where else could she go? Her brother couldn't keep her forever. His house had little walking space; his family was growing, his wife being again with child. He worked as a salesman in a shoe store tucked in a narrow lane in Lucknow. "Brother will send you word," Kulsum said, and Ismail released her hand.

VT station's high roof, buzzing with pigeons, gradually pulled under the darkened sky. Tall windows filed past; tube lights and fans leaned from billboard-plastered walls. The passengers in Kulsum's compartment were on their feet and queuing before the exit. The old man who'd sat beside her was gone. The luggage racks were picked clean. Kulsum looked out the window. A sea of people stood inches from the train. Even before the train groaned to a halt, an army of turbaned coolies climbed aboard and scrambled for luggage. People on the platform craned their necks to scan the arrivals. Some people were embracing, others were waving, laughing, or crying out names. Loudspeakers made an announcement that was barely audible above the noise. From outside the station rose a chorus of car horns.

Ismail was not to be seen. He had not come, perhaps. Stretchers and wailing ambulances flashed through Kulsum's mind. She leaned into the window and pressed her cheek against the grill. Hastily, she searched the crowds. Coolies were balancing columns of suitcases on their heads, baskets of fruit on their hips. Perhaps he was standing elsewhere. There were so many people, so many compartments after all. When, minutes later, the crowds began to depart from the train, Kulsum was alone in the compartment, wringing her hands. It was not like him to send a telegram and not meet her. Kulsum's throat felt dry. She shifted in her seat. Something was wrong, she decided as she prepared to leave the train.

She stopped and sat still. On the platform, a familiar-looking young woman—slender, elegant, dusky-complexioned—was threading her way through the crushing crowds. Men were stealing glances at her as she headed towards Kulsum's compartment. She paused at a nearby window and looked in. She wore a shiny green *salwaar-kameez*. Her plaited black hair was thick and reached the small of her back. How beautiful, Kulsum thought. Younger and more fashionable than she appeared in her photograph. Without thinking, Kulsum waved. The woman saw her. She approached Kulsum's window. At once, she said *salaam*. She wore a gold nose ring, a large pink rose behind her ear. "He could not come. Not feeling well," she said softly, with sincerity. Like a curious child, she peered into the train, curling her fingers around a bar.

Kulsum's heart pounded. She tried to smile. As she looked into the woman's kohl-lined eyes, she hoped she would kindle a sisterly fondness for her over time. It would be hard, she knew. Already sour thoughts were coming to her mind. How would she live day after day with the woman, this girl framed neatly in the window? Kulsum groped for her suitcase. Her fingers clutched its handle. She rose to her feet and prepared to ride home with Nazia, her husband's new wife.

— II —

It seemed to Nazia the wall clock had been reading twenty to six for quite a while. She was lying on her side on the living-room floor, her head against the settee, the old radio an arm's length to her right. She wondered if the clock had stopped working, joined forces with the world that was teamed up against her. She lowered the volume of the radio. The clock was ticking, she decided, and cranked up the volume again. A patriotic song, a big hit of three years ago, was on. "O workers of India," singer Raj Mohan sang, "come, let's touch our foreheads to the soil, to fertile Motherland." Nazia switched the set off. The words were unnerving her. She had entered the living room no more than ten minutes ago, having spent a good part of the day pacing in her room. She could stand it in there no more. The walls, she'd felt sure, were closing in on her. She read the wall clock again. Twenty to six, it read as before.

Ajay would be coming at six. He said he'd wait under the coconut trees three buildings away. When she emerged with her suitcase, he would drive his scooter up to her. Quickly, she would hop on and they'd be off, to Aurangabad, where a relative of Ajay's friend had arranged provisional lodgings. "Better come out at six," Ajay warned when they held hands at the far end of Chowpatty Beach three afternoons ago. "They will have the police looking for us in no time." She nodded, placing his hand in the gulf between her breasts. "I hope I'll have the courage," she wanted to say, but assured him instead she'd be there.

Nazia studied her trembling hands. She balled her fists. She was directly below the whirring ceiling fan. Warm air circulated slowly in the room. The curtains leading into the balcony yawned while the heat from outside seeped in through the walls. Nazia's neck and arms glistened with sweat. Her clothes—a pink satin *salwaar-kameez*—lay damp against her skin. She thought of getting up to speed up the fan but something held her to the floor, gnawed away at her strength and will. She read the wall clock once again. She drew up her knees and set her chin on them.

She wished she had never been born. Never never never been born. She'd just been married, she told herself. She was supposed to be happy. Instead, she was questioning fate, weighing the consequences of escape. Fickleness had been tormenting her since the escape plan was drawn with Ajay two weeks ago. One moment she'd be feeling like smashing glass or clawing some delicate fabric to shreds, and then suddenly, as though she were riding down the crest of a wave, she'd feel fine, her mind having wandered to a calmer place. Absently, Nazia switched on the radio. A film song was fading to its end.

By Allah's mercy, First Wife was in her own room. It was just as well she kept to herself each day. Whenever she came out, she made Nazia restless. First Wife's hair was loose and straggled over her face. Her sari was always ruffled. She said such strange and silly things. "I am like your older sister," she insisted one day, her fingers kneading Nazia's palm, an unsettling smile flickering on her face. "I know there is a good, loving person inside you," she dared to offer last week. Didn't she know Nazia didn't care if she, First Wife, lived or died, or that she, Nazia, remained silent and respectful in her presence only because age and rank dictated she did? Didn't the woman realize by now Nazia would never in a thousand years take a liking to her? What a creature this First Wife was. Disingenuous in her behavior. Fulsome and sugary with her words. Nazia lifted her hands and fanned open her fingers as though to ward off images of First Wife stacking before her mind. She'd had enough of her. Enough enough enough.

As for Husband, what was there to say? His brow was perpetually furrowed. Not once had she heard him laugh. Even when he was with her, sprawled on the bed, his mind was far away. He frightened her, this truck of a man. The sight of his burly build crippled her voice. The image of his sharp, gold-filled teeth seldom left her mind. When she pressed his legs some evenings, her arms felt rigid, under scrutiny of his heaving, rotund belly. When he moved his fingers up and down her cheek, she could hardly breathe. Of course he did not love her. She wondered if he loved even First Wife.

The man was married to his hardware store. Hinges, handles, and screws swam in little schools in his mind. She could picture him pulling down the corrugated shutters of the store at day's end, his briefcase by his feet, his kerchief dabbing his eyes. "My beloved shop, I'm sorry I have to leave you now," Nazia imagined him saying. A knot would build in his throat, choking him on the local train home. Oh how wicked she was being today. The poor old beast. He would come home in a few hours, weary and spent, to find her gone. Flown out of his stifling cage. Nazia laughed. He wouldn't blame her when he unfolded the note on his pillow. Perhaps he would even understand. Who would not flee from here, he might ask when he'd put her letter down. Of the twenty days since First Wife came back from wherever she'd gone, Husband had spent eight nights with Nazia. Or seven and some more, to be correct, for what about that night when, feigning sleep, she saw him leave her side and steal out of her room, slippers in hand? He'd gone to First Wife, no doubt. Now he could spend all his time with her. In a short while—twelve minutes—Nazia would be unshackled, free, out of his hands and fleeing the city.

Had Ajay's mother accepted her, none of this would have happened. Nazia would be in their home today as daughter-in-law, attending to the family as she had when she assisted in their cooking, scrubbed their utensils, and washed their clothes. They paid her well. They let her eat leftovers in their kitchen, even allowed her to take some home to her father. Last *Diwali*, Ajay's mother, a petite wiry woman, presented Nazia with an old sari of hers. "Take, take," she said. "Don't feel shy. It will look nice on you." She would have been less giving had she known her only child Ajay, a medical student, a poet, gathered Nazia into his arms earlier that day. Nazia was pressing his shirt when he came to stand beside her.

"I didn't sleep last night," he said, drawing her toward him, his breath fluttering on her lips. She stood motionless, her hands pushing back his chest. She tried to pull away but he held her by the waist. "Speak to me," he said. "You love me. Don't be afraid." She said nothing, having heard such lines from vendors and roadside cobblers on her mile-long walk to work each day. "Emotions speak for the God inside us," Ajay told her the next day. "Give Him rein." He sat her down on the armrest of a chair and explained the virtues of being open, honest, unashamed of true feelings. "Touch me wherever you wish, whenever you want," he said. Two days later, she did. Thereafter, they met in the evenings at an abandoned bus stop in Mahim and drove on his scooter to Band Stand and Worli Seaface, he reciting romantic couplets against the wind, she covering her face with her veil. And now, in minutes, they'd be on his scooter again, her cheek pressed to his back, her arms locked around his waist.

"This is All India Radio," a man's voice boomed, stirring Nazia from her thoughts. She clicked the radio set off. Ten minutes to six, the clock read. She rose to her feet. She ran down a list in her mind: clothes, money, two pairs of sandals, folding umbrella, small mirror, two *parathas,* two guavas, four bananas, a towel, hairbrush, soap. Yes, everything was packed; she was all set to go. She proceeded to the balcony, grimacing as she waded through the heat. A woman in the opposite building was draping a sari over a sagging clothesline. She paused to look at Nazia. She smiled. Nazia looked away. There was neither need nor time for nonsense like that. She flicked her eyes up and down the street. Few people were in sight. It occurred to her she had better not stay outdoors. She stole a glance at the woman with the wash. She was still smiling, nodding affectionately now. "Yes, Inspector sahib, she stood on the balcony," Nazia imagined her saying. "I saw her clearly. I smiled many times at her. But she didn't smile back." Nazia's heart beat faster. The woman was waving at her now. Just what did she think Nazia was? An exhibit? Some pitiful child? Soon she would find out. Along with Husband and First Wife, this woman, too, would know what Nazia, half their age, could do. She turned her back to the buildings and retreated indoors.

"Say yes to his offer, Daughter," Father had pleaded one night about two months ago. He dissolved into tears which, since Mother died, came easily to him as though on demand. "My days are few. I must see you settled before I go." He wept like a boy, patting her head with his gnarled fingers. His *kurta,* reeking of liquor, had fresh stains of *dal.*

Earlier that day, Husband had come to their one-room house. He sat cross-legged with Father on the straw mat and explained his case, point by point, counting his sentences on his fingers. Nazia, peeping from behind the curtain that partitioned the house, heard all he had to say. He was an honest businessman. He worked hard, six days a week. His shop was small but in a busy part of town. He earned well. He was buying a color TV soon. The stoves of his house were lighted each day. But his wife, as was Allah's wish, was childless, he said, raising his hands and shaking his head. Nazia saw her father nod understandingly, compassionately. He clicked his tongue in sympathy. He patted Husband's arm. He knew what Husband meant, he said. No need to go on. At the door, a monthly allowance to Father was offered, bargained, shaken hands on.

Of course, Husband had come briefed on her situation. He feigned obliviousness, expertly in fact, but Nazia read him easily. He was aware of how Ajay's mother had stormed into the tenement block one evening, screwing up her nose and chopping the air with her hands. He'd been told of how she had sacked Nazia and demanded to know what had made her think she'd take in a non-Hindu like Nazia for a daughter-in-law, and—*Hai Bhagwan!*—a Muslim servant-girl at that. Husband knew, too, of how she'd cursed all the way to her car, of how she'd ranted about "gold-digging" girls vying like vultures for her son.

Yes, Husband *knew.* Men like him kept a watchful eye for scandals to see what gains could be distilled from them. He'd come with his offer as a result, to rescue her, to restore her good name. But Nazia would not be fooled. By marrying her, he thought he had won, didn't he? But did he know nothing had changed between her and Ajay? Did he know they held hands and kissed in secluded parks even now?

Nazia entered her room. The curtains were drawn, the lights off. The note lay folded on the pillow. She moved her hands in circles over the wall. She realized she wouldn't see the room again. The house—her eyes danced to the window, the bed, the dressing table, the ceiling—was the best one she had lived in. Who could tell what they would find in Aurangabad? Nazia sighed. Was she being foolish by leaving? She was secure here, there was food to eat, water didn't need to be carried to the house in buckets from outside. She sat on the bed beside the suitcase. How would the scooter carry two people and her suitcase? And Ajay's valise as well? Nazia clasped her hands. She rested her forehead on them and closed her eyes.

The doorbell rang. She sat bolt upright, her fingers poised like claws on the suitcase. Had he come up to the house? What was the time? She sprang from the bed, sending the suitcase crashing to the floor. She raced into the living room. The clock read a minute short of six. Hadn't she told him she'd be there? Didn't she say several times she couldn't wait downstairs with a suitcase in her hand?

Nazia flung open the door. An old woman, shriveled and spine-bowed, stood smiling outside, leaning against the wall.

"Salaam, Second memsahib. Come to collect money for milk," she said.

Nazia felt faint. Images of screeching vehicles formed and splintered in her mind. "What milk?" she said.

"What milk?!" the woman said, and cackled with laughter. "Second memsahib is sweet and funny. *Arrey*! What else but the milk I leave outside this door, right here, every morning at five!"

Nazia stared at her. "Come tomorrow. I have no money," she said and closed the door. The doorbell rang again. Nazia cursed and swung open the door.

"First memsahib will pay," the woman said, her face long and serious now. "She keeps full account."

Nazia proceeded to close the door. "First memsahib is not at home," she said.

The woman thrust her hand forward. "But," she said, her toothless smile returning, her eyes lighting up, "First memsahib is right here." She pointed to Nazia's left and began to titter like a child.

Nazia turned around. Kulsum stood behind her, rummaging through her purse. Nazia glanced at the wall clock. It was six. Her pulse racing, she slipped away and hurried down the passage that led to the bedrooms. When she got to her room, she shut the door, placed her ear against it, and listened. Kulsum coughed. The milk woman spoke. The front door closed. Seconds later, Nazia cracked open her door to listen. Kulsum was still in the living room. She was blowing her nose. Nazia's heart sank. She cursed the milk woman in her mind. "Drown yourself in your milk and die!" Perhaps now the best thing would be to go down to the street without the suitcase, and signal to Ajay she'd be late, that he should wait longer. Suddenly, the woman with the wash surfaced in her mind. "Yes, Inspector sahib, I saw her run to the gate. She made signs to someone and ran back upstairs." Nazia clutched her forehead. She'd risk it, she decided. She slipped out of the room and tore down the hallway. She found Kulsum seated on the couch in the living room, her fingers pressed to her lips. When their eyes met, Kulsum rose to her feet.

"Sister, why did you say I was not at home?" Kulsum said. She sniffed into her kerchief. Her eyes appeared red and swollen. "Please tell me. Why do you pretend that I don't exist?" She stepped forward and stood between Nazia and the door.

Nazia worked her way around Kulsum. It was past six o'clock.

"I am talking to you so nicely and you are walking away from me," Kulsum said, holding Nazia's elbow. "What have I done? Why don't you like me? I must know to improve. I am speaking to you. Please turn around and at least look at me. I have nothing against you in my heart, Sister. I wish you well. I want us to live peacefully together. But first we must talk to each other, don't you think? But how can we when you run to your room and lock your door each time you see me, when you eat at odd hours only to avoid me? At dinnertime, you pretend I don't exist. He may not notice but I do. I never know what you are thinking. Don't ignore me like this because it hurts. Come, let's sit on the couch. Come, Sister. Please."

Nazia wrenched her arm out of Kulsum's. She opened the front door and flew down the stairs. What should she tell Ajay? How much longer, he would want to know.

"Sister!" Kulsum screamed from the house. "Where are you going? Listen to me."

When she reached the building gates, Nazia saw the woman with the wash peering down from the balcony. Nazia stepped out on the pavement, barefoot, and looked down the road. There was no one on a scooter under the coconut trees. She bit into her fingernails. Was he late? Had he waited, decided she had backed out, and returned home? That couldn't be. She was only a few minutes late. Perhaps he was apprehended while leaving his house. They'd caught him with rolls of money in his pockets. Perhaps he was in a van sirening towards a police station now. There, they would beat him with a belt, slap his face, hurl him hard against the wall, punch him again and again in the chest . . .

"Come upstairs, Sister. Don't be childish. We'll begin again. All is forgiven."

Nazia turned around. Kulsum was puckering her lips, making soft kissing sounds as though to coax a cat. She reached for Nazia's elbow. Nazia gritted her teeth. She started to speak but her teeth would not unlock. In despair, she raised her hand to strike at Kulsum's face but then drew it back to cover her own mouth instead. Suddenly, she began to cry. She drooped her shoulders and sank her face in her hands. "No!" she told herself but tears proceeded to gather in her eyes. "No," she said again, crouching little by little, until she was down, sitting squarely on the ground.

— III —

"I'll take more," Ismail said, and at once Kulsum dug the serving spoon deep into the bowl near her to heap his plate with rice. "This is a home," Ismail went on in his gravelly voice as though the two ideas were closely related. "I come home tired from work each day and what do I find? Your long faces. Enough of this. Put *dal* on the rice." Nazia obliged, the steaming *dal*-bowl being closer to her.

They were seated cross-legged on the living-room floor, forming a triangle on a mat Kulsum spread open at dinnertime each evening. Plates and bowls, bordered with intricate flower designs, lay arranged before them. Nazia had been silent all through the evening (she usually was) and Kulsum had her eyes locked on her own plate for the most part (she usually didn't). To Ismail's exasperation, this was how dinners had gone for three days in a row.

"All right. Tell me in few words. What has happened between you two?" he said. "Kulsum, you speak first."

Nazia rose to her feet. Knots of rage tightened somewhere in Ismail's chest. He considered pulling Nazia down by the hand but decided against it, remembering he'd sworn not to touch one wife in the presence of the other. He didn't know what would follow if he did, but suspected it would be unsavory. He certainly wasn't going to find out today. After eleven hours of work, during which a loyal client had returned purchases worth Rs. 4,700, he was in no mood to attend to bickering. Let her go if she wants to, he decided, as he saw Nazia whip across the room. Coarsely, he mixed the *dal* into the rice on his plate with his fingers.

What was the matter with the two of them? Why couldn't they just . . . get along? Guldip Singh had returned the brass hinges for the first time in sixteen years. He'd given no reason. "Not right for me," he said, not meeting Ismail's eyes. Ismail demanded to know what was not right with the hinges—were the dimensions off? weren't they working as smoothly as the hundreds he'd purchased in the past?—but Guldip Singh only smiled sheepishly and shrugged. "Not good for this hotel I am working on," he said, tapping his fingers on the tall column of boxes his helpers had carried into the store. "Why 'not good'?" Ismail asked as he worked out a refund, but Guldip Singh offered no more. The bastard. For sixteen years he'd found the hinges "par-fect, ax-cellent," and suddenly they were not good for the lousy third-rate hotel he was furnishing this time. "Go to hell," Ismail muttered under his breath as Guldip Singh was leaving the store. Guldip Singh may have heard him, for he stopped and turned around. Ismail reached for the telephone and punched numbers at random. Then, as soon as Guldip Singh was out of sight, he slammed the receiver down.

"You should speak to her," Kulsum said as she gathered the rice grains on her plate into a little mound. "She does not speak to me. She pays me no respect. Only if you beat her good and sound, she will learn to obey." She rose to her feet with her plate in her hand. "See? She didn't take even one dish to the kitchen sink, not even her own plate. She thinks I am her father's servant. I will not take hers today."

"Take it now. Enough of this."

Kulsum made a face and kneeled to collect the dishes. "She has no care about what people say," she said. "She goes out every afternoon, Allah only knows with whom and where. Just because she studied up to class four she thinks she is better than me. She thinks she need not tell anyone where she goes to loaf." Kulsum rose, balancing two bowls and several plates in her hands. "She'll bring ruin and shame to this house. Mark my words. If I were you, I would teach her our customs." She retreated into the kitchen, cursing her backache.

Ismail didn't feel like eating. There was food on his plate and he was still hungry but he pushed it away. He had not reckoned matters would molder like this. His late uncle in the village had two wives. Everything worked so smoothly there. The women got along well in their quarters, the *zenana;* the men were content to spend their time in the *mardana*. He remembered how, when he stole into the *zenana* as a boy, his two aunts fought over him and hugged him together like one woman with four loving arms. But here it was turning out . . . differently. Naturally, there was no *zenana* or *mardana* in his small, modern, two-bedroom flat. As a result, the air was constantly sparking with tension, Ismail thought. He furrowed his brow. The wives ought to be more than pleased with his arrangements. What more did they want from him? One, he'd laid down the rule that they would have dinners together, an unthinkable proposition in his uncle's house. Two, he wasn't stopping them from moving freely in the flat. Three, he hadn't outlawed their going to the cinema together or even to the local market once in a while. And what was he asking in return? Only that they live amicably and leave him alone. Ismail rose from the floor and went, empty-handed, to the kitchen. He found Kulsum stacking the sink with dishes. When he approached her, she moved aside to let him wash his hands.

She cleared her throat. Ismail ignored her. She cleared her throat again and spoke. "The new boy I employed last week said his mother is ill," she said. "So he will not be coming to work tomorrow. Who will buy the food, who will cook it, I ask. Tell me who is going to wash all these pots and dishes piled like the Qutb-Minar here? *I.* That is who. No one else does anything in this house. That one does not lift a thing. But why will you believe me? You don't care."

Ismail stared at her. Kulsum had never spoken to him like this. It was as though someone else had returned from Lucknow, one who was becoming an incensed stranger with each passing day. He wiped his hands with the napkin she offered. "I had a difficult day," he said, examining his fingers for stains. "A good client of many years returned a large consignment of materials this morning. Later I learned he took his order to Pran Lal & Sons in the next lane. Tomorrow someone else will, too, if you don't keep quiet. Because of your quarrels, I don't have peace of mind and the business is suffering. Enough of your troubles for today."

Kulsum played with her bangles. "As if I have peace of mind here," she said, twitching her mouth corners. "I talk to her and what does she do? She shows her back to me, her elder. I knock on her door, I call out, 'Sister! Sister!' but she never replies. The other day she told the milk woman I don't live here anymore. And then—you won't believe this—she ran down to the middle of the street, without even covering her head, and in front of all the neighbors she—"

"Enough, I said!" Ismail yelled, raising his hand like a policeman to halt the battery of her words. He turned away from her. "Do whatever you want. Both of you."

Later, ensconced in the cane chair in the balcony, Ismail felt alone. The business had begun to slack off over the past month. Two of his best salesmen were requesting more pay. A box of aluminum towel rods disappeared from the store some days ago. Now a collapsible steel ladder he had been painstakingly working on was soon to be marketed by Pran Lal & Sons. The image of Ranjit, his new employee, took shape in his mind. Was the young upstart pilfering from the store? Selling goods illegally from his home? Perhaps even selling Ismail's ideas in the next lane? Did Ranjit have something to do with Guldip Singh's decision today? In the shop this morning, he'd caught them looking obliquely at each other in a way that suggested there was some sort of an agreement between them. Ismail rose from the cane chair. He took a deep breath. He gripped the balcony railing. He would decoy Ranjit and catch him red-handed. Then he'd show the rascal what sort of boss he was dealing with. Into the busy street he would drag him and smash the scoundrel's knuckles against a dozen passing cars until his rotten, thieving hands fell to pieces from his wrists. Ismail drummed the railing with his fingers. Sloppiness he could tolerate perhaps. Dishonesty, never.

He fixed his attention on the street below. The street lamps were on, showering dusty, yellow light on the few people still milling about. A group of teenage boys sat idly on the building wall, swinging their legs, teasing young women walking past. A rickety bullock cart entered the street, groaning, hauling slabs of sawdust-covered ice. A garland of bells around the ox's neck jingled merrily in the warm night air. Ismail listened intently. The driver was clicking his tongue. He had his arm around a little girl sitting beside him. She was instructing the ox, prodding it along with a stick of sugarcane.

Ismail's heart swelled. It was the longing for such moments between father and child that had made him take a second wife.

Over the years this yearning had grown, at times intensifying to a cutting pain. Without a vent to his parental desires, without the happiness of listening to heartbeats in one's own creation, could fulfillment be gained? What was the use of anything? He swept his eyes around—the buildings, the street, the trees, the sky. Without children, when he died, no part of him would still pulse with life. Ismail studied his hands. Ephemeral and futile. He'd been given life, a body, a chance. He *had* to return the favor. Or the labor invested in his making, in the nurturing of his soul, would go to waste. It would be a disservice to his lineage, to Almighty Allah Himself. Ismail lifted his eyes to the sky and marveled at the stars. They, too, must multiply somewhere, he thought.

About a year ago he'd dreamed he was dying. In the dream he was sprawled on his back, his legs lifeless, a stack of old photo albums towering on his right. There was a single moon-washed cloud in the sky. It rocked gently from side to side. The sky was dark, he remembered. Silent. It rotated by slow degrees. Then just as the pictures from the albums rose and spiraled up to the cloud, gray sand dunes crowding the horizon undulated toward him.

He'd awakened, sweat beading his brow. Roughly, he shook Kulsum awake. "What? what?" she said, sitting up, her eyeballs gleaming like marbles, her hands crossed over her heaving breasts. "Nothing," he told her, looking away. "Go to sleep." When, in seconds, she did, he concluded he was alone, even with her by his side; at forty-one his life was a hollow, silent shell. He listened to Kulsum breathe. He scanned the room in the dark. He decided then, lying down gently on his side, that to impart meaning to his life he would have to wed again.

He turned to leave the balcony now. He entered the living room, and stopped. It seemed as though a long time had passed. The floor was cleared of dishes and utensils. The walls and the furniture were silent, yet in communication with him. Ismail stood still. He was considering sitting on the sofa, to appreciate the moment, when, from the kitchen, Kulsum entered the living room, wiping her hands with the loose end of her sari.

"Will you take tea?" she asked. Ismail brushed aside her offer with a quick handwave, hoping that would send her away. He waited in silence, he took a step back, but the tranquility he'd just sensed was gone. He steered himself around and reentered the balcony that now seemed fuller of the night. He heard Kulsum's footfall behind him. He saw her settle into the cane chair on his right. Briefly, she met his eyes. He could tell she was angry. She wouldn't leave him be, he realized, unless he heard what she had to say.

"What is it?" he said, sighing.

Kulsum cleared her throat. It occurred to Ismail she had rehearsed what she was going to say. "A young, very handsome man came up to the house this morning," she said, scratching at the chair's armrest with her fingernail. "To meet her, of course."

Ismail narrowed his eyes. He took a step toward her.

"She never answers the door, so naturally I had to. Even before I could ask, he told me he was her cousin. Of course he was lying. I saw right through his act. But I asked him to wait. I shut the door. I went inside and knocked on her door. I told her a cousin had come. Then I returned to my room. Minutes later, I heard them arguing in the living room. Something about a scooter in an accident. I don't know. At one point, I think she slapped him. Then I heard her cry. There was some talk about a journey on a train. They are planning to travel somewhere. When I could not hear them, I left my room. I entered the living room and found them gone. You should ask her who this man is and what he wants and how he can come up to our house in broad daylight. What will neighbors think of you if she runs away with him? We will lose whatever respect that's left. If you don't teach her our ways, shame will fall on us. If you want, I will teach her. Give me permission."

Ismail considered her words, her tone. Not once in their eight years together had he heard her speak like this. A change had come over the demure woman he had set eyes on for the first time on the day of their arranged marriage. Someone else sat before him now, hissing words of venom.

"If she is beaten once, she will learn fast," Kulsum was saying.

"Go inside," Ismail said, keeping his voice stern. "You are tired."

Kulsum rose. A door clicked shut somewhere in the house. They exchanged glances. Ismail bolted into the living room. Kulsum followed. Nazia emerged from the inside passage, a small suitcase in her hand.

"What is going on?" Ismail said. "Where do you think you are going with a suitcase this late at night?"

Nazia did not answer. She set the suitcase down. Eyes downcast, she stood stock-still.

"She is going wherever she goes every day," Kulsum said.

"Go inside," Ismail instructed Kulsum.

Kulsum proceeded past Nazia and into the passage. She hung in the shadows in silence.

Ismail held Nazia's arm. "It is late," he said. "You are angry now. In the morning you will feel better." His eyes locked on Kulsum's but he didn't let go of Nazia's arm. Kulsum turned around and proceeded toward her room.

Nazia twisted her arm to free it from Ismail's grip. "Let me go," she said, her face contorted with pain.

"Enough. Go inside."

"Let me go. I will not live with her."

Ismail dragged her into the passage. Ahead, Kulsum slammed shut her door. Nazia struggled to free herself. Her sandals drummed the floor. Suddenly she fell and slipped from Ismail's arms. She sprang to her feet and darted into the living room. Ismail ran after her. He locked his arms around her waist and pulled her back. She fell against his chest. He spun her around. He clamped his hands on her shoulders and drilled his gaze down her almond-shaped eyes. At first he thought she alone was trembling, but then he found his hands were shaking as well. She was grunting, breathing hard. Suddenly her head scarf slipped to the floor and a fragrance, that of lilies, rose to him. Without another thought, he drew her closer to him. Nazia gave a sharp cry. Ismail let go of her and watched her cover her face with her hands.

"I cannot love you," she said, speaking into her palms. She lifted her face from her hands and locked her fingers together. "I beg you. Please let me go."

He slapped her so hard she reeled back and collapsed on the couch. He stood open-mouthed, his hand stinging, not sure what had occurred. He hadn't intended to strike her. He had intended to touch her earrings, her cheeks, her lips. He saw her leave the couch and reach for her suitcase. He saw her wipe her tears with her forearm. He tried to step up to her but his feet were riveted to the floor.

He watched her reach for the front door and open it. When, in moments, she was gone, he cried, "Nazia!" and shot after her. Down a flight of stairs, he caught up with her and grabbed her hand.

"Where are you going?" he said. She did not answer. "When will you return?" he asked, and stopped. He let go of her hand.

He saw her fly down the stairs. He found himself chasing her. She was hurrying across the building compound, her suitcase held before her chest like a shield. The boys sitting on the wall turned to see her. One of them whistled and said something. The others slapped their thighs and laughed. They all turned silent when Ismail drew near.

Outside the building gates, Ismail seized Nazia's arm. "Enough of this. Everyone is looking at us," he said under his breath but she went on to hail a taxi. To his horror, one screeched to a stop. "I said enough," he roared, gusting his breath on her ear. He dug his fingers deep into her arm. Nazia screamed. The boys dropped off the wall and stepped up to them.

"Need help, begum?" one of them said. The others sniggered. "Your father is hurting you?"

Ismail wheeled around and threw his arms on two boys. He struck a face twice with his fist. He saw a lip bleed. He saw the boys stagger back. They cursed and made obscene gestures at him. Ismail ignored them. When he turned back to Nazia he saw her climbing into the taxi. Before he could take hold of her arm, she slammed the door. "VT," he heard her tell the driver. "Hurry!" As she rolled up the window, Ismail reached for the door. He missed, and the taxi pulled away.

He stood as solid as a pillar even when a fist smashed into his jaw. It was only when a blow landed on his temple that his world flickered and blackened for a while. He felt his heart tighten. It seemed to soar up his chest. When he came to, he was on his knees, buckling under a volley of blows. He struggled to get up from the pavement but the boys were pummeling his back. Someone tried to kick him in the groin. Ismail got hold of the foot but he soon lost his grip and fell smack on his hands. He sat up quickly and flailed his arms. He thought he heard a man in the opposite building shout for help. Then he saw the man clap his hands as though he were trying to scare some birds away. Suddenly the sound of running feet came from both ends of the street. A rock-hard fist plowed into Ismail's neck. He gave a cry of pain. He heard the boys take to their heels. He saw them jump over the building walls like cats. An elderly couple was the first to hold Ismail under the arms. He tried to get up but couldn't. An incessant hammering had commenced in his head, exploding tiny bulbs of pain. The light was turning dim, the world hazy and faint. He was sitting on the footpath, he noted. There had been a bloody struggle. There had followed a chase down some stairs. After that, he'd held someone in his arms. Ismail looked around. Who were these people grabbing his arms? He tried to break free but they wouldn't let go. If only his feet would move. He met the eyes boring down on him. Someone was calling for an ambulance, another for the police. Suddenly, a flustered woman emerged through the thick crowd. She saw his face and screamed. She instructed some men to carry him up the building behind them. Ismail resisted with all his might but four or five men hoisted him easily on their shoulders and whisked him across a compound. Up a narrow staircase they climbed and carried him into a flat a hundred stories above the ground. The clock in the house was ticking like a gong. There seemed to be much confusion. Everyone was shouting orders at once. At last, they were lowering him. He descended a hundred stories and lay on his back on the ground. He was in the *zenana* in the village, he remembered now. He'd fallen again from the mango tree. The mango had been pink and ripe and just out of his reach. Soon his aunts would sit on either side of him. They would scold him and nurse his wounds with iodine solution or mercurochrome. He could hear the jangling of their anklets in the courtyard. Why weren't they beside him already? Who were these unruly people craning their necks over shoulders to look down at him? And why, for that matter, was this wide-eyed woman kneeling so close to him? She wasn't even his aunt and yet she was beating her breasts. "Y'Allah! What did she do to you?" she was saying. "I knew you would come back to me. But not like this!" She was bending over him. She was lifting his head onto her lap. "Why is everyone standing here uselessly?" she shrieked, turning to the crowd. "*Arrey*, call the police, call the police. Go catch her, someone!"

# Bombay Talkies

**"I THINK WE WILL GET THERE** on time," Salima said, and her father, standing beside her in the bus, read his wristwatch and wagged his head in agreement. They had managed to get into the crowded bus after a long wait in the hot sun, and now struggled to keep their balance as the bus rocked from side to side, working its way laboriously along Bombay's potholed roads.

Father and daughter were on their way to Bombay Talkies, a dilapidated cinema house in the northern sector of the city, to see a movie Salima had been wanting to see for weeks. Ruby Azam, India's top actress, had become Salima's role model over the last few years. Salima studied how Ruby dressed. She watched how she carried herself on-screen. So well did she copy the graceful inflections of Ruby's speech that before long, many of Ruby Azam's screen mannerisms found their way into Salima's own delicate gestures.

Her father, Hakim Khan, on the other hand, had no similar passion for modern Hindi films, dismissing even Ruby Azam as a poor imitation of Nargis and Madhubala, the movie queens of yesteryear. He was accompanying Salima this afternoon only because there was no one to go with her to the cinema anymore, her one and only friend—Shabnam or Shabana or whatever her name was—having left Bombay to marry into a family in Lucknow, miles and miles away. Salima herself would be leaving Bombay soon. In less than a month, she would be in Hyderabad, four hundred miles to the southeast, where a good match for her had already been arranged. But the main reason Hakim Khan had taken the time to see a film with his daughter today was that in her numbered days with him he was keen to create a favorable impression on her. He wanted her to leave his home with at least one good memory of him and with the recognition that beneath all the cold and hard layers that thickened him was lodged a measure of fatherly love.

"The newspaper mentioned the movie begins at three," Salima said, her voice so soft that at first Hakim Khan thought she was speaking to herself. He watched her peer out the window perhaps to ascertain how much distance the bus had covered. "What time is it now, Baba?"

Hakim Khan felt both pleased and surprised. Salima hardly spoke to him at home. Yet now in the crowded bus, in the midst of so many strangers, she was addressing him with much excitement in her voice. He leaned his body to one side and wrung his arm out of the mass of bodies packed densely around them. He cursed the city, her ever-growing population.

"Two-fifteen," he announced, shifting his gaze to the bus standees around them (all men), two of whom, he noticed, were throwing quick glances in Salima's direction, adeptly shifting their positions now and again to steal larger glimpses of her.

Salima had recently turned eighteen. She was blossoming into a beautiful woman, Hakim Khan observed. Her kohl-lined eyes were large and brown like those of her late mother. Her hair, neatly plaited under the scarf draped around her head, was thick and of good length. Though he was able to afford no formal education for her, there was, nonetheless, a refinement in her manners, an elegance associated with her demeanor, which Hakim Khan saw only in Bombay's educated women and on-screen in actresses Nargis and Madhubala of the good old days. Salima was also a good cook and housekeeper, and there was no doubt in his mind she would make an excellent wife for the Hyderabadi man. After her departure, there would follow no complaints about her. Of this, Hakim Khan felt sure. He looked at her closely again. Like her oldest sister Naseem, she, too, had a mole on her chin. This feature the girls shared had drawn them close to each other, Hakim Khan had decided several years ago. The two sisters had bonded solidly, like mother and child, since their mother's death from tuberculosis nearly eighteen years ago. That explained to him why Naseem had made such a fervent search for a good match for Salima. Two months ago, her letter from Hyderabad arrived in which she had someone write for her that she'd found a decent man for Salima. Everything went smoothly after that, Praise be to Allah.

Salima turned abruptly toward a seat near them. A passenger was showing signs of rising. She moved forward as the passenger rose, but her movement lacked the aggressiveness and speed necessary for seizing empty seats in Bombay's buses. A man cut in before her and lowered himself into the seat with a sigh. Salima, having moved a little farther from Hakim Khan, looked down and then out the window at the cars and the people moving at nearly equal pace outside.

Hakim Khan found himself studying Salima's profile. Her nose was straight like that of actress Nargis, and even her chin jutted out slightly the same way. How strange, he thought, that he should notice these things about his daughter only now when she was soon to leave him. Suddenly, she looked up at him and threw him a questioning glance. Her long earrings swung back and forth. Hakim Khan shook his head to indicate nothing was the matter, and stroked his beard. He looked away, choosing to focus his attention on the two men standing close by, their fingers outlined in the pockets of their trousers. He decided he would prevent them from edging any nearer his daughter with his steady glare.

He wondered if he loved Salima, loved her the way a father should. He decided he didn't. Now he wondered if he loved any of his four children—all girls. Hakim Khan had wanted a son, someone to carry the family name. He had even chosen a name for him—Raza Sher Khan. He had chanted the name in his mind like a prayer on each of the four occasions his wife went into labor. When Salima was born, his patience had withered, his disappointment transforming into bitterness and hate. Not only did he not love Salima all her life, he thought now, but he also wondered if he despised her for her sex at birth, for her difficult birth that had wrenched the life out of her mother.

Yes, he didn't love her. Indeed, once he'd beaten her badly. He'd struck her tear-stricken face with the flat of his hand for some trifling misdemeanor he could not recall later. He dragged her across their small, one-room house by her hair and flung her against the kitchen wall where she slumped to the floor, taking down a whole line of brass utensils with her. Seconds later, she was wrapped in Naseem's shaking arms. He wondered if that incident had made her shy and reticent with him. This daughter lacked confidence. She had no friends. And look at her now: so scared among strangers.

"Ticket, ticket."

The bus conductor had arrived, a puny disgruntled man wearing the symbol of Bombay's working class: a scowl. His uniform was shabby, his hat was tilted at a careless angle, his shoes were worn down to holes in places. One of the city's frustrated millions, Hakim Khan assessed. Fed up with his job, with his life at home, with the corruption in the country. As one of Bombay's longtime citizens, Hakim Khan knew that feeling well. He responded now to the furious clicking of the conductor's ticket-puncher by extracting a ten-rupee note from the pocket of his *kurta*.

"Two tickets. Bombay Talkies," he said, and was a bit alarmed minutes later to hear the same words from one of the two young men standing near him. Both men were still furtively glancing at Salima. They snapped their eyes at her lowered face or her hips from time to time. City loafers, Hakim Khan branded them. Jobless ruffians. Bombay was full of them—young men with bright-colored kerchiefs tied jauntily around their necks, shirts unbuttoned, trousers skintight, their mouths stained a betel-juice red. Had he been younger, stronger, he would have hammered both scoundrels. For staring at his daughter, he would have smashed his rock-hard fists into their shoulder blades, into their lecherous faces. He'd have hoisted them off the floor of the bus and hurled them out the windows. But today he was sixty, past his prime, a grandfather three times already. Why, on some days, he could hardly carry the bucket of water from the common tap to his home. His strength had depleted to the point that, last year, he had had to relinquish his job as a butcher of halaal meat. He was reduced now to waiting for money orders his three married daughters took turns sending his way.

The bus jerked violently and a piercing screech of metal followed. Someone announced one of the tires had gotten punctured. Several people muttered complaints. The driver yelled everything was fine. To his horror, Hakim Khan found that both the young ruffians had used the opportunity to move closer to Salima, one of them having touched her back and hip.

"Just a pothole," the driver shouted. "Nothing serious."

Hakim Khan's face turned crimson with rage. His arms shook and he clenched his teeth to put an end to his shaking. "Don't you have a mother or sisters at home?" he was about to yell at the men but stopped when he suddenly recalled the woman who had shot that line at him in his bachelor days. He could still see her face in his mind's eye, see her painted lips spit out the words at him. It was a line used frequently in Hindi movies, and, like a villain in one of the films, he had guffawed and shaken his head plaintively at the cross woman, lamenting that not only did he not have a mother or sisters but he was all alone in the world. Yet now, here he was, enraged at the hoodlums near Salima for doing to her what he himself had done to scores of women in buses in his younger days. As the bus came to a halt at a bus stop and the floor beneath them groaned as more people crammed in, Hakim Khan recalled the days when, just like the men near Salima, he would push himself into crowded buses only to brush his arms against women's breasts, or work his hands around their hips, or grind his pelvis into them when they struggled to move past him.

Yet now for Salima, whom he had decided he did not love, for whom he harbored no paternal affection worth noting, he was burning with fury. He had defected to her side somehow. Could this mean beneath his coldness and roughness, he had a small fondness for her, even a bit of love? Hakim Khan looked at her and took in her delicacy with moist eyes. Seeing her gazing out the window like a helpless lamb, he remembered his wife and how she'd wait up for him each night, how she had wordlessly accepted his numerous vices. Recalling the details of her face now, Hakim Khan was overcome with such a surge of emotion for his wife and then for their daughter standing before him as she held on to a seat's headrest for support, that he reached out for her, drew her toward him, and promptly exchanged places with her.

•  •  •

Salima understood why her father had pulled her away from her spot. She had sensed the two men closing in on her, had felt their eyes traveling over her body. She knew which of the two men had grabbed her hip when the bus had plunged its wheel into the pothole. In those brief moments, she had felt fingers run over her back and then move down to her hips. She had felt the man give her flesh a gentle squeeze. A part of her had enjoyed it, had even wished her father were not by her side. Her heart thumped furiously. She could still feel the warmth of the man's hand. She felt sure his sweat had left an imprint on her silk *salwaars*. She sized up both men from the corners of her eyes. Hakim Khan had his eyes on them, too. Salima saw both men grow fidgety under his supervision. She studied them carefully. Both sported dark stubble. Their shirts were stained yellow at the armpits. Their lips were pursed as if they were whistling. They peered out the window and one of them pointed to a woman outside.

Salima shifted her gaze to Hakim Khan. He was grinding his jaws; his lower lip trembled. The man whose stentorian voice terrified her, whose occasional words to her at home arrested her actions and froze her thoughts, was protecting her like a dutiful father now. Salima wondered if Naseem and her other sisters feared him as much as she did. They had all gotten married in their teenage years. Was it to get away from him, this man for whom his daughters were sometimes less important than the mounds of goat meat he once worked with daily? Was that why Naseem wanted to see her married off as early as possible?

A hand touched Salima's right thigh. She felt the hand slide up a little. She didn't move away. Somebody was finding her attractive and she decided she would enjoy the attention she was receiving. She imagined whoever was touching her would whisper into her ears that she was beautiful. She imagined him saying he'd like to kiss her lips, take her in his strong arms, and marry her the next day. She would turn around and kiss him back, then press her head against his chest. She remembered now that her father was with her and she moved away from the hand pressed against her thigh. She missed its warmth immediately. This is why she'd squeeze herself into packed buses and trains while her father hacked goat meat in the market in his working days. This is why she slipped away from home and into crowded places whenever her father visited his friends now.

There was supposed to be a scene fairly early in the movie they were on their way to see in which Ruby Azam is approached in a bus by the film's hero. They fall in love and begin to sing the song that was now on every Indian's lips. It was said Ruby Azam wears a revealing dress in the bus scene, showing her cleavage and exposing her thighs. Rumor had it that she unbuttons the hero's shirt and writes "I love you" on his chest with a lipstick. Salima found the hand was back on her thigh. She let it travel to her hip and imagined she was Ruby Azam all alone with the man touching her in the bus that was rolling on, rocking and rattling as it headed slowly for Bombay Talkies.

Her adventures on Bombay's buses and trains would end when she left for Hyderabad, she realized. She would miss these encounters, she knew. They now constituted the only entertainment in her life. The man her sister Naseem had selected for her, whom she had met with for an hour in Hyderabad last month, was polite, gentle, not like the heroes in Ruby Azam's films, not like the two hairy-chested men in the bus today on whom her father was still keeping watch. Unlike her husband-to-be, the two men near her had hard, muscular bodies, they wore colorful kerchiefs around their necks, and they weren't shy about indicating to her that they found her attractive. Her husband-to-be was an administrative officer in a small company, earning a decent salary, and he belonged to a class higher than hers. Salima couldn't imagine him touching her boldly the way one of the men on the bus just had. She couldn't imagine him with a hard, stubbled jaw that he'd graze against her neck as did the leading men in Ruby Azam's films. Would he even smell like the kerchiefed men, of betel-juice and perspiration? Salima threw a sideways glance at them. Her heart leaped and swelled. She looked out the window to think about other things. Cars were streaming by, their shrill horns competing with one another in the afternoon air.

She edged away from the hand touching her. If her father realized she was complicit in the bus adventure, he would kill her. He'd be right to do so, she thought. She risked her reputation each time she stole out of the house and got into buses to see how far men's hands would go. She wondered if Naseem had felt a similar attraction for such men. Was it in a bus she'd been caught one day by their father several years ago? That day, Salima had entered the house to find Hakim Khan looming over Naseem, his beard nearly grazing her chin, his huge hands clamped on her shoulders, the sleeve of her blouse ripped, her palms joined together. She was pleading to be let go. Seeing Salima, Hakim Khan let Naseem go, kicking Salima in the shin on his way out of the house.

The bus braked suddenly and the passengers were jolted. Someone shouted an abuse, someone else uttered a cry. The bus was so crowded now it was skipping stops, halting a few paces ahead of designated bus stops when passengers wanted to get off.

"Bombay Talkies, next stop," the conductor said, although Bombay Talkies was still some distance away. Hakim Khan read his wristwatch.

"Will we make it in time?" Salima asked. Hakim Khan showed her his watch. They wouldn't be late, Salima decided. They had enough time for a wait in line for tickets, enough time even to select two good seats in the map of the auditorium the management sometimes displayed to patrons at the window.

"We should move toward the exit," Hakim Khan said, steering his body around. He threaded his way through the bus standees, one hand locked around Salima's wrist. No sooner had he dragged her after him than Salima felt a weight pressing behind her. She knew it was one of the two kerchiefed men leaning on her. She could feel his hardness against her hip; she felt spurts of his warm breath on her neck. His hands were placed gently on her waist now, pretending to guide her toward the exit, but she realized he was positioning her before him. He was humming a Ruby Azam song, pressing his hips against hers harder than before. The bus stopped at a red light and suddenly he was gone. Moments later, the weight was back on her, but with an unusual roughness. Salima's heart thumped faster when she realized the men had switched places. The second man rubbed his thighs so furiously against Salima that she staggered forward and fell hard on Hakim Khan's back. He turned around. His eyes fell on the men. His jowls shook when he saw how close they were to his daughter.

"Motherfuckers!" he yelled, and tried to reach for their shirts. In defense, the men threw Salima at him. She landed in his arms. He nearly lost his balance.

"Bastards! Dogs!"

"Hoy, hoy!" the bus conductor roared from somewhere near the exit. "What's going on there?"

"We don't know, Conductor sahib," one of the kerchiefed men said. "This old man is crazy."

Words rushed to Hakim Khan's lips. His lips fluttered as he held the words back. Making public what had just happened would bring shame on his daughter. Instead, he slammed his fist toward one of the men's faces. It missed by more than a foot. One of the men shot his fist into Hakim Khan's cheek.

"All right. All of you, get out!" the conductor said, working his way briskly toward them. "Come on. Out, out!" He shouted to the bus driver to keep the bus standing at the lights. "This is Bombay Talkies. No arguing with me. Come on now, out. All four of you."

Hakim Khan and Salima alighted and were once again in the blazing sun. Standing on the road beside the stationary bus, they watched it while adjusting their clothes, and waited.

"I'll break their bones," Hakim Khan said. "Just let them come out. I'll smash their heads together with my hands." He rolled up his sleeves and tightened his fists. The veins on his arms stuck out. His body shook.

"Please, Baba, forget it," Salima said, pulling at his arm. "We'll be late for the movie."

"Just let those swine come out!"

But nobody else got off and the bus moved away. Hakim Khan trembled with rage. Tears sprang to his eyes. As they walked the distance to Bombay Talkies, he dabbed his kerchief against the bruise on his cheek.

"Baba," Salima said, shuffling her feet faster toward the cinema, "can I ask you something? Why did you strike that man?"

Hakim Khan stopped walking. He stared at her. The naivete of her words! He peered into her face and registered the innocence written on it. "S-Salima," he said, and shook his head. He took her hands in his and drew her toward him. "My innocent girl. This city, this dirty city, is far too wicked for someone like you."

•  •  •

When they reached Bombay Talkies, they found throngs of people outside. It hadn't occurred to them the show could have sold out. Their steps grew shorter as they approached the noisy crowd. Seconds later, father and daughter merged with it. A sign outside the ticket window cried in bold letters that all tickets for all shows that day were sold out. Salima's heart sank as she saw ticket-holders pushing their way noisily through the cinema entrance.

"We'll have to buy tickets at the black rate," she said. She clutched Hakim Khan's arm. He was surprised by the way her nails dug into his flesh. He had never seen her so agitated and impatient. Her eyes sparkled with the kind of excitement he hadn't thought was possible in her.

"Black rate?" he said.

They stood still for a long time, sensing defeat, visualizing their journey back home. A scuffle broke out at the cinema entrance. Voices in the crowd rose.

"Fifty rupees one ticket, Chachaji. Want ticket? Two tickets is hundred rupees."

A young boy in khaki shorts stood before Hakim Khan and Salima. His beige shirt had a school badge pinned on its pocket. A schoolboy, Hakim Khan observed. Having to pay his school fees this unfortunate way. Forced to make money for his family by selling tickets illegally in this hopeless, ruthless, shameless city. He spat on the ground.

"Fifty rupees?" he said. He wiped his mouth with the sleeve of his *kurta*. "Too much."

"Not too much," the boy said. "In ten minutes, it will be sixty rupees. This is a Ruby Azam movie, Chachaji. Super hot film. Good songs. One long waterfall shot of Ruby Azam. Famous bus scene with short, short dress. Only two tickets I have. Last chance."

"Let's buy them, Baba," Salima cried, distracted by the crowds moving in, her eyes taking in the gigantic billboards in front of her that showed Ruby Azam in a cleavage-exposing dress. "Let's buy them before somebody else does."

Hakim Khan paid the boy a hundred rupees, several times the official rate. They had come this far and it would, indeed, make little sense to return without seeing the film. Salima, soon to leave for Hyderabad, would never forgive him. She'd leave his home with this ugly memory, hold it against him for life. He took the tickets from the boy. Seats K13 and K14 they said in large black print.

Inside the theater, they had difficulty locating their seats. The light was dim, the commercials were on. Nearly every seat seemed occupied. With people yelling and bustling about, father and daughter couldn't tell where Row K was. Without warning the lights dimmed further. There was a scrambling for seats, a frantic calling of names. People could be heard making themselves comfortable in their seats, ripping open bags of snacks. A hush descended on the house. Hakim Khan and Salima were plunged in darkness.

"Where are those useless ushers?" Hakim Khan said. "Call them. Ask someone, Salima. I can't see anymore."

Salima looked around for the usher's flashlight. The movie started. Music filled the auditorium. The usher was nowhere to be seen. The titles were up on the screen now. There it was: Ruby Azam's name in thick red letters, Bombay's Marine Drive providing a busy background. Someone from the seats behind shouted at Salima to stand aside. She pulled Hakim Khan closer to her and they moved a few paces away.

"Where are those idiotic ushers?" Hakim Khan said. "Go, Salima. Go find one!"

Ruby Azam was on the screen, emerging slowly into a cone of light spilling from a street lamp. She had on a pink, hip-hugging dress, a high ponytail. A pink handbag hung over her shoulder. She was turning onto a dark and isolated street now. Only two other people were around. The background music was building to a crescendo.

"Look, there's an usher!" Hakim Khan said, and Salima rushed toward the usher's flashlight, her attention still on the screen. Ruby Azam was swinging her handbag to and fro. Salima presented the tickets to the usher. He returned them and told them to follow him. He flashed his light on the red carpet to help them see their way. He escorted them up the steps and stopped at Row K. He shone his flashlights on seats K13 and K14. Salima saw the laps of two women there.

"Let's see those tickets again, Madam."

Salima surrendered the tickets to the usher and fixed her eyes back on the screen. Ruby Azam, in a revealing dress, was boarding an empty bus now. The bus conductor and driver were exchanging glances.

"These tickets are counterfeit," the usher said.

"What?" cried Hakim Khan and Salima together.

"Fake," the usher explained, examining the tickets with the flashlight. "Not worth the paper they are printed on."

"Impossible," Hakim Khan countered. "We just bought them. Five or ten minutes ago."

"Maybe. But they are still fake. It's a big racket in Bombay. I have to ask you to leave."

"Leave? But we paid good money for our tickets!"

"Speak softly, please. As you can see the movie has already started. Did you buy these tickets at our window?"

Hakim Khan was taken aback. "Of course. Where else would we buy them?"

"Not possible," the usher said.

"What do you mean 'not possible'?" Hakim Khan snapped. "Are you calling me a liar? Rascal, third-class fool!" He took a step forward and jabbed his own chest with his thumb. "I am telling you we bought these tickets at the window, so now go and find us our seats," he roared, while Salima, her eyes not leaving the screen for an instant, skipped down the carpeted steps. On the screen, she saw the hero poised to take Ruby Azam in his arms.

# A Change of Lights

**SHE BOUNCED HER TWO-YEAR-OLD** child lightly on one arm and used the other hand to wipe the trickling sweat off her brow with the loose end of her sari. As she did, the single crutch held under her right shoulder shifted a little, sending mother and child nearly off balance. The mother was named Lajwanti, the shy one, but none of the other pavement-dwellers addressed her by her name. Instead, they called her Lungree, the lame one. Lajwanti had heard it was June, the month that supposedly marked the beginning of the monsoons in Bombay. But one look at the cloudless bright sky convinced her she had misheard. It simply couldn't be June, she thought as she stood roasting in the sun by the side of the city's main road. She frowned and alternately fanned her face and Bharati's, the child's, with her free hand.

Why this incinerating heat, she wondered, shading her eyes from the blazing light with her elbow. She brushed off the strands of hair sticking to her forehead, pinched her nose in disgust, and cursed. The heat, intensified by the humidity, seemed to have descended inexorably on the city from the sky, covering it like a thick prickly blanket. The near-paralysis it produced in the city's inhabitants was so devastating that even Lajwanti, despite the frantic pangs of hunger pounding her stomach (now caved in), was tempted to give up working at the intersection of S.V. and M.G. Roads. But when she turned to look at Bharati struggling weakly to escape her arm, she knew she would *have* to find some food. Except for a half-eaten moldy loaf of bread, Lajwanti's efforts in digging into trash bins this morning had proved futile. Now it was afternoon, way past the city's lunch hour, and Lajwanti could feel sharp jabs of pain in her abdomen. It felt as if her insides had begun to knot up in their craving for food. She knew Bharati was suffering just as much, perhaps more. The child's fragile body was shriveled to the bone. That would be good for begging, Lajwanti thought. Fleshless children, she had noted at the traffic lights, brought their parents good money. She hoped Bharati would be an advantage to her today. Today would be the final test, Lajwanti decided. Carrying her on the rounds was getting to be cumbersome. If Bharati didn't fetch her more than five rupees by evening, she would have to do something about it. About her. She scowled at Bharati's slender bony form draped over her arm and cursed again.

"*Bojh!* Burden! Why don't you run away the way your father did?" she hollered. "Why didn't that rascal take you with him when he abandoned me? That shameless swine." Lajwanti knifed the air savagely with her hand, her long black nails poking the child's parched face. Bharati gurgled weakly and stared at Lajwanti's twisted lips with beady unblinking eyes. "Burdening a cripple like me with one more mouth to feed!" Lajwanti shouted. She spat out a long stream to her right, aiming it close to a startled stray dog that, like them, had been reduced to a mere skeleton. The dog yelped, cowered for an instant, but then boldly approached Lajwanti, running its nose up and down her solitary naked foot. Lajwanti struck the dog's head hard with her crutch, sending it scampering away from her, whimpering in pain.

She turned to look at the cars swishing by in front of her on S.V. Road. She knew she had to earn enough money from them today not only to pay for half a bottle of country-liquor her body could no longer do without, but also to feed Bharati, who had miraculously survived two days without proper food. With the four rupees she had made the previous day, Lajwanti had sacrificed the liquor and bought herself a small bowl of lentil soup, two slices of bread, and a banana instead. Her mouth watered as she recalled how she had savored each bite of her favorite fruit, chewing it slowly, patiently, making the most of each mouthful. Such a shame she had had to sacrifice half the banana to Bharati. Only that had stopped the child's cries of hunger. What a drain on her meager resources this child, this *bojh*, was. Lajwanti shook her head and waited with growing impatience for the cars to stop whizzing by in front of her. She glared at the signal lights above. They glowed green at her in defiance.

"Go red, you bastards," she snarled at them. As if the signals had heard her foul language, they blushed and turned red. The cars screeched to a halt, and within seconds Lajwanti had before her about twenty cars to select from. She struck her crutch on the road, hoisted her weight around it, and began a day of work. With Bharati riding on her left hip, Lajwanti hobbled to a motorcar in the row farthest from the curb. That was the strategy she used, unlike the other beggars who would pounce on the first available automobile. Lajwanti had discovered through various permutations that by attacking the last row and working eventually to the row of cars closest to the curb, she tended to accumulate maximum loose change. The only disadvantage she had as compared to her colleagues was her mutilated right leg: she lost much time making it to the last row. She had also learned from experience that the signals on S.V. Road remained red for either a minute and a half or for three minutes, depending on the traffic flowing perpendicularly on M.G. Road. Quickly, she studied the motorcars moving there. She would get three whole minutes this time. She worked her way to a Mercedes-Benz, reputed to provide good earnings.

"Memsahib, just one rupee," she begged in a disconsolate tone. "Daughter and I have not eaten for two days." She forced herself to cough irritatingly, using the phlegm in her throat to create repulsive sounds. That, she knew, brought the money out of the purses faster sometimes.

The woman at the car window swung her elbow inside, pulled her painted mouth off the straw of her cold drink bottle and belched. She leaned away from the window to study Lajwanti. She pinched her puffy face in disgust; flakes of facial powder rained down her blouse.

"Two days, huh?" she said, looking over Lajwanti with scorn. She turned to the man beside her. "Tell me, isn't it amazing how these creatures have never eaten for *two* days?"

"Yes, darling. It is."

"I mean it's never three or one. Always two."

"You're so observant, darling."

"Memsahib," Lajwanti whined, "this baby is hungry. See?" She pinched Bharati's skin, lifting it as far away from the bone as she could. "Very weak. No flesh on her at all. One rupee. Please, memsahib."

The woman closed her mouth over the straw again and sucked in a healthy fill. Lajwanti stuck her free hand inside the car through the window. The woman drew back and glared as if it were a piece of rancid meat. Assured of attention, Lajwanti withdrew her hand and poked Bharati's stomach. "Not a grain in here, memsahib."

"Oof, I tell you!" the woman said, slapping her brow. "We have to get out of Bombay now. Before these ugly beggars take over our city."

"You're right again, darling."

The woman shook her head from side to side. "Can't even have a cold drink in peace nowadays without this shit . . . these filthy animals surrounding you. Don't we pay enough taxes as it is? Why can't they just sweep these types out of sight?" She flicked open her purse, extracted a twenty-five paise coin and dropped it into Lajwanti's extended palm, making sure she made no contact. She clicked her tongue and rolled up the window, a torrent of abuse gushing from her mouth. Whore, Lajwanti branded her. "Bitch," she said and hastened towards the next car. Another foreign one, a model she had never seen. Before she could wail her rehearsed plea, the passengers in the car rolled up the windows. "Pimps. Eunuchs!" Lajwanti yelled, and deposited a frothy pool of spit on the car's trunk.

An hour later, Lajwanti was standing in the middle of the road, a stream of cars flowing before her while another stream raced by in the opposite direction behind her. The signal lights had turned green on her suddenly while she was working on a Honda, leaving her no time to hop back to the pavement where the others were. She had sought refuge on the raised divider in the center of the road, reaching it just in time. She rocked Bharati absently now, keeping an eye on the green lights glowing above the rush of cars. She had gone through two Toyotas, six Fiats, three Ambassadors, and a couple of Maruti-Suzukis with little success. Not only the humidity, but also selfishness, had gripped Bombay. Something had come over Bombayites. Today they were parting with no money at all. Lajwanti peeped into the pocket she had made with her sari around her waist. Eighty-five paise. A record low. It must be the sweltering heat. It was dulling everyone's senses, hardening their hearts. Lajwanti couldn't recall it ever being *this* hot.

She looked at the traffic halted on M.G. Road. She could see some of the beggars were working there, too. With her condition, she was incapable of working overtime and scorned those who did by calling them greedy dogs. She looked up at the signal lights again. They still shone green. She hated this waiting. It tired her instead of resting her. Often she would be filled with such impatience at the end of the wait she would accost as many cars as she could, and usually so rapidly she ended up with almost nothing in her hand. In these summer months, she couldn't keep her bare foot too long on one spot, for the tar on the road, sticky in patches because of the heat, burned her sole. Patience, she told herself, is also what I have to work at. Learn to stand by their car windows till they get sick of you.

Lajwanti gathered the shreds that together made up the loose end of her sari and wiped away the rivulets of sweat coursing down her hands and neck, and those of Bharati, too. The child began to cry on being rubbed. Lajwanti slapped her hard across the face. When Bharati's caterwauling increased, Lajwanti decided to quit after the next round of begging. She would head back to the pavement and spend the rest of the day under a tree. Bharati was proving to be totally useless.

"Oy, Lungree!" she heard someone shout across the motorcars. Lajwanti craned her neck, cracking open her eyes just a fraction to avoid the blinding reflection of the sun from the tops of the moving cars.

"What is it?" she shouted back, rocking Bharati faster to stop her crying.

"You two all right there?" asked Sudha, one of the beggar-women.

Lajwanti nodded yes. "Couldn't get back to the pavement in time."

"Be careful," Sudha shouted, cupping her mouth and leaning forward. "You better not lose another leg!"

Lajwanti could see the others were snickering. They always made fun of her. Made nasty jokes at her expense. At the expense of her missing leg. She hadn't lost it on purpose, had she? As far as she knew she never had one. Even Baba, the old man who had raised her since she was two, didn't know how or where she had lost it. He told her he had found her by his side in that condition upon awakening one morning on the pavement. The note tucked inside the towel she was wrapped in had only said "Lajwanti."

Lajwanti missed Baba. He had looked after her well, she recalled as she adjusted Bharati on her hip. She had given a man with no one in the world a purpose in life. How he had slogged for her sake, working each day as a door-to-door bread deliverer. And yet, he had nothing saved when he died. Lajwanti, then fifteen, illiterate and naive, had looked for employment only to discover no one wanted to employ a lame girl. "*Arrey?*" they would say and hold their chins. "But you are a *lungree*," they would add bluntly and wave her off. When by accident she approached a brothel for work, she was cause for much laughter. "We would have to pay *them* to sleep with a one-legged," she was told and shooed away.

The lights were still green on S.V. Road. Lajwanti looked at them grimly. A black crow, cawing at the sun, was perched atop the lights. Cawing in hunger, too, Lajwanti imagined. But crows were lucky. They didn't have to go through the humiliation of begging. They could swoop down boldly to pluck at whatever they fancied. No pleading, no asking. They could also fly away from this wretched, selfish city whenever they wanted.

Lajwanti wanted so much to get away from Bombay. She didn't object to the crowds—the more, the better for begging—nor did she mind the deafening noise. What she hated was the heat, the scorching, debilitating heat that gnawed at you, cooked you gradually until your mind was ablaze and you went around yelling and bickering about nothing for no reason at all. Lajwanti would love to flee to some place cooler where one didn't perspire so much, where clothes didn't weld to one's skin. She had heard there were parts of India that enjoyed cool climates and had once even sneaked into a bus headed for such a place. However, she, along with Bharati and her crutch, had been hurled mercilessly out of the vehicle minutes later when she had been unable to purchase a ticket.

One on occasion, she had decided to travel free of charge on the roof of a goods train that left Bombay each night, but changed her mind on approaching the railway station. She had a feeling she'd be caught, or worse, that she would roll off the roof and the train would run her over. She never thought of trying the trains again after that night. Their sharp whistles, in any case, always frightened her, chilled her spine.

To her delight, Lajwanti now saw motorcars queuing up before her, their tires grinding against the hot road. The signal lights, she noted with relief, had finally turned red. She staggered toward a Fiat, but swung away from it when she noticed the car's only occupant was a uniformed chauffeur. Drivers were poorly paid, she'd been coached. Waste no time on them. She scanned the other cars around her. Her heart jumped. She had spotted a BMW, the prized one. She simply had to get there before someone else beat her to it. She lumbered hastily toward the driver, a balding middle-aged man looking straight ahead. His icy eyes were half open, his bushy eyebrows partly raised. Lajwanti launched into her yammering at once.

"Sahib, this baby's not eaten for three days," she lied and cupped her palm to form her begging bowl. She swung it from Bharati's belly to the window. She found not a sign on the man's face that suggested her words had registered. She would have to ululate louder. Make herself more irritating. She thrust Bharati forward, letting her drum out a muddy progression on the car's gleaming polish. There was still no effect on the statuesque man behind the wheel. Bharati was so useless, thought Lajwanti. Absolutely no asset. Not at all like Sudha's son Munna. Across four rows, Lajwanti could see Munna slung lifelessly over Sudha's shoulder, his only arm and only leg dangling. Why did she bother to carry Bharati with her at all, Lajwanti wondered. No one believed her when she said Bharati was starving. Although she was light, bearing her on one leg and a crutch was a burden. A *bojh*.

"Sahib, only one rupee," Lajwanti cried again. She joined her palms in supplication.

"For God's sake, do something, Raj!" a female voice from the car said. Lajwanti bent down to look inside. There was a young woman next to the man. She seemed to be breathing heavily and gritting her teeth. Behind her on the backseat, Lajwanti could see a plump little boy giving long lazy licks to an ice cream cone.

"Memsahib, only one rupee for this baby."

"Raj, shut her up for God's sake!" the woman said, pressing her brow.

"Ignore her," the man said, still staring at the cars in front of him.

"But how can you stand her voice?" the woman said. "At least roll up the bloody window." She looked over her shoulder. "And you, Chintoo, stop those slurpy sounds."

"Memsahib, see your boy. So nice and big like a balloon. And now see this baby. Pity, memsahib. Pity."

"Raj, *roll up the damn window!*"

"Stop it!" the man yelled. "What's got into you? We can't have pavement-dwellers dictating what we do."

"Oh, sahib. One rupee."

"Well, give her something to shut her up."

The man gave a snort and turned to Lajwanti. He stared hatefully at her face for a while, but then moved his eyes down her neck, letting them slide down her dusky glistening skin until he reached her breasts. He looked up into her eyes again and parted his lips to show her his tongue, now peeking shyly from the corner of his mouth.

Lajwanti shifted the sari from her left breast so that the man could see it clearly. Her blouse was in rags; with just a little stretching, she knew she could reveal her nipple to him. And if she showed more, he would compensate her better for her service. She positioned herself carefully so that the man's head obstructed the woman's view. She hooked her finger under her blouse. Slowly, she peeled it off her breast. It poked out in relief, fully exposed. Lightly, she danced her fingers around the nipple. She rubbed it, pinched it, stretched it close to the man to bait him. When she saw him roll his tongue over his puckered lips, she let go of the nipple. It shot back to set her breast bouncing joyfully in the hot sun.

Lajwanti heard the jingling of coins. The man was digging his hand into the pocket of his trousers. Now he reached out for her palm, brushing her breast as he did. Quickly he slipped coins into her hand and winked at her.

"Only this, sahib?" Lajwanti said, leaning closer to the car. "Twenty paise? That's not even a quarter rupee. No, no, sahib. This won't do."

The woman in the car sprang forward. "I don't believe her audacity," she said. "Good God! She's half-naked too! Chintoo, look this way at once!"

Lajwanti adjusted her blouse and clung to the windowsill. "You touched it, sahib," she said.

"You what?" the woman cried.

"What are you listening to these guttersnipes for?" the man said. "You know I'd never do that."

"I saw it, I saw it," the little boy sang now, flaunting his cone like a trophy. "Daddy touched her. Daddy touched her."

The woman let out a scream and lashed the man's chest with her fingers. He tried to roll up the window. Lajwanti clamped her fingers over the mounting glass and pushed down with all her weight. She found the window climbing steadily. As she shifted her body to press down even harder, she lost her grip on Bharati, who began to slide down her thigh, one limb after another.

"Sahib. Please, sahib," Lajwanti said, and yanked her fingers away from the window at the last moment. She could hear the man and the woman arguing. She thumped the top of the car frantically with her hand. She spat twice on the window. Lajwanti was about to strike the side of the car with her crutch when she noticed cars slowing down on M.G. Road. In panic, she moved away from the BMW. The lights were about to change, she realized, and hopped hurriedly for the safety of the pavement, one hand locked around Bharati, the other clutching the crutch.

When she reached the pavement, she was out of breath and Bharati took to shrieking again. What was she going to do, Lajwanti wondered as she wiped away the sweat beads from their burnt-brown skins. How would she survive another night without her booze? How would Bharati survive without food? What if even today the city trash bins had been scavenged before she could sift through them? Lajwanti trudged toward a shady tree nearby and set her crutch against the trunk. Balancing on her leg, she lowered Bharati carefully on the stony ground. The dog that had come up to her before took a sniff now at Bharati. Lajwanti hopped to her crutch and smacked the dog's belly hard with it. It scuttled off toward an empty cold drink bottle, its dry tongue seeking the final drops.

Lajwanti sat down and threw her back against the tree. She looked at Bharati and shook her head. Bharati had failed her yet again. Carrying her as a measure of their despair wasn't working.

She couldn't understand it. Bharati had been denied food for two full days and was now so weak and light Lajwanti had had to remind herself at times during the rounds that Bharati was still bent limply over her arm. How much worse could she make Bharati look?

Lajwanti reached for her crutch and used it to rise from the ground. She knew she had to return to those damn cars, to those tight-fisted motorists. The ache in her stomach would allow her to sit under the tree's leafy canopy no more. She decided to leave Bharati behind this time. She plodded toward a tall wooden box that lay unclaimed not far from them. She fetched it, prodding it on with her crutch, and placed Bharati on it. That would keep the dog away, she figured. She brushed the dirt streaking down Bharati's face. She put her hand on the small heaving belly. It felt much too warm, she thought. She would have to feed Bharati well today, she concluded, and stumped her way to her spot by the green lights.

Lajwanti could see Sudha exhibiting Munna on M.G. Road for better payment. Many motorists were putting coins in Munna's hand that Sudha held out. Was it time Bharati was maimed, too, Lajwanti asked herself. Maimed to become more profitable? Bharati could have another chance this way, put through one last test. What harm was there anyway in chopping off just one of Bharati's legs? She wasn't being beheaded, was she?

The lights above switched to red. Lajwanti's eyes hunted for a foreign car at once. She spotted one two rows away from her. The car was festooned with flowers. Balloons on the car roof quivered and the streamers fastened all around fluttered merrily in the wind. Lajwanti moved toward the car, planning how she would sever Bharati's leg. She thought of taking her to the railtracks late that night. The goods train would slice off the leg instantly. After that, if Bharati still fetched her no money, she could abandon her. Dump her outside some temple or mosque when there was no one around. Or some night she could take her to another section of the city and leave her beside somebody asleep on the pavement. For Bharati's sake, she would select someone who looked reliable. As a mother, she would do this much for her. Why, if Bharati was lucky, she would find someone as kind as Baba.

She was before the wedding car. Instead of sticking her hand out, she stared at the car absently. Something was happening to her, to her mind. The hunger was numbing her brain, she thought. Why else did it feel as if she had already enacted her plan? A bejeweled hand suddenly emerged from the car window, a crisp five-rupee bill held between two ring-studded fingers. Just then the lights turned green; a minute and a half had passed. Lajwanti reached out for the money. But before she could get to it, the car sped off. The bill flew several car rows behind her and smacked against the windshield of a passing car.

Lajwanti stood frozen amid the flowing traffic now, one hand slapped across her heart. Some motorists shouted names at her, some shook their fists. Oblivious to their threats, Lajwanti studied the remains of her severed leg stretching out from her hip. Had she once been the victim of her plan herself? Motorcars honked to get her out of their way. She heard in their horns the shrill whistles of a train. She shut her ears. The crutch slipped out from under her armpit, leaned back and banged violently against a car. It snapped at once, its two ends flung rows apart by the traffic.

Bharati was going to be spared the fate of that cycle, Lajwanti decided. Spared no matter what. Riveted between two rows of speeding cars, Lajwanti reached down to stroke the stump of her leg; her shoulders began to shake with her sobbing. Then above the roar of the traffic and the din of car horns, she cried out for Bharati, for forgiveness, for a change of lights. She hoisted herself on her toes to see the box on the pavement on which Bharati lay still. Wanting nothing else now but to be with Bharati cradled in her arms, Lajwanti looked up at the signals, then back at the pavement, and found once more she could hardly wait for the lights to go red.

# Ramadan

**HIS BEST FRIEND VENU** first mentioned the affair to Farid. The boys were sitting on the compound wall of Farid's building, swinging their legs, giving each other a nudge each time a girl passed by on Mehta Street, when, suddenly, Venu cleared his throat and said, "I'm really sorry, *yaar*."

Farid's brow knitted slightly. "What for?" he said.

Venu had behaved strangely all week. In school, Farid had caught him glancing at him time and again. Had Venu gathered more information on the scandal involving Ms. Pinto, the new Geography teacher, and Mr. Cooper, the Physical Education instructor? Or perhaps he had new gossip about other teachers that would have tongues wagging in Bombay.

"Please, Farid," Venu said. "Don't pretend. You must know what I mean."

Farid shook his head. Glancing at his wristwatch, he noted it was nearing 6:30 in the evening. His eyes traveled to the third floor and then onward to the fourth floor of Ajanta Palace, the building towering before them. He could see neither Shilpa nor Niloufer on their balconies. They weren't coming down to chat this evening, he decided. Yesterday, Shilpa had groaned about a calculus test, one on partial differential equations that was worrying her. Of course, if she wouldn't come down today, it was no use waiting. Her friends Niloufer, Nayab, and Binafshee would be staying indoors as well.

"What are you sorry about?" Farid said, trying to will Shilpa to emerge in her window. "Spill it. Stop the riddles. And stop that fingernail-biting. You want to be called a sissy or what?"

Venu read Farid's face. He stopped biting his fingernails. "So you, like, don't know then?" he said. He shifted in his seat. "Amazing." He held his chin. "What my mother said is true. The family always learns last."

"Learns what last? Whose family? Kill the suspense and spill it, man. I've got to go home in a bit."

"All right. Cool down. I'll tell you. But only because you ask and only because you're my friend." Venu looked left, then right. "It's your father," he said, leaning toward Farid. "Everyone's saying he's having an affair."

Farid's mind absorbed the words. He watched a taxi jouncing down Mehta Street. It was only when the car disappeared around the bend that his heartbeat began to race. He jumped off the wall. On the footpath he had to steady himself. It wasn't rage that was rising in him but shame, thickened with chagrin. Chagrin, not because Venu, his classmate and lifelong friend, had stained his father's reputation, but because he, Farid, had never considered the possibility of an affair. Now, of course, it all made sense—his father's mounting caprice, and his leaving for work at the bank earlier than he used to. Farid had assumed the stretches of silence that strained their dinners lately were due to the stress of Ramadan, the holy month of fasting that affected you even if you didn't keep the thirty fasts. Now on this twenty-ninth day of fasting, it was all coming together, making sense. He clasped his hands and brought his thumbs to his lips. Venu could be right. But how strange. An affair? Papa? Ridiculous. With whom?

"*Yaar* Venu, I've got to go," Farid said.

"One sec," Venu said. He climbed down the wall and stepped up to Farid. He dug his hands into the pockets of his trousers. "I hope I didn't, like, upset you. I just thought, you know, that you knew."

"No worries," Farid said, clapping Venu's shoulder and managing a smile. "Stop acting all crazy like a sissy. Of course I knew." He bit his lower lip. Why did he say he knew? If he'd known, Venu must wonder how come he, Farid, hadn't cared all along, not said a word about it to Venu, whose look of concern was now transforming into one of confusion. "*Yaar*, it's nearly time to break my fast," Farid said, his eyes on his *chappals*. "I've really got to go."

When he reached home, a two-bedroom flat on the second floor of Windmere Apartments, Farid was breathless, having run up the stairs. He had trouble getting the key into the lock of the front door, for his hands were shaking. He shut the door behind him, flung the keys on the settee, and made for his parents' bedroom. He found his mother Bilquis seated cross-legged on the bed, her back against the headboard. She was reading aloud a verse from the Qur'an. Sensing his presence, she raised her hand to break his advance. Then, only after the verse was fully recited, did she lift her eyes.

"What is it?" she said, holding the book closer to her breasts as if to prepare herself for whatever Farid had barged in to say.

"Ammi," he said, his fingers fluttering before his lips. "How do I say this?" He walked straight up to her, then stepped back, paused, and headed for the window to her left. He held on to the grill. He stared at Mehta Street below. "It is Papa," he said. "Ammi, I just learned that—oh no, I can't. It will break your heart." He turned to face her and threw his back against the grill.

Bilquis's eyes shifted from his face to the darkening sky unfurled behind him. When Farid approached her, her worry began to abate. She returned to the Qur'an and drew the book closer to her eyes.

"You won't believe what Venu just told me," Farid said. When she didn't respond, he drew closer to her and sat on the bed. He reached for her elbow. He shook it. Silence grew between them. Bilquis paid closer attention to the text before her eyes. Farid shook her arm again. When she still didn't respond, he sprang to his feet and drew away. "Y'Allah!" he cried. "You know! You've known all the time." He bent down to examine her face. "Is it true? Ammi, is it true? Don't tell me the whole world knows except me. Why, of course. If Venu knew, all of Mehta Street and school must know."

Bilquis shut the Qur'an, kissed it, and set it on the chiffonier beside the bed. "That's enough, Farid," she said, now meeting his gaze. "Yes, I know. I've known for quite some time."

"What? Since when?"

Since the day your papa and I hired her to come to our home to teach you Marathi three evenings a week, Bilquis wanted to say. Since the moment your papa's eyes fell on hers and hers lingered on his face for an instant longer than necessary. I knew since then, Farid, Bilquis would have liked to add. Instead she said, "I knew just before this Ramadan began," relieved and regretful that the month of self-denial and discipline would, after one more day of fasting, draw to an end. "Your papa told me a day before you and I began the fasts this year."

This was true. Although she'd known for months, it was only the day before this year's Ramadan commenced that Kasim had sat her down on their bed. He'd held both her hands in his that morning, fallen to his knees, and taken to shuddering and weeping like a boy. Bilquis wanted to rise but he wouldn't let go. "I know who she is," she finally said, feeling the pressure ebbing at once from his grip. "I know who it is this time."

He stopped weeping then. "Oh, Bilquis," he kept whispering after that and sniffling. "She has done something to me. I try not to think of her but she has spun this . . . this web around my mind." He threw his head in her lap. She leaned back on her hands and shifted beneath him so that he raised his head and lifted his eyes. "I can't fight her spell on me any longer," he said. "I'm finished, helpless. Yes, Bilquis. I am weak. Say it to me. Go on. Look into my eyes and say it to my face." He paused to dab his tears on the sleeve of his bush shirt. Again, she tried to get off the bed. Again, he wouldn't let her. "Bilquis, try to understand. I need her. I've fallen in love with Devika, I think."

She stiffened. She hadn't prepared herself for that. She managed to wrench her hands out of his. She raised her fists in the air and for a moment it seemed as if she were about to strike him when, in fact, she had wanted to beat her breasts a dozen times. She unclenched her fingers, and sank them into her loose and disheveled hair.

"Devika does not leave my thoughts," she heard Kasim whisper. "I'm sorry." His eyes were downcast. Tears no longer marked his cheeks. "Curse me if you must. But please let me go to her."

She looked straight at him. Where in him was the man she loved? When he met her eyes, she had to turn away. She cast her gaze on the wall, at the picture there of the Ka'aba, the sacred stone house built in Mecca by Prophet Abraham and his son. The Ka'aba stared back at her, a cube draped in black, an island circumambulated by an ocean of pilgrims performing their prayers. "Say something," Kasim said, and her thoughts left the Ka'aba and Mecca and she grew aware first of him crouched by her feet, and then of his warm hands on her thighs. The nerve, she thought, clenching her teeth. He'd mentioned Devika by name in her presence for the first time. She looked at him, watched how he proceeded to clutch her wrists like a bewildered child, shaking them back and forth as though he wanted *her* to urge him to go to his newfound love. It had been "Farid's teacher" or "Farid's tutor" three years ago when Farid was in sixth grade. When, last year, Venu chose French instead of Marathi, Farid insisted on taking French as well. There'd been arguments between father and son.

"Who cares about French in India?" Kasim argued. "Marathi is the city's language. Who in Bombay will employ you if you don't know Marathi?"

"But Venu found out French is simple. Just *le, la, les,* some *avoir* and some *être.*"

"Venu is an oaf, a bad influence. No more Venu for you from now on."

"Venu's my best friend, but you have no friends so how would you know what that means?"

"Enough! He's your father, this is your son," Bilquis cried, but they went on and on anyway. They stopped only when she stepped in between them, an empty glass in her hand. She hurled it into a corner of the room. Days later, Farid chose French, Kasim spoke nothing directly to his son thereafter, and Bilquis became the messenger between them. At the start of Farid's new term, Devika was let go, and the words "tutor" and "teacher" were not mentioned in the house again.

"Say I can go to Devika," Kasim said several times that morning before this year's Ramadan began.

"When have I stopped you in the past?" Bilquis said at last, hoping her tone assured him that for months she'd known he was seeing Devika each day, hoping, too, her expression, or the lack of one, was convincing him that pooh! not once had she cared.

Kasim let go of her hands. He rose to his feet. He swept back his graying hair with his palms. Then, without a word, he left the room.

Bilquis wished Farid would now do the same. She had gone through what he was suffering, and with just one fast remaining until it was Ramadan Eid, the Festival of Fast-Breaking, she wished not to revisit any of it again. There was *halwa* and *mithaee* to make, sisters, brothers, and in-laws to visit.

"But Ammi," Farid said. "How can you be so calm? Don't you at least want to know who the woman is?"

"What difference will that make?" Bilquis said. I used to care one time, she tried to tell him with her eyes. And did it do me any good? I couldn't tell anyone then. To keep social status, I can't tell anyone now. If he'd asked me to leave, where would I have gone? If he asks me to leave tonight, there's still no place for me to go.

"You are strange and puzzling, Ammi," Farid said.

Bilquis agreed. She prepared to leave the bed. What was the use of such talk? What was the point of discussing Kasim's affairs? The previous two, the only ones he'd confessed to, had been short; neither had lasted more than three weeks. She had told no one in order to keep the family name. She knew when his affairs began. She knew exactly when each one spent itself. At the end of each, Kasim was not unhappy it was over but elated and relieved. He would come home early from work for several days thereafter. At night, he'd lower his head into her lap or hold her for long in his arms. He'd lift her chin and tell her he was the most blessed man in India to have a wife as lovely and noble as she. But the Devika affair had persisted past three weeks, much longer, one year, one month, four days, to be exact. This time, although she could pinpoint the day it began, she couldn't tell when he'd whisper in her ear that she, his wife, was one in a million, that he was the luckiest man alive. The spell, or whatever he called it, was especially strong this time. Maybe he was truly helpless, weak, and defeated like he'd said.

"I will never, *never* speak to that man," Farid said, gritting his teeth. He turned away from Bilquis and faced the wall. "Now I won't even look at his face."

Bilquis rushed toward him. She struck his arm.

"You bear no right to speak of your papa that way." She shook her head. Her long earrings swung and slapped her cheeks. "How soon you forget all he's done for you." Farid stepped away from her. She reached out and held his arm. "He is a good man inside, Farid. We both know that. He's a caring, providing father."

"Ammi, *bas*, enough!" Farid said. "If only you could hear what you say. Papa hardly talks to you. He bears no feelings for me, he doesn't even—"

Bilquis brought her fingers to his lips. "You will pelt your own father with stones? No. No son of mine will do that. Your papa loves you. He's told me so many times. His present situation is temporary," she said.

"Situation?"

"Yes. We should see it like that. He has succumbed to such indulgences in the past. But this one, like the others, will, when it's over, deliver him to us."

"There have been others?"

"Keep faith, Farid. Believe in your heart this one will pass."

Farid considered grabbing her shoulders and shaking them hard. "I don't understand you," he said, holding his brow. "There have been others, Ammi? I don't know what to say. Why is there no anger, no jealousy in you?"

Bilquis looked around the room for a wall clock. She remembered the room didn't have one. "What is the time? I had better warm the food for breaking the fast," she said. "Enough of this."

"Ammi, how can you be so calm?"

"No more on the subject. Go perform your ablutions. It is nearly time to say the evening prayer."

"But how can you—"

"Farid, go, I said!"

•  •  •

It was well past nine when Kasim came home that night. He found no one in the living room, or hall, as the family called it. He set his briefcase on the floor, took off his shoes and socks. He considered sitting on the couch for a while, but went to the bedroom instead. There he found Bilquis in bed, her back to the door, her brown cotton sari settled over her body like a low range of hills.

"Bilquis," Kasim said. She did not stir. "Bilquis," he said again, louder than before. As though he were waking from sleep, he swept his hand over his brow, over his cheek, and down his beard. The weight of the day, of many turbulent days, seemed to bear down on his heart. He went to the creaky almirah and opened its doors. When Bilquis turned on her back, he unfastened his necktie, flung it into the darkness of the almirah, and shut its doors.

"Good. You are awake," he said, approaching the bed.

She sat up, rubbed one eye with the heel of her hand. "Y'Allah. Is it morning? What time is it? When did you come? Shall I warm the food? I thought for a moment that I slept through the alarm."

"I ate," he said.

He wasn't keeping the fasts this year. He had stopped keeping them now for two years in a row. One Sunday before last year's fasts he announced to her he would fast no more. His words stunned her. She stood before him, shaking, unable to summon her voice. The Day of Judgment, she struggled to say. When it comes, my love, what will you do? Her remonstrations continued all through the day, but he countered them with grimaces. When she tried to hold his arms, he brushed her hands away. "I've done my share," he declared. "In fact, I've done far more than my share."

She came to stand before him. She said she wouldn't let him pass, she couldn't let him fall in His eyes. He chuckled and walked straight into her. She tried to push him back. Finally, he lifted her with both hands and set her aside.

"What have all the years of fasting brought me?" he asked her in bed that night. They lay on their backs, their eyes on the ceiling. "What good has it done me or you? I'm still an assistant manager at that hopeless Progress Bank. You are still a simple housewife in this stupid tiny flat. So why the penance? Why did we deprive our bodies of food all these years?" She turned on her side and showed her back to him. She couldn't think of what to say or where to begin. She hoped he'd stop, but to her dismay he went on. "Why food in any case? Why not abstain from something else? Music, for instance. Or love, work, books, perhaps. But no, it has to be food, someone merrily decided. Well, it's rubbish. You have anything to say to that? Of course you don't. And you know why? Eh, Bilquis? Well, I'll tell you why. Because you practice faith blindly. You refuse to question. But I use my mind and I *do* question and I've had enough. So I've decided there'll be no more fasts for me. You, too, needn't fast by the way. You have my consent."

Bilquis switched off the night lamp. Her eyes remained on the dresser in the corner. Slowly, she made out its tall oval mirror in the dark. "But Farid," she said, hoping the boy's name would make him reconsider. If the father won't fast, why will the son?

"He also needn't fast," Kasim said. "You can tell that son of yours that I, his father, said there's nothing to be gained." He heaved a sigh and shut his eyes. Three hours later, wrecked by insomnia, Bilquis was sitting up, arms folded, her feet lowered to the cold dark floor.

"Where did you eat?" she asked him now, sitting upright in bed, regretting her query already. She was relieved when he did not reply. She watched him unbutton his shirt, watched how when he looked down, his belly protruded and his chin disappeared, how his raised eyebrows deepened the lines on his brow. How suddenly their bodies had aged. She grew conscious of her own. Once their bodies were young and supple, and then, one day they weren't. She lifted her arm and examined it. How soft and loose her skin had become.

"We had another late meeting at the bank," he said, removing his cuff links, offering no details. Everything in the room seemed to acknowledge the battle raging in him, a vicious and devouring battle that was tearing him, insisting he submit, comprehend his place in the universe and come to terms with himself. He'd always been indecisive. He'd always wondered why he had to be satisfied with just one thing. "Once those idiots Mistry and Narayan start yapping at the meetings, no one, not even the bloody Prime Minister of India, can shut them up," he said.

"There is some *khichdee*," she said. "I can warm it for you. It won't take long."

His fingers stood still for a moment over his cuff link. He began to scratch at a spot on his sleeve. "I told you I ate," he said.

Bilquis lay down on the bed and stared out the window at the sky. When would he stop fabricating stories for her? Late meeting at the bank, it was some days. Delayed trains on others. She was a gullible fool, he thought no doubt. This woman, with only six years of schooling, will believe anything I say. Didn't he realize she knew where he'd been, that in spite of knowing she wasn't going to care? Perhaps he expected her to care. Perhaps he wanted her to challenge his claims of meetings and traffic jams and have a heated argument.

She felt his hand on her ankle. She drew up her foot and raised her head to stop him with her eyes. He had come to sit by her feet and was now staring hard at the floor.

"Bilquis," he said, his voice hollow, a strained echo from across a hundred Arabian Seas.

"Yes?" she said. "What is it?"

He seemed to be collecting his thoughts, seeking an order in the disquiet and disarray that now defined his life. "Nothing," he said first, and then, "How are the fasts going?" surprising her with his concern, his eyes avoiding hers.

She brought her head down on the pillow. She searched for a star in the slice of sky caught in the window. "They've felt longer than last year," she said. "Tomorrow, by the way, is the last one this year."

"Yes," he said, responding, it seemed to her, to some question of his own. He placed his hand on her knee. "Why do we do what we do?" he said.

Bilquis sighed. From the contemplative nature of his tone she could tell he wouldn't let her sleep.

"Like fasting, you mean?" she said, and wondered why she had spoken, why she had bothered to offer anything at all.

Her suggestion intrigued him. "Maybe," he said, wrinkling his brow. "Maybe fasting." He turned to face her. Something was amiss, Bilquis decided. Something had happened between him and Devika, she could tell. "I don't know what to do, how or why I should go on," he said. He jabbed his heart. "This thing inside me, Bilquis. It grows and grows and grows."

"Grows?" she said. "What grows?"

He scratched his forehead, and she waited while he fished for a word in the confusion pooling in his mind. "Emptiness," he finally said, and, lowering his head, turned away.

She remained still, wide-eyed. Almost every three nights this Ramadan he'd come home with some curious phrase for her. "Sorrow and futility" it was last week, "contrition and martyrdom" it was three or four days ago, and now "emptiness." Who knew what he'd lay before her next. If she said nothing tonight, he would stop and let her be. He'd let her sleep so she could awake at five to prepare the predawn meal. "Keep the last fast," she suggested to him.

He let go of her. "Is that all you can offer? God only knows how many times I have told you that that is *not* what I need."

"You are right," she said resignedly, keeping her voice low, hoping to calm him. "Sorry. My mistake. You don't need it. I forgot you've done your share. Well, it is late. I have nothing more to say and, please, I need to sleep. Has Farid returned from Venu's place?"

"It's not Ramadan fasts I need, Bilquis. It is you I need. I want you to help me not go to her," he said.

"Kasim, please. It is late. Not now. I must rise early."

"It's become a war I can't win by myself. I'm asking you to stay by my side."

Bilquis clutched her brow. He took both her ankles in his hands. "I mean, why did I ever go to Devika when I had you and Farid? Why didn't you try to stop me all along?"

Bilquis covered her eyes with her elbow. She felt him draw closer to her. He hooked a finger under her bangles and gently began to tug.

"Maybe if you had said, 'Kasim, don't go, I need you here with me,' I would not have gone."

She lifted her arm and turned to him. "All right," she said. "Don't go. Don't go to your whore."

He released her bangles and rose to his feet. He showed his back to her and stepped away from the bed. He mumbled something she couldn't follow. "You think this is easy for me," she finally heard him say. "You think I enjoy this, don't you? You believe I went to her because it made me happy." He laughed, silently. "But you know nothing," he went on. "How little you know about life, Bilquis. You keep silent now because you think you know everything about my life, your life, Farid's life, everyone's life, but let me tell you, let me tell you once and for all, that you don't know a bloody thing. That's right. Not *one* thing."

He trudged out of the bedroom. He was still talking to her from the hall when she read the alarm clock. It seemed to her several hours had elapsed. She pulled the blanket over herself. As it settled over her skin, she took a deep breath. Her mind soared into the clouds and beyond, past tomorrow's crescent moon of Ramadan Eid and into the silent gulf of space, and from there back to earth, past the dormant Arabian Sea and onward to Bombay and to the early hours of the next morning, to what she would prepare for herself and Farid. She wondered again if the boy had returned. She considered telephoning Venu's house. The thought loosened and slipped from her mind. He'll come home soon, she told herself. He always did. Farid was no child, she reminded herself, just as a door closed somewhere in the universe yawning open in her mind. He was home. How wonderful both father and son were home, under one firmament, one roof. In the name of Allah, the Compassionate, the Merciful, Bilquis thought, then said, and within moments sleep came.

• • •

She felt relieved she was finally on her way to Devika's flat. She would have had to go to her sooner or later, so why not today, this last day of Ramadan? She could have told someone before she'd stepped into Mehta Street and hailed a taxi. Or at least scribbled a note for Farid. But then he'd wonder why she was going to meet his ex-tutor, suddenly, after all these years, and he'd know, he'd put it all together. Bilquis folded her arms. So what if he knew? Why shouldn't he know what his dear Marathi teacher was up to?

"Driver, faster," Bilquis said.

"Too much traffic, Sister," the driver said. He lifted his hands. "How can I drive faster than this?"

She sat back in the taxi. She grabbed the upholstery on either side of her. Only minutes ago, she had telephoned Devika and, on hearing her voice, had put down the receiver. Perhaps she should have informed Devika that, like it or not, she was on her way. What if Devika had been about to leave her house? What if Kasim had skipped a day of work and was with her? In her arms. Perhaps lying on her bed. Bilquis covered her eyes. She brought her fists down on her lap. There was so much honking, so many cars and buses roaring outside. She raised her wrist to read the time. She'd forgotten to wear her watch, she realized. She asked the driver the time. He told her it was a few minutes past four. There was still an hour for Kasim to leave Progress Bank. It would take him at least an hour more to reach Devika's flat. Bilquis leaned forward. "Little faster," she said. She should have set out sooner. Left immediately after the afternoon prayer and not one full hour later. She'd better turn back. What had made her leave her home so rashly? How could she have set out without telling a soul? Perhaps it wasn't too late to return to Mehta Street, to ask this man to turn his car around.

"Driver," she said.

"Sister, please calm down. I told you I cannot go faster. Do you not see all the buses and cars? Don't worry. I will take you to Tilak Road one way or another."

Bilquis looked around. He was right. Motorcars surrounded the taxi so closely, so menacingly, she thought it would be impossible to open a door let alone turn a car around. She threw back her head against the seat and shut her eyes.

Ramadan would come to an end today, and tomorrow it would be Eid. She didn't want to ever awake at five. Why, she almost didn't get up today. Had Farid not stirred her leg at 5:15 who knows when she'd have opened her eyes.

"Ammi, get up," Farid had said. "Only one more fast to go."

Both she and Kasim had sat up together. They breathed fast, in unison, like one person split momentarily into two, their hands held firmly over their hearts. Seeing them like that, Farid had backed away. "It is 5:15," he said, softly, proceeding out of the room.

"Come, it's late," she told Kasim, the words coming from the memory of Ramadans gone by. He sat still while she tore their blanket away from herself.

She'd made it out of the room. She'd had to reach for the wall in the darkness several times. Will you fast, she had asked Kasim indirectly, God knows why, and by saying nothing he had refused. His silence stung her. It seemed to swell in the room, to prod her gently out of there. How silly of her: "Come, it's late," she had said, having expected him on this last day of Ramadan to rise with her and seek out Farid.

The taxi gained speed and turned left on Tilak Road. The traffic was lighter here. A breath of cool air gusted past Bilquis. A minute later, she asked the driver to stop the car. He brought the taxi to a halt, leaned toward the meter and read out the fare. She did not react, but sat still, like the driver, and listened to the sounds of the street converging inside the car. "Seventy-eight rupees, sixty paise," he said again and turned around to find Bilquis in tears.

He faced the steering wheel again and watched her in the mirror. "What is the matter, Sister?" She smeared her tears with a shaky hooked finger. "Did you not want Tilak Road?"

She told him she did. She said nothing was wrong, that the building she was seeking was called Diamond Hill. He said he knew where it was, look! there it stood, only a few yards away.

Outside the building's gate, Bilquis stooped before his window and paid him the fare. "Sister, you will be all right?" he asked, folding the bills around the coins and tucking them into the pocket of his shirt. He rested one hand on the steering wheel and stuck the elbow of the other out the window. "If you want," he said, "I will wait here for some time."

She shook her head. "You are a kind man, Brother, and I am grateful. But I have to do this by myself." She smiled and struggled to suppress a fresh bout of tears. "Go, go. There is no need to wait."

She was in the lift. She must have told the young lift attendant the floor she desired for he seemed to know where she was going. When the lift came to a stop, he drew open the gates. "This is sixth floor, memsahib," he said. Bilquis stepped out. The lift clattered, hummed, and gently sank out of sight. Bilquis proceeded down the corridor, toward a door polished to a dark chocolate brown and bearing no name. She stood before it for some time. She listened for sounds. She saw the doorbell but chose to knock instead. She counted to five. She knocked again. She counted to three. She knocked one more time. Her heartbeat raced. She looked down the empty corridor. She knocked harder and harder. With each knock, she found herself hoping no one would answer the door.

• • •

"Oh!" Devika said upon seeing her standing outside. "Bilquis!" She swung open the door wider and stepped aside. "Come in, come in please. My goodness. I don't know what to say. This is such a surprise."

With hesitation, Bilquis stepped into the flat. Only once had she come here before, long ago, when Devika had slipped on some stairway and bruised her knee. Devika couldn't come over to teach Farid, so Farid had had to be escorted to her place. Bilquis scanned the room, as she had then, pausing on the picture frames still cluttering the walls, on the television with enormous indoor antennae, the fake plants, and finally on the lace curtains ballooning with the breeze.

"It's been so long," Devika said, shutting the door. She had lost much weight over the years. Her arms were so thin her bangles traveled nearly to her elbows when she moved her hands. Her beauty had matured somehow, in just three years, the lines around her eyes marking the passage of time. She stepped around Bilquis and motioned her toward the couch. "How nice to see you. Will you take tea? Biscuits? Pastries?"

It bothered Bilquis that Devika seemed happy. Bilquis shook her head. It is still Ramadan, she wanted to say. This is the ninth month of our lunar year and I shouldn't be here, in this vile house, before a woman as fallen in His eyes as you, but it being Eid tomorrow, the most auspicious day of the Islamic year, I am driven to your doorstep to ask you to hand back to me what is mine.

"How is Farid?" Devika asked, directing Bilquis toward the couch again.

As if you don't know, Bilquis thought. As if Kasim has not smuggled photographs of my son into this flat. How well you pretend, sweeping your almond-shaped eyes all over my skin, stretching your painted lips into a slippery smile as though we are old friends.

"Don't stand, Bilquis. Sit, sit. Please."

"This is no social call," Bilquis said, relieved to have located her voice, finding herself advancing toward the couch. She stopped herself, remembering why she had come, deciding quickly it would be more appropriate to stand. "I am not here to visit you. I believe you know why I am here. But I will say it anyway. I've come to ask you to return him to me."

Devika settled into the armchair opposite the couch. Her eyes danced over the floor. She reached for an earring and seemed surprised to find one there. "I have nothing to give you," she said. "Please sit, Bilquis. We have not seen each other in many days."

"And that surprises you? I suppose you expected us to meet, to sit on each other's laps perhaps in spite of all the harm you have done."

"I do no harm. And when I said, 'We haven't seen each other in many days,' I was referring not to you and me. I have not seen *him* for long is what I meant. The last time we saw each other was many evenings ago. He stood just where you stand now, glaring at me with the same bitterness that now fills your eyes. Earlier that morning, I told him that in a dream I saw the end of my life from a point in time after my death. I saw my life-journey had no place for him. So I told him to stop coming here because our friendship was cursed, doomed, that like some crippling disease it would lead to nothing, nowhere."

" 'Friendship?' Is that what you call it now? I know women like you. Don't smile, Devika. Believe me I do. What I don't know, however, is why he comes to you, what men find in women like you."

"What they must not find in you," Devika said, lifting her eyes. She rose from her chair. She rearranged the pendant of her necklace, and folded her arms. "Look, we can discuss this situation like mature women or we can resort to name-calling like schoolgirls. I have not taken him from you. Not once have I asked him to come to me. Today he and I are good friends, that's all." The windowpanes rattled. The curtains rose and fell. A gentle breeze swept across the room. When it died, Devika proceeded toward the window. She stopped halfway. "When he comes here, he is happy, like a child. But when it is time for him to leave, he becomes remorseful first, then annoyed. I always believed it was leaving my home that troubled him each time, but then one evening he said he was angry at himself for having come at all to my door. What a horrid thing to say! I told him a hundred times afterwards that he needn't come; if visiting me upset him so much, he should stay at home, with his dear wife and son locked in his arms." She wrapped her sari snugly over her shoulders. She approached Bilquis, sighed, and smiled. "Sorry. I lost my temper there. How is my darling Farid? Does he remember his Marathi? Does he ask about me? I didn't mean to sound upset. Please sit, Bilquis. There are other things we can talk about." She reached for Bilquis's arm but, changing her mind, drew her hand away. "Well, all right. Stand if you prefer. But if you don't mind, I will sit on the couch." She waited for Bilquis to reconsider, to take the seat beside her. When Bilquis didn't move, she went on. "Farid was a son to me. Of course, you won't understand what it means to have no children. You don't know how much I've wanted to see Farid sometimes. Yet I didn't. I kept my word. His father told me, 'Farid is all his mother has. Promise me, Devika, you will leave Farid and Bilquis alone.' "

"Enough!" Bilquis said, her face pinched, her lips quivering. "Farid is my son, our only child. You bear no right to speak his name. You have driven a knife between father and son. What more do you want? Will you step now between mother and child?"

Devika rose to her feet. "I think you are too upset to discuss anything sensibly today," she said.

Bilquis backed away from her. "When Farid was a little boy," she said, "his father would carry him to the terrace of our building on the eve of Eid. He'd hoist him on his shoulders, and say, 'Son, can you see the crescent moon of Eid?' Those days are not spoken of now, their memories poisoned by your name. I am ready to leave now. Set him free. For his son's sake. Tomorrow is our Eid. That is all I have come here to say."

Devika sighed. "I've told him he needn't come here. What more can I say? If he is not with you, I don't know where he is. If you can't keep him with you, if you can't give him what he seeks . . ."

She stopped speaking, for Bilquis, having put her hands over her ears, was making her way toward the door.

"Yes, leave," Devika shrieked, following her. She ran up to Bilquis and seized her arm. "Like him, you come here on your own, without my invitation, and when you feel ashamed for having come, you vent your rage on me. Cowards! Get out. Go away from my house and from my life." She flung open the door. Bilquis hurried out. "Run, Bilquis. Run! Yes, faster! And tell your spineless eunuch of a husband this tonight: Stay away, stay far away from me."

· · ·

Outside Diamond Hill, Bilquis found the taxi parked exactly where she had left it. Anger surged through her, then retreated, making way for a calming sense of relief. She approached the car, saw the driver reach over his seat to open the rear door. She held the folds of her sari in her fist and climbed in.

"To Mehta Street?" the driver asked.

"Yes," she said, breathing hard. "Hurry." She pulled the door shut and folded her arms. She had a feeling that not only the driver but all of Tilak Road was watching her from the rearview mirror. No sooner did the car advance than Bilquis asked if there was a faster way to get to Mehta Street. "The traffic," she said, "may still be heavy on the road we took before."

The driver said there was a way, in a city like Bombay there was always another way, such as the route via Danda which, by his estimate, was two or three kilometers longer, nothing more.

"I see. Then it doesn't matter," Bilquis said. "Take any road you want. I don't care. Drive me back to Mehta Street, that's all."

He chose the Danda route, which soon pleased her because she had forgotten this route afforded a brief near-panoramic view of the Arabian Sea. She could use the view now. Indeed, especially now.

She would have him stop the car for a while so she could step into the wind and listen to the crash of waves.

She would evict the meeting with Devika from memory, set it free in the wind, or drown it in the sea, even though Devika's face kept resurfacing in her mind. Had she imagined it all, she wondered. Or had she gone and kneeled at Devika's doorstep like a mendicant today? Bilquis looked out the window. Each balcony in the sky-rises sailing past on her left seemed to be following her progress down the road. Of course she'd met Devika. Of course she had confronted her, for now here she was, housed safely in this rumbling taxi that was shielding her from the turbulent world outside.

Bilquis touched the car seat before her. If only she could stay inside this shell forever, if only Kasim and Farid were with her now, on her either side. She had held out cupped palms today and Devika had, in effect, spat on them, cast her out of Diamond Hill with words Bilquis would take to her grave.

The stench of drying fish soon filled the car. Bilquis rolled up the window and asked the driver to follow suit. They inched their way through Danda's busy open-air fish market where on either side of the narrow and curving road stood a succession of bamboo stilts. Tiers of fish curtained the space between the stilts like folds of a drape catching the fading light of the sun. The car rumbled on, cleaving through the smell and roar, moving past an army of shirtless *dhobis* whipping bedsheets in unison against a bed of rocks. Bilquis rolled down her window, for up ahead, emerging gradually from the left, was the grayish blue expanse of the Arabian Sea. The road soon swung left and her heart leaped when the sea filled her view.

Her thoughts revisited Farid, how he'd kept all the fasts this year, and how for his happiness she had ventured to Diamond Hill. His respect for his papa was essential. Harboring resentment for his father, no son could grow. She had made them shake hands, made them embrace many times in the past but these had served as mere gestures in the end. Vain and empty rituals. "What has aroused such antipathy in your heart for your papa?" she asked Farid in the kitchen once, point-blank. "Hatred for anyone, especially for one's father, is unpardonable, Farid." As before, he said nothing at first. When Bilquis persisted, he swung around and yelled, "But look how he treats you." He took his eyes off her and fixed them on the carpet. His eyebrows had risen, corrugating his brow. "A man who cares not about himself cannot care for you or me."

Not true, she had blurted. Papa does care about you. But Farid, leaning farther from her, wrenched himself from her arms. She let go of him.

"You can't make me like him, Ammi," he said, departing, not looking in her direction. "You can't make me love someone who's never around."

She could counter that with nothing, for even when Kasim was home, he made little effort to talk to the boy. But now that she'd braved Diamond Hill, the tension at home, she hoped, would die. *Every hardship is followed by ease.* That line in the Sura "Comfort" in the Qur'an was written for her. She said it to herself again. *Every hardship is followed by ease.* She'd make sure the situation at home would change, return to how it once was, how it should be. It is never futile to hope for reconciliation, she thought. Though thick walls have risen between father and son, separating boy from man, I will tear each down, brick by brick if necessary.

She asked the driver the time. He informed her it was ten minutes past five.

Kasim could be on his way home. He was on the train from Dadar to Bandra, or maybe it was Khar he got off now and took a rickshaw or bus to Tilak Road. How strange of Devika to say they'd not met in days when clearly that couldn't be true, for where else could he be going, with whom was he spending his evening hours?

The driver cleared his throat and spat out the window. Bilquis watched him in the rearview mirror. How strange it was, too, that she and the driver, two people who had never met each other before today, could feel so bonded, like siblings, as if every moment they'd lived had worked solely to realize this encounter. Imagine! He had waited for her in his taxi, this man whose name she didn't know, who had understood without her telling him that despair was choking her heart.

"Brother," she said.

"Yes?" he said.

"What is your name?"

He seemed surprised by her question. "Ram Prasad," he said.

"Why do you ask?"

She couldn't think of what to say. "Do you like driving? Driving this taxi, I mean. I mean, do you drive it every day?" she asked.

He met her eyes in the mirror. He nodded and said it was the only thing he was qualified to do in the city, the only thing that let him send money periodically to his wife and daughter back in Ratnapur.

"Ratnapur?" Bilquis said, aware that Ratnapur was far away but uncertain of where exactly it was.

"Yes," he said, and looked away. "They want to come to Bombay but where do I make them stay? We are six taxi drivers sharing one room in Mahim. What can one do? I have not seen them for . . . let's see . . . sixteen months now."

They drove on in silence, the road suddenly free of cars and tracing the foamy rim of the sea. She would die, she thought, if miles or months were to separate her and Farid. Bilquis stared out the window. Clouds had gathered like surf near the horizon, clearing up the rest of the sky. In the distance she made out a lighthouse. She leaned toward the window and let the breeze rush past her face.

"Stop the car," she said. "For just two minutes."

He kept the meter running while she walked across the wide footpath, toward the wall that rose to her knees. The wall ran the length of the road, separating sea from land. Far off, Bilquis saw a couple abandon it to stroll away from the sea.

Why do we do what we do, he'd asked her last night, as if she alone held the answers to his swelling tide of doubts. Bilquis watched the waves leap over the rocks. She liked how the rocks simmered white, how with each wave's demise their dark hue would show. She stepped forward. She clasped her hands and leaned into them. Here lay the answer to his question, she thought. We do what we do for the same reason the waves now advance toward the shore. She turned to the horizon. No barrier marks where our selves end and where the earth begins. She paused for a while on that thought. He wouldn't understand it. He would throw his hand on her shoulder and chuckle at her theory. She could see him shake his head, hold his brow, and leave their bedroom.

When the taxi sounded its horn, she remembered the meter was running, and turned her back to the sea. She came to stand before the car. She asked the time and learned it was almost 5:30. Bilquis considered this while eyeing two vacant rickshaws parked under a coconut tree a short walk away. She'd take one home, she decided. She'd stay just a little longer by the sea.

"How much do I owe you?" she said, flicking open her purse.

"But Mehta Street?" the driver said. "Don't you want—"

"No," she said. She could feel his eyes reading her face. Suddenly she felt the need to explain herself, tell the driver who she was, what had made her ascend Diamond Hill, and why she wished to stay by the sea alone and never return to Mehta Street. She said nothing. It would be silly to unburden her thoughts on him. She'd enjoy confiding in him. She'd gain his sympathy. But then at night she'd bite into her fists, ashamed, curled up tearfully in bed.

"Brother," she said while he counted out her change, "you are a good man. But go now. I will be fine."

She took the change and faced the sea again. The wind grew so strong she covered her mouth with the loose end of her sari. She could allow no salt it bore to reach her tongue. "Neither grain nor drop from dawn till dusk" were the instructions she'd memorized as a girl. "In Ramadan, no food, no water while the sun is up," her mother and aunts would warn. "Remember, Bilquis: Even a smell inhaled deliberately may break your fast."

She was back at the wall. She sat down on it. She turned to the road and found to her surprise the taxi had not moved. She gestured to the driver to leave. The car did not budge. Bilquis wondered if he was looking in her direction. She waved to draw his attention but again he didn't respond. Bilquis wrapped her sari around her shoulders and turned toward the sea. She figured that, like her, he was enjoying a break from the ceaseless turmoils of the day. She glanced once more at him and decided he wasn't watching her at all.

• • •

Everything had gone well; she had managed to maintain her composure even in Devika's home. Yet now here she was, suddenly trapped among idling cars and blaring horns, and still in Danda. Ram Prasad's taxi had moved no more than inches in ten minutes. Bilquis covered her mouth with her hand. This was no ordinary traffic jam. No doubt something terrible had happened a few cars ahead. Why else would so many pedestrians be rushing there?

"Can you tell what is going on?" Bilquis asked.

"No," Ram Prasad said. "Accident, maybe."

They waited in the taxi for a while, neither of them moving or speaking, as if they'd agreed to preserve the stillness within a car that had become a tranquil island in the ocean of mounting confusion outside. There was a familiarity to this moment. Some fragment of memory, jammed in the back of her mind, was being coaxed out, a memory of Kasim and herself in a traffic jam in Danda. On this very road. Years ago. It was the evening when they were last in Danda together. Bilquis folded her hands only to unfold them seconds later. They had gotten into a taxi and were returning home, she remembered, when the motorcar in front of them had braked without warning. A child had nearly been run over. The child's guardian, the grandmother possibly, screamed from the footpath just as car after car came screeching to a halt. The man whose car nearly knocked down the child verbally lashed at the grandmother for her negligence. A foul quarrel commenced. Invectives followed. Abundant curses were exchanged. Finally, ignoring pleas for a truce from onlookers, the grandmother sat the boy and herself in the middle of the road. The traffic stood still in both directions for an hour.

Perhaps something similar was happening now. If only she had not asked Ram Prasad to stop by the sea . . .

"This is my fault. I am sorry," Ram Prasad said, rupturing the silence cocooning Bilquis. "I should not have taken this road today."

"You did not know," Bilquis said. "None of this is your doing."

She expected him to speak. Instead he opened the car door to step outside. He walked a few paces to get a better look down the road. Bilquis craned her neck toward the window. "Can you see what has happened?" she cried. Ram Prasad shook his head.

Bilquis watched him walk away until he disappeared into the thickening crowd. She turned to the people huddled on the footpath, all facing the cause of the commotion. Danda was not what it used to be. None of the people reminded her of herself and Kasim years ago. She thought of the many strolls they had taken in Danda, his favorite location for spending the evening. How they would hold hands and let go whenever someone walked past . . . Six evenings a week they came to sit on the wall, to face the glassy sea, giving the wind no space to cruise between them. They'd stopped their Danda walks shortly before Farid's birth, Kasim's question to her on their last evening here marking the end of their trips. She'd been in a pensive mood that evening. She had wanted to go home. She'd been about to suggest that they hail a taxi when Kasim asked, teasingly, who she was thinking about.

"What do you mean?" she said. She blinked at him. "Why, nobody," she said. She turned to face the sea. "Who could I be thinking about?"

She felt his breath on her neck. "Not even of me then?" he said.

She'd pushed him away. In truth, she had been thinking of their child she was carrying. When he asked again, she rose from the wall and insisted they go home. He rose, too, apologizing. "All right. Let's go home," he said after moments of silence. "We'll come back tomorrow." She said nothing. In the taxi he held her arm and asked what the matter was. She told him the wind was too strong for her, that at this stage in the pregnancy, wasn't it best she remain indoors? The little boy ran across the road just then, Bilquis recalled. The grandmother screamed and cars braked in time, sparing his life. "No more evening walks for me," she told Kasim then, one hand on her belly, Kasim squeezing her free hand. When he said over dinner that her refusal to join him meant he'd have to go to Danda all by himself, she sealed her lips for the rest of the day. She remembered he came home late from work one evening a few days later, and the first of his affairs began.

Ram Prasad emerged from the crowd. Bilquis leaned forward, relieved to see him making his way toward her.

"Yes, accident," he pronounced, and seated himself in the car. "Ambassador and a lorry. Ambassador is finished. Front of it is totally gone. Two schoolchildren are still sitting inside."

Bilquis clicked her tongue. "Are they hurt?"

Ram Prasad shrugged. "Don't know. By God's mercy their driver was saved." He glanced at his wristwatch. "An ambulance is coming. The traffic jam will clear soon."

Bilquis shifted in her seat. "I hope so," she said. "I have my fast to break."

Ram Prasad met her eyes in the mirror. "Fast?" he said. "You are Muslim?" Bilquis weighed the implications of her answer in her mind. Because of the Hindu-Muslim riots in the city no one asked such questions. She nodded. Ram Prasad rolled down his window some more. His door hadn't shut fully, so he opened it and shut it hard.

"Today is the last fast," she said. She leaned into the window to search the sky. "Tomorrow is Eid. The new moon will be sighted today."

Ram Prasad joined her in scanning the sky. "I don't see the moon," he said. He turned around to look at her and lifted a steel tiffin-box that must have lain by his side. "There is one *chappati* in here," he said. "Nothing more. If you want you may—"

"Oh no, no," Bilquis said, arresting the box's advance with her hand. "That is very kind and thoughtful of you, Brother. But my son is waiting for me. I must reach Mehta Street before 6:10. There is dinner to warm, prayers to say."

Ram Prasad read his wristwatch. "Actually, unless the traffic clears very soon, we will not get to Mehta Street in time."

"Oh," Bilquis said. She rubbed her throat. "Then please turn the car around."

Ram Prasad shook his head. "It will take us even longer to reach Mehta Street that way."

"I see," Bilquis said. She sat back and tried to relax the tightness she felt in her arms. "Insh'allah, we will move in a minute," she said.

They didn't. They sat in silence for several minutes. Finally, an ambulance siren bled through the air. It grew louder, but then subsided like a wailing child lulled at last into sleep. The van had arrived to rescue the two children, Bilquis thought. The pandemonium increased. The victims were somebody's children. She hoped they had a mother. She thought of Farid, of the temerity with which he sometimes raced his bicycle down Mehta Street, letting go of the handlebar to throw his arms skyward whenever he found her watching him from the balcony. He'd roar with laughter when she'd shout his name or wag her finger at him.

"I should not have chosen this road," Ram Prasad said. "There is always some delay here. My mistake."

This was Devika's revenge, Bilquis told herself. She could have gone to Diamond Hill later, anytime after Ramadan.

"The matter, you see, was such," she said, her voice just above a whisper, "that, Brother, I felt it had to be settled before Eid."

Ram Prasad turned his head slightly in her direction. "I do not follow," he said.

She told him. She let things run out of sequence. She missed significant details. She found herself out of breath and held on to the back of Ram Prasad's seat. She paused to sort her thoughts. Then she gave voice to her mind even faster, the words colliding, fracturing, and competing against one another. By the end, she was gasping and in tears. Ram Prasad listened to her in silence, staring straight ahead, his knuckles white against the steering wheel. When he thought she was calmer, he leaned back in his seat and dropped his hands on his thighs.

"These things happen, Sister," he said. "Such is life." He looked down and then straight ahead again. "I also have something I want to share. May I tell you?" He took her silence for assent, and paused to watch someone pass in front of the car. "Last week, a businessman rode in my taxi. I recognized him in two seconds. He had had a heart attack in my taxi some four or five years ago. It was I who drove him to Bombay Hospital. He held my hand as they took him into the emergency room and said he would always be grateful to me. But he did not remember me last week. How do you forget someone who pulled you from the arms of death? But then I said to myself, 'Such is life, Ram Prasad. These things happen.' People forget or don't want to remember. I said, 'Forgive and forget, Ram Prasad. Pretend it did not happen and you'll be happy.' In any case, why expect gratitude? What can it mean to give with one hand and, at the same time, expect to receive in the other?"

Bilquis wrapped her sari tightly around her shoulders. She hadn't expected him to speak with such candor, so intimately, so freely. The space between them had somehow dissolved and taken with it the protocol that had set the terms between them. She felt close to him, closer than she wanted to feel toward him or anyone else at this time. It occurred to her his question wasn't rhetorical; he was waiting for an answer, perhaps for words to alleviate the disappointment he was feeling that had him hunched over the steering wheel now.

"What . . . ," she said, chafing her brow. "What is the time?" She regretted her words instantly. Ram Prasad was sitting erect in his seat. How inconsiderate, indifferent, and insensitive, he was saying to himself no doubt. My feelings, my experiences, my history, mean nothing to her. I am not a person. I am someone providing a service. Bilquis felt her arms grow taut again. She sensed her mind closing in on itself. She struggled to cleave it open, to search for language that would convince him of her empathy. But Ram Prasad, she observed, had already read the time and was watching her in the rearview mirror. Bilquis stared back while he reached for something by his side. She was still attempting to summon her voice when he brought his tiffin-box into her view again.

"Sister," he said, turning around. He opened the box and offered the *chappati* to her. It lay rolled on one side of the box. "You will need this now. It is not much. I will stay outside the car while you break your fast. Take. Do not refuse. Please take."

• • •

What Bilquis would remember for years afterward was the sight of Farid and Venu running towards Ram Prasad's taxi just as it stopped outside her building. "Ammi!" Farid cried, as she stepped out of the car. Bilquis paid the driver. She didn't look up, feeling certain all of Mehta Street was watching her. "What happened?" Farid said. "Where did you go? Venu and I have gone house to house in search of you."

Bilquis drew Farid close to her. "My son," she told Ram Prasad. Farid looked at him and then at Venu.

Ram Prasad smiled and started the car. Bilquis held her silence until he drove away. She saw Farid and Venu exchange more glances. When Ram Prasad's car was no longer in sight, she said, "There was a traffic jam. That is why I am late. That driver helped me break my fast. Did you break yours, Farid?"

Farid nodded. "But where did you go?"

Bilquis started to cross the street. She waited for two auto-rickshaws to pass. "I must go upstairs now. I have to warm the food."

"Papa is home," Farid said. "I think he's ill."

Bilquis looked up at the flat. "I see," she said. "Come upstairs for dinner in five minutes."

She wondered as she ascended the stairs why Kasim was home early. Perhaps Devika had spoken the truth when she claimed they hadn't met each other in days. Bilquis laughed silently. How readily she was condoning his trespasses, how willingly she was washing away his sins. She laughed at herself again, and shook her head. Just because he's home early the first time this Ramadan.

She entered the house and went straight to the bedroom. He was in bed. She advanced toward him. He lay sprawled, arms flung outward on either side, one sock dangling from his foot, the other sock coiled on the floor. She approached him in silence. He heard her, and propped himself on his elbows. Bilquis stood still. "Where did you . . ." he said, and lay down again. How aged and beaten you look today, she thought. Never have I seen you like this. She set the house keys on the dresser, arranging the keys into a small fan.

"I came home early today," he said. "I'm tired, Bilquis. So tired I think I will need your and Farid's help just to rise from this bed."

She said nothing. Where have *you* been, she had more right to ask than did he. She approached the mirror and took off her earrings. She saw her hands were shaking, that her brow was tense. Dropping the earrings on the dressing table, she continued to watch her face.

"I must know," she said. "I must know if it is over."

She leaned closer to the mirror and peered into her eyes. They were red in the corners, probably from the pollution in the city, she thought. She knew he was studying her face, hoping she would continue to speak so that he wouldn't have to.

"Yes," he said some seconds later. He turned on his side, showing his back to her. "It is over. Everything is over. Pleasure, purpose, motivation, fulfillment. All over. My passion for work has died too. I got nothing done today. Diligence, I thought, was one way to heal. It's not working for me. I don't know what I should do." He turned on his back and patted the mattress beside him. "Sit here. Close to me."

She left the mirror and proceeded not to the bed but to the window near it instead. She had to cling to the grill to steady herself. He had shut the windows. She reached above for the latch and managed to pull it loose. She was about to push the window open when, in its pane, she made out Kasim's reflection. He wasn't watching her as she'd presumed, but was staring at the wall in front of him.

It might be the picture of the Ka'aba he was concentrating on, she thought. She flicked her eyes toward the wall. "Sit here, next to me," she heard him say. He was watching the black stone, she realized. Perhaps his eyes would move now, pilgrimlike, around it. One revolution, two revolutions, three . . . She pushed the window open. Mehta Street below was abuzz with life. People were returning home, some from work, others from the bazaar. Couples were taking their strolls. A man and woman she did not recognize were about to cross the street. They stepped back to let a speeding taxi pass.

She would accept him as she had before. She would believe him no matter what anyone said. Believe, Bilquis, she told herself. Believe the affair is over, that he has been working long hours at the bank the past few days. She swept her eyes over the balconies in the surrounding buildings. People were leaning over the railings or seated on chairs. I don't care what any of you are saying, Bilquis thought. It is over, he just told me, and now when I will sit by his side and take his hands in mine, I will know that Devika was his last.

Despite the noise outside, she heard Farid's voice below. When he and Venu came into view, Farid was pointing at something down the street. For a moment, he seemed much older. She pictured him as a young man with a wife and children. She saw herself with them now, the children having linked their arms to form a circle around her.

"I nearly forgot," Kasim said. Bilquis heard him stir in bed. "*Eid Mubarak*, Happy Eid. Someone on the train said the moon was sighted today."

She didn't turn around. She would have to be strong, would have to contain herself when she stood before him. But poised delicately on the sharp edge of control she felt close to breaking down. It was Eid finally and yet she felt no joy, no relief from the month of fasting. She could fast another thirty days, she thought. Another ninety. Even more.

"Farid!" she yelled. "Farid!" He looked up at her and waved. "Come on upstairs."

He was still talking to Venu. Finally Venu turned away from him, looked up at her and waved. Bilquis did not wave, finding that her hands would not let go of the grill.

"How much more of your silence will I have to bear, Bilquis?" she heard Kasim say. "You and only you are the most important person in my life."

Farid had paused before the street, she noticed. He was looking left, now right. He took a step forward but then drew back at once. Bilquis's heartbeat raced when a lorry loaded with sheets of bouncing plywood passed by.

"Will you keep silent forever?" Kasim was saying. "It is over, I promise you. It is Eid, Bilquis. And I am home. Early. To be with you."

She took her hands off the grill. It is not over, she cautioned herself. This one is, but there will be another. And then yet another. I will know they are over when you won't have to tell me they are.

"Sit here. For a moment. I am so fortunate to have you with me."

All right, I will sit beside you. I will speak to you. You will break down like you did before on such occasions. After months of waiting I will take you in my arms.

"It is over, Bilquis. I promise. It will never happen again."

Yes, it is over, Bilquis thought. Our marriage is over, Kasim. You can keep the Devikas. One day Farid will keep me.

Farid was halfway across Mehta Street. Bilquis stood still, watching him, willing him to move away from the center and closer to her. He waved at her. She stretched out her hand. "*Eid Mubarak,* Farid," she whispered, stretching her hand farther. "*Eid Mubarak,* my son." Kasim was saying something. But she wasn't listening. She was trying instead to recall the day she first saw Farid cross Mehta Street alone.

# Trivedi Park

**RADHIKA KILLED HERSELF** six Sundays ago.

Sumiti and I were in our bedroom, reclined on the bed, listening to Lata and Rafi's *Golden Duets* on the gramophone, when the doorbell rang in a way it hadn't rung before. Sumiti started and I sprang to my feet. I ran into the living room to answer the door. It was Manukant Parikh of the fifth floor. He was bent forward, panting. His hands clamped his knees. This puzzled me, for I thought: He could have taken the lift up the two floors, couldn't he? And, in any case, where's the need to run up to our door?

"Arun!" he cried, not like a man of fifty, but like a terrified boy of ten. He straightened himself and held his brow.

"What is it?" I said.

"Radhika," he said, his fingers shaking, a tremble rending his voice. Radhika . . . ," he repeated but his voice failed him again. His forehead was creased. His eyes were wide open. A bead of sweat ran from his temple to his jaw. I wondered what he could want from my daughter, and I was considering not telling him she was in her room, studying for a trigonometry test scheduled for the next day, when Sumiti shrieked and Parikh and I dashed inside the house. I didn't know where to turn, for the cry seemed to have come from both bedrooms at once. Together, we burst into Radhika's room. There we found Sumiti alone, slumped on the bed, her face white, a look of horror in her eyes.

"Sumi, where is she?" I said, my heart thrashing against my ribs. "Where is she?" I said again as I scanned the room. I approached Sumiti. Her lips were fluttering like petals in a storm. She stood up, reached for my arms, and dug her fingers into my flesh. It was clear from the way her teeth were locked she couldn't say a word. In the other room, Lata and Rafi began a new song. The next instant,

Parikh's fingers were on my elbow. When he pointed at the window, I shook Sumiti's arms away. The white curtains were billowing gently with the breeze. People were flocked on the balconies in the building opposite ours.

"*Hai Ram*, no," I said, whereupon Sumiti began to wail.

I approached the window, leaned out, and gave a cry, for there she was, my precious girl, our only child, prostrate on the concrete seven stories below, a crimson halo expanding around her head.

I turned to the sky. It stared back at me. Parikh hauled me away and I fell into his arms.

She had lain like a blown flower, this girl of mine, her legs locked together to form the stem, her arms winged out like hollow leaves on either side. The blood, spreading in all directions from under her head, opened like a rose.

About a month ago, at six in the morning, I lay in bed, awake, aware of footsteps in the house. I turned to Sumiti on my left. She was asleep, resting on her side, her folded arm forming a second pillow under her cheek. I kept still for a while. I watched Sumiti breathe. Then I rose from the bed and threw on a shirt. Radhika's room was still and quiet. Yet, I sensed something shift and come alive, and a breath of energy rolled through the room. She was there, I know. She was to my left and to my right, and in front and back of me. Out the window, I saw the dome of night receding, pushed upward by the first traces of dawn. I approached the window. I pulled down the latch. I threw the window open, and waited. The footfall soon died and I knew that Radhika was gone.

It must require something more than courage to leap out a window, I thought that morning as I held the wooden sill. A bird flew past, daring a turn quite close to me. I thought, Radhika would have gazed out the window one last time before she died. She would have seen the forest of TV antennae crowning the shorter buildings. She would have seen, too, the steeples of St. Peter's Church in the distance straight ahead. She would have heard the rustle of the coconut palms, their patulous fronds twisting and swaying between the buildings of Trivedi Street. She may have looked right, I thought, and seen the iron gates of Trivedi Park where she played with her friends as a child. And then she would have looked away to stare long and hard at Trivedi Street below . . .

I backed away and shut the window. I fastened the latch and turned around. I haven't touched Radhika's window since that day.

Without Radhika, the house bears a funereal gloom. The buildings of Trivedi Street have become tombstones in my eyes. I sit now in the living room, alone on the couch. It is a little after five this wet Sunday evening. Outside, the rain is descending in torrents, washing Bombay clean. The TV is on but I've turned down the sound. A woman, wearing an enormous *bindi*, is reading a letter aloud to a boy. Her nose ring twinkles. Her eyes are baggy and lined with kohl. As she reads, her eyes shift from side to side like twin clocks keeping time.

If only I could accelerate these hours. If only it were already tomorrow. I can't do a thing in the house. I have midterm tests to grade—twenty booklets are piled by my side—but since yesterday my energy has lingered low. Like Sumiti, I am seduced by sleep. I have to dodge and outrun its widening snare. I try not to dwell on the pleasure of stretching out on the floor, or of giving myself up to this couch or of surrendering head-bowed and on my knees to the soporific ticking of the clock on the wall. I think I ought to get out of the house, thus wean my mind from the lure of sleep. But where should I go? Where *does* one go in heavy rain?

Sunday has become my dreaded day. It affords me no reason to flee the flat. My week begins when, at the railway station, I elbow my way through the Monday crowd and jump into a southbound local train. I get off at Churchgate, the train's final stop. I walk westward to Jai Hind College where, this term, I'm teaching Introductory Physics II to two sections that, together, meet five times a week. This semester, Saturdays are free but I still commute to the college by the eight o'clock train. Students stop by my office; I attend to administrative matters accrued through the week; I search for ways to eclipse the boredom of Sunday's impending hours. Saturday ends with a stroll along the crescent of Marine Drive. I watch the rush-hour traffic crawl by. I envy the birds riding the salty breeze. I sit on a bench amid a party of pigeons, and listen to the static and roar of the Arabian Sea.

There is nothing more painful than losing one's child. A part of you dies each day or falls into a permanent slumber. Wherever I look, I hope to see her face. Several times some days, I feel consumed by her presence, and then it's only her voice I hear faintly in my mind. Radhika would have turned fifteen (at 3:25 p.m.) today. All of last week, Sumiti and I pretended we didn't remember, that it held no importance, that neither she nor I really cared. At 3:25 p.m. this afternoon, Sumiti lay in bed, one arm slung across her eyes, the other over her belly. I stood beside the bed, watching the rain writhe down the panes. Then I sat by Sumiti's feet. She knew why I was with her then. She knew why I began to press her legs.

Sumiti has spoken little since Radhika died. We are careful with our words, as though we are neck-deep in waters churning around a whirlpool close at hand. When we speak, we use few, measured sentences, for we are conscious of how, each time, we draw closer to discussing our child. Sumiti worries me. She picks at her food, she wears the same sari all week, she does nothing but lie in bed all day. Soon after Radhika died, she made our room into her cell. "Silence placates me," she explained. "Solitude is good for the grieving soul." Sumiti has become a victim of lethargy, one could say. She will not respond when I point this out to her. She'll gather her brows and blink at the ceiling when I tell her she is defeating herself. At times she'll block her ears and shut her eyes as though these are crevices in the walls that separate her from the world.

The picture on the TV screen has faded. A commercial for Dazzle detergent has come on. A family, beaming in a courtyard, is draping spotless white garments over a clothesline linking two trees. I can't bear to watch them smile, their parade of delight all shallow and fake. I rise from the couch and proceed to the bedroom. Sumiti is in bed, awake, in only her petticoat and blouse. The fan spins above her, clicking, its rhythmic groans sounding like heartbeats in the room. Sumiti's sari lies coiled on the floor, the hills and valleys of its folds wriggling with the breeze. Her hands are stiff and pressed to her sides. Pivoted at the heel, her right foot rocks from side to side like a car's wiper fending off rain.

"Do you want tea?" I ask.

She does not answer. Her foot continues to swing.

"Sumi?" I say, louder than before. "I said shall I make some tea?"

Her foot stops shaking and she narrows her eyes. She lifts her head to stare not at me but at the bare wall to my right. "What is it now, Arun? Don't you have work to do?" she says. She throws back her head on the pillow and heaves a sigh. Her thumbs run over the tips of her fingers, again and again, as though to keep score of something repeating in her mind. I turn around and return to the living room. I sink into the couch and embrace my knees. I didn't want to drink tea in any case.

Sumiti will not see visitors, she has made known. When the relatives and neighbors stopped by she hardly said a word. Now she seldom leaves the flat. I don't know and don't ask what she does at home when I'm away. Meena, the girl who comes to cook and clean, has told me that some mornings she must ring the doorbell several times. When Sumiti lets her in, she instructs Meena on what needs to be done, then retires to our room. "Memsahib never answers the telephone," Meena confirmed for me this morning. "She said I had better not touch the telephone either." I told Meena we receive many wrong numbers. I lied, too, that the memsahib cannot sleep at night, therefore, she tries to rest during the day. Tomorrow, I told Meena, I will pluck the receiver off its cradle before I leave for work. I expect it will stay detached, asleep on its side, until I return.

Sleep approaches like a lengthening shadow. All day it has lurked behind me, stalked me through the house. Soon it will want to scale my back, surf over my shoulders, and trickle down my limbs. It will want to seep through my skin and siphon my resolve. But I shall not yield the way Sumiti has. My strength will not abate. I will sit here, my back straight, my knees joined, my senses on full alert. I will grade the students' tests. I will regrade them. Again and again, if necessary. I will score them until I've triumphed over sleep, until the test booklets are wrung free of all their errors. Until they are speckless. Clean. Like sheets that rise and fall. Lined side by side for drying in the sun . . .

"I wanted to say that I don't want tea," I hear Sumiti say.

I open my eyes and sit up on the floor. I walk on my knees and climb back onto the couch. I can't remember when I fell, when gravity gathered me in its arms. I shake my head. I lift my eyes to find Sumiti astir. She has slipped out of the tentacles of our bed at last. She stands in the hallway like a somnambulist, her long hair loose, her brow furrowed, her dazed eyes roving here and there. Sumi, there's nothing to fear, I want to say. Be brave. Come, step into the room.

"The volume is down," I hear her say as she points at the TV to her left. "What use is the picture without the sound?"

I lock my fingers behind my head. I return my gaze to the screen. The picture melts and another fades in, of a Rajasthani man in white flapping clothes, walking in the shadow of a camel in tow. As they plough down a dune, the wind sprays sand over their footprints, softening the creases moments after they are formed.

"I spoke rudely," Sumiti says. "I didn't mean to. When you came in, I was thinking of I don't know what at the time."

We watch the screen. The sound of the sibilant rain floods the room. I consider abandoning the couch and entering the balcony, where the floor has become a sputtering pool, where I see the railing and the plants are dripping with rain. In the opposite building, a boy and a girl stretch their arms out a window to collect raindrops in their palms. A man stands on the terrace of their building, his head thrown back, his hands trying to touch the clouds. When I return my gaze to the TV, I find Sumiti gone. I focus on the screen. Then I lean forward to listen, my forearms on my thighs. At first, only the patter of the rain fills my ears. But soon I pick up a cough and then the creak of the bed, and I know Sumiti has returned to her shell.

I spring from the couch and reach for the TV. I switch the set off and pace the room. I scour my chest and face with my hands. Languor is effaced by activity alone. The faster you advance, the farther it recedes. So I drive my feet into my slippers. I pace the room again. Then I rush for the main door and leave the flat. The door slams behind me as I tear down the stairs, the handrail along the wall squealing protests against my hand. The stairs roll and gallop and fly beneath my feet. Lower and lower I plunge, spiraling headlong down a helix that appears to have no end. On what seems to be the fourth floor, a woman shrieks, reels back, and then quickly says a hello. I lift my hand and utter a grunt while racing down the stairway two and three steps at a time.

At the bottom of the stairs I realize I have nothing to shield myself from the rain. I wait until the pain in my chest subsides. Then, diving into the downpour, I lift my face to the sky. Clouds have collected to form a gray, turbulent roof over Bombay. The rain bathes my arms and neck and face. It filters through my clothes and pastes them to my skin. I throw open my arms and turn around. I have driven drowsiness miles and miles away. Cool drops dribble down my cheeks to collect under my chin. I leave the compound drenched, my heart drunk with rain. A taxi chugs past, dragging four wings of water, spitting out jets that leap and crash against my feet. Turning right, I swash down Trivedi Street. The Asoka trees, once the footpath's towering sentinels, are stooped like willowy reeds, crooked into arches that hiss and sway with the breeze. Far down, someone navigates a bicycle in ankle-deep water, shuttling his weight from one pedal to the other. Water surges and swells wherever I look. It rinses compound walls. Sheet after sheet ripples down the street. The gutters on either side bear full-throated currents that gush toward the drains.

No sooner do I take my next step than familiar fingers feather my wrist. I pull my arms up to my chest and lower my head. I want to quicken my pace but I halt instead and grope for the trunk of an Asoka tree. She has returned, I know. Radhika is by my side again. I think of the rain dancing on my neck, of the runnels twisting down my chest. Water has streamlined into gurgling parabolas around my feet. Matchsticks spin and dance in the foam some yards away. You must not follow me, I warn her in my mind. Go to Mummy. Tell her to leave her room. I let go of the tree and resume my walk, an Asoka leaf strangled to pieces in my hand. If I steer my mind somewhere far from here, I know she will go away. I picture Churchgate Station. Jai Hind College rolls open swiftly in my mind. I think of the Coriolis force I will discuss in class tomorrow. Due to the curvature of a rotating earth, I will begin, an object in motion will veer from its path in direct proportion to its velocity. The force deflecting the object in the earth's frame of reference is called the Coriolis force. It's a pseudoforce, I'll say. Magnitude zero at the equator and maximum at the poles. I increase my strides. She increases hers. When I slow down, she does the same.

Daddy, wake up. It's five, she used to say.

I will have to listen to her again. The murmuring will not cease otherwise. I pitch the leaf into the gutter and watch it hurtle toward the drain. I remember how she would stir me awake at five in the morning, how her hand would rock my thigh. I remember sitting bolt upright in bed, my head hurting, my hand clamped over my mouth, my heart throbbing recklessly in the dark. I picture Sumiti turning on her side, clucking her tongue. It is early morning. The sky is silver-gray. The wind whispers gently in the fountains of coconut leaves. Radhika steps closer to me, rubbing her eyes, having come to lead me to her room, to her homework piled on her desk. We listen to Sumiti grumbling under her breath. We see her take my pillow and pull it over her face. "Won't even let me rest," her muffled voice says. "From now on, why don't you sleep in her room?" Radhika turns to leave. I follow her into her room where the desk lamp is on, where her shadow climbs over her bed and travels softly over the walls. We sit side by side, bent over her books. She writes slowly, painstakingly, her fingers pinching her pencil, the tip of her tongue visible between her lips. My forehead rests in my hand, my elbow on the desk. Radhika glances at me from time to time. The desk rocks when she swings her legs. "Sit still," I say as I read each word she writes. We'll spend two hours at her desk, as we've done each school day, continuing her lessons from where Sumiti gave up last night. I'll bob my head when her answers are right. I'll sit back and slap my thighs when her answers are wrong.

Send me to the special school, she tells me now. I attend to my walk. Send me to the school in Poona for stupid girls like me. There must be a way to suppress this voice, to uproot it from my mind. I kick the water left and right. Mummy says if I don't fare well, she'll tell Meena to dust the suitcases for my journey to that school. I run, squishing the water under my feet. I have to stop again. I hang my head, clench my teeth. I give up, Radhika. You have won. You have me out of breath. I cover my ears. I hum a tune. The girls poke fun at me, she says. Daddy, I don't want to be near them again. Where is she? Why won't she let me be? You don't need a special school, I want to shout. You are not like the children there. I drop my hands and double my fists. I can hear my heart hammering away.

I consider turning around and charging up Trivedi Street. I could bound up the building's stairs and seize Sumiti's arms. I need to tell her what is happening to me. I want to hold her hand over this pounding in my chest. Sumi, she won't free me, I will say. You've seen how I work, morning to night, minute by minute, but what she'd tell me some mornings keeps repeating in my mind. We were wrong, I will add, taking Sumiti's joined hands in mine. Wrong to worry who would one day match their son with our child in matrimony if everyone knew she was slow. Radhika was deficient, I will say, looking straight into Sumiti's eyes. We may as well lift the veil before the world now. A girl at fourteen should burn with shame when caught naked before her father. A girl at fourteen doesn't ask where her father "met" his sisters, why he had lived with them as a boy and not with the neighbors. You explained. I explained. Yes, she nodded, but kinships made no sense to her. Our child couldn't cope, Sumi. And we wouldn't accept that. So say it once. With me. "Radhika was slow." There's nothing to it. The neighbors and relatives have surely said it. You remember her school principal said it. The tutors we hired for her said it God knows how many times.

The street has bent slightly to the right, and Trivedi Park, to which the street is tangential, has inched into sight. Gone are the *bhel-puri* carts and the beggars that usually gather outside the entrance, the rain having driven them away. Gone, too, are the four-carriage giant-wheel and the small merry-go-round for toddlers. I don't recall when the park's entrance was vacated like this, when the street was thus deluged. For a moment it appears a storm has tunneled through the street, moistening it, whisking all life away. I tread with mounting difficulty toward the park, which is small and circular, fenced in by a hedge and a cordon of fruit trees. The narrow road skirting the park has become a shallow moat this evening, transforming Trivedi Park into a lush verdant island, its entrance into an abandoned harbor. A dozen buildings surround the park, facing a lotus tank that marks the park's center. A woman emerges now from a building straight ahead, the stem of her umbrella clamped between her neck and jaw, her sari bunched in her hands. She ventures forward, bracing her arm against the wall, probing the ground with her foot. Now she stops in her path. She glances at the clouds, turns around, and retreats indoors.

I pull open the gates and enter the park. The gates close with a dull thud behind me, sealing Trivedi Park from the world outside. The park is deserted, as though evacuated in a hurry, its patrons driven into their homes by the daylong rain. A hushed silence hangs over the ground, removed from the wind ruffling the tops of the trees, from the gray clouds that roll and play. With each step I take, it gets more silent, more becalmed, as though tranquility here is tied mathematically to the radius of the park. I stop to listen, to look around. This must be what desolation means. This must be what Sumiti is seeking in the confines of our room. I proceed, the smell of the ground carrying to me, and I feel certain that years, going backward, are being washed away, their memories, diluted by the rain, are forming my trail. I feel cleansed, free, in communion with the park. No one will stop me here and pat my arm. No one will solicit me for details on how Sumiti is coping with our loss. Like a ten-year-old, I hop a puddle, my feet together. I turn to the clouds and stretch my arms. I hope it rains and rains. I hope it pours forever.

The swing lies motionless to my left, the slide to my right. I feel as if I'm discovering a lost playground, invading a forgotten world, as I proceed down the path that ends at the slide. I reach for the slide and run my fingers down its slope. The water coasts down the incline in jagged wavelets. For a moment, it seems the slide is dissolving, changing to its liquid phase. I turn my hands on their sides, thumbs pointing at the sky. How easy it is to disrupt the flow. How soon the water piles by the dams I've made with my hands on the slide. The slide frightened her for months, I remember. "She screams and kicks when Arun sits her at the top," Sumiti would announce at parties, provoking everyone to laugh. "Down below, I snap my fingers. I call her name. But she won't let go of his hand."

I step out of my slippers and mount the slide's rungs. The metal feels cold, the past feels near, the ladder has become a conduit to the years gone by. It is more than a decade since I last scaled the slide. Then, Radhika's chin had dug into my shoulder. Her arms were flung around my neck. Her legs were wrapped around my back. In spite of the years since then, the rungs feel familiar, this climb habitual, as if I am back, after a short separation, to complete a task left unfinished in the past. I survey the park, my eyes above the slide. Trivedi Park is a lake of glass, mirroring fractured images of the clouds and trees. The wind bellies down to where I stand, whistling softly through the winking leaves.

"Help me," I hear someone say.

I keep still for a while, my arms stiff, my back erect, my feet stuck to the slide. The park feels smaller, the slide suddenly taller. When I look over my shoulder, I make out a blue raincoat and hat.

"Who is it?" I say. A boy steps forward, his hands clasped behind him, his eyes fixed on me perched on the slide.

"My watch fell in the water," he says, pointing toward the tank. "Can you give me a hand?"

I climb down the slide and step into my slippers. I nod, motioning him toward the tank. The silence stretches between us, straining, deepening the lead he's gathering on me. I consider asking him his name but instead I watch how his feet scoop water in the air, how the splashes announce each step he takes.

"It fell here," he says, running toward the tank to accuse a spot way out of his reach and mine. He is short, gawky, perhaps in his early teens. The ends of his trousers are tucked into his rubber boots. A stream of water spouts off the rim of his hat.

The ground here is strewn with pebbles that increase steadily as one advances toward the tank. The tank itself is circular, its moss-grown wall protruding a foot above the ground. I kick aside the pebbles and get down on my knees. With my hands on my thighs I lean over the wall. The tank is dark, the lotuses are in bloom, the water level has risen to just inches below the top. The rain, though abating, still craters the water, the rings colliding in a kaleidoscopic dance. The ripples are forming a veil, I think. They are united in denying my eyes all access to the depths. I move aside a lotus to broaden my view. I hold still and look hard for some time.

"See it?" the boy asks.

I shake my head and rise to my feet.

"It's no use," I say. "Why don't you return when the rain is gone? Come back when the sun is up. Your watch will become visible then."

He turns to the lotuses, ruffling his brow. He approaches the tank and sits on the wall.

"It will be safe," I say. "No one else knows it is here. Go home now. You shouldn't even be out on such a day."

"And you?" he says, showing me his wide eyes. "Why are you out with neither raincoat nor umbrella today?"

"My daughter used to play here when she was a child," I say. "This lotus tank wasn't even around at the time."

He holds his chin and blinks at the ground. He looks up at me. He turns away, pensive now, and stares at the trees. "I like this park," he says. "It seems very old." He turns to me. "I had left my house for a walk in the rain. But when I returned home, I realized I forgot the keys. So I went for another walk and that's when I found the park."

"You must have friends," I say. "Someone you could visit for a while?"

He shakes his head. He looks away. "I have no friends here," he says. "We moved to this neighborhood only four days ago. I'll have to stay outdoors until my parents return."

"I see," I say, and step up to him. I stand stock-still when he turns to me.

"This is a nice park," he says. "I sat on the swing. I threw pebbles in the tank. Then the watch came off and, before I could catch it, it fell in the tank." He rises to his feet. He steps away from me, his brows knitted, his eyes lowered as though from embarrassment at having spoken too much.

I step closer to him, uprooting pebbles with my feet. "A girl died in this neighborhood six weeks ago," I say.

He stoops to collect a pebble. "I know," he says, as he shakes the pebble loose. "I heard she tumbled out a window and landed on her head. Some even saw it happen. They saw her head crack open. She had a screw loose, they say."

I step back and cover my face. My legs feel heavy, my head feels light. I drop my hands and look around. They're whispering about her. Huddled in their homes, they're all gossiping about my child. Like a ripple, the word of her fall spreads. Sweeping through home after home. Never to die. The oblique glances on the streets, the icy stares on the train, the flickering smiles from my students will have to be borne for the rest of my life.

"You are shaking from head to toe," the boy says, rising.

"She didn't just fall," I say, stepping toward him. "They'll tell you soon she killed herself. But what they'd have done in my place, they will not say. 'If detained again in standard eight, student will be expelled from school.' Wouldn't you have read the note to her? Wouldn't you have threatened to punish her if she failed?" He stares at me, lips parted. The words, risen like a river from deep inside me, ascend to the sky.

"I have to leave," he says.

"No, wait," I say, reaching for his shoulder. "We can talk about something else. I've spoken very little today."

He sets aside my hand and backs away. I throw myself at him and grab his wrists. "Don't touch me!" he shouts. He fights to get away. "Please don't touch!" he yells.

"Wait. Don't be afraid. Look, the sky is clearing. Soon the rain will stop. We can retrieve your watch. Whose son are you? What is your name?"

"Look, mister," he says. "I am sorry your daughter died."

"What would you like to talk about? I teach Physics. Do you like Physics?"

"Let me go," he cries. "I have to leave. Look there. Behind you. People are watching. They're all pointing at us."

I swing him around and exchange places with him. The balconies are bare, their wet walls the only witnesses to this scene.

"All right. What do you want?" he says, his dark eyes welling with tears.

"You know what I was thinking this morning?" He shakes his head. "I was thinking about frames of reference, of how a body in motion would seem to be at rest to an observer sitting on it. I was thinking she is at rest while her mother and I are moving in time. Could her voice in my mind be a call then? A cry that she's being left behind?"

He breaks free. I ball my fists. He staggers back and falls.

"Go away!" he yells. "Don't take another step." He grabs a handful of pebbles and hurls them at me. They miss, plunging into the tank like solid drops of rain. He springs to his feet and runs from me. He scrambles down the path between the swing and the slide. "Help!" he cries as he pulls open the gates. "He's after me. Somebody help!"

"Go!" I yell as loudly as I can, my fists trembling, my chest burning, my heart thumping hard. "Run! *Run!*"

He runs from the park. A few steps later he stumbles and falls. He picks himself up and hunts me with his eyes. When he meets my gaze, I am far away, beaten, fallen to my knees. "You killed her!" he keeps shouting until he slips out of view, shaking his fist in the air. "Murderer."

• • •

The rain has ceased. The wind is down. The bent Asoka trees are still. I enter my building compound and lean against the gates. The lights are on in some of the apartments. People are emerging in balconies and windows here and there. I proceed, not toward the lift but to where Radhika had lain, where a lucid pool of water has collected now. I crouch to my feet. I touch the ground. There is nothing but hard concrete beneath the water. The ground feels warm. Its texture is coarse. Gently, I move my hands around. It is here I had rocked her head that evening in my arms. It is here I had stroked her brow. You didn't tell anyone what you intended to do. You didn't even give us a sign. Didn't you know you had many years ahead of you? Didn't you know your fall would kill us too? Where are you now? Speak to me. *Speak*, you stupid, silly girl of mine.

I lift my face. I rise to my feet. My eyes climb the building, reversing her fall. When they reach the seventh story, my heart begins to race. Radhika's window is flung open and Sumiti leans over the sill, watching me now. I shade my eyes with my hand. I wave to her with the other. When she withdraws inside, I hasten toward the lift.

Up on the seventh floor, she's waiting at the door, my towel held open in her hands. She stands aside as I enter the house. She shuts the door and follows me into the living room. She unbuttons my shirt. I stare at the floor.

"I saw where you went," she says, drying my chest. "From her room I saw you enter the park."

She dries my face. She dries my neck. Then she peels the shirt off my skin and drapes it over her arm. I lower my head for her to dry my hair, the susurration of cloth against skin the only sound in the room. When she stops abruptly, I look up. Then before she can leave the room, I gather her in my arms.

"Arun, no," she cries, but I don't let go. "Arun," she says and I hold her closer to my chest.

I feel her resisting, retreating, her feet edging from mine, her fist pushing out my arms. I lock my hands and draw her toward me until, finally, my cheek lies pressed to her hair.

"It's her birthday today," I say.

When Sumiti's shoulders begin to shake, I break down as well. We wail like two children, calling each other's names, uttering words that make no sense, our cries louder than they were six weeks ago. Without warning, she attempts to flee to our bed again. I don't let go. I keep her close to me, letting her tears roll down my arm, letting her yield little by little to me.

Listen, I want to say when she puts her ear against my chest. Sumi, I think she is saying something she's never said before.

As she listens, my heart swells. I realize, as we stand together as one, that the love I had judged was lost between us is now awaking, rising, set to consume us full force. We listen in silence, our eyes closed, bracing our hearts for its return. Patiently, we wait for it to arm us for the journey still ahead.

# Mango Season

**"YES?" SAID THE YOUNG WOMAN** at the information desk at Khar Telephone Exchange, and from her icy tone Aman Lal could tell that the half hour he had reserved for business that sultry Thursday afternoon would soon be insufficient. His wait in line, for one thing, had already consumed twenty minutes.

"Yes, what do you want?"

The woman blinked at him from behind thick circular glasses in a way that suggested an intolerance, an absolute abomination, for small questions. Her face, round and puffy, registered no smile. Her teeth protruded slightly.

"My line got cut," Aman Lal began. "Yesterday morning my phone was working nicely but then last evening just as I was—"

"See Varma, Solkar or Dasgupta. Room 36. Third floor, fifth room from the lift," the woman said in a monotone and let her eyes sweep past Aman Lal's face to rest somewhere above his left shoulder at the customer waiting behind. "Yes?" she called, blinking again, her plump hand extended to reach for something, her brusque demeanor insisting that Aman Lal take his skeletal body someplace else. Indeed, Aman Lal did find himself edging away, moving sideways as if he were on a smooth conveyor belt. He stopped. The woman's words had begun to flicker and juggle in his head.

"Excuse me. 'Third floor, fifth room,' did you say?" he asked, the words barely audible, his voice hollow and frayed. The woman did not answer. Her head swung mechanically from side to side as she read some document that had found its way into her hands. Her well-oiled hair caught the room's fluorescent lights as her head continued to move. Her brow—broad and sporting an enormous red *bindi*—was creased. Her lips fluttered slightly as she read. A young man, hunched obsequiously before her, sniffed and cleared his throat. Some people behind him were grumbling, pointing at their wristwatches. "OK. This will do," the woman announced and slapped the form atop a stack of sheets on one side of the desk. "Come back in three weeks." The man acquiesced and, hunching his shoulders, drew himself away. "Yes?" the woman called again and someone promptly took his place.

Aman Lal hunted for the lift. Third floor, fifth room, she'd said. He stopped walking and held his jaw. People were hurrying in every direction. Fragments of conversation flocked to where he stood stock-still, marooned. He could still hear the woman at the information desk. She was explaining something at the top of her voice, rattling sheets of onion-paper in the air. Third floor, fifth room, she had said. Or was it third room, fifth floor? Aman Lal wondered if he should stand in line again, pretend he'd just arrived at the exchange. But the line was too long, beginning now to snake all over the floor. Varma, one name was. Room 36, she'd said. Why couldn't they write things down for God's sake? Could they not see from his walk, from the way he talked and the way his left hand shook, that he needed special assistance? Or was he the only seventy-year-old in Bombay today? Perhaps he should ask the woman exactly that. Thump her desk three times with the flat of his hand and demand to know if she knew anyone older than her miserable self. "Wretched woman," Aman Lal said under his breath and stepped forward woodenly. He bumped into someone dashing past him and was forced to stop again.

"Lift," Aman Lal mumbled moments later to people breezing past him. One young man met his gaze, smiled and looked away. A woman, wheeling a cart of white boxes in his direction, was the one who finally stopped. An oval badge pinning her sari to the shoulder of her blouse said "Staff, KTE" in fine yellow print.

"Lift? You want lift? Go straight down that corridor. Then turn right. After you pass a big wall clock, which doesn't work, turn left. You'll see a long line for the lift there. Stairs will be faster today. Take them. Stairs are next to the lift. Understood?"

Aman Lal found the line outside the lift and stood at the end of it. He would have to be more assertive, he decided. He used to be a math and science teacher at St. Michael's Boys' High School, he reminded himself. Not some run-down shack such as the woman at the information desk had no doubt attended. Standards eight, nine, and ten he had taught for thirty-five years. His voice, once authoritative and booming, made the boys sit up, straight and wide-eyed, their wrists firmly on their desks, their pens copying down algebraic equations. "Yes, Masterji," "No, Masterji," was all they dared say. Now, since his retirement some years ago, his voice had lost its bite, its volume, its audience.

He had to get the telephone working right away. Last evening, he called his house from Taj Mahal Restaurant, a seedy establishment down his road, with the hope of jolting the phone back to work. He'd heard a dull ring drowned deep in crackle and hurried home at once. The dial tone, however, had not returned. On Saturday, his seventieth birthday, Deepa would be calling him from Darjeeling. She said she'd call at three. "You will be home, won't you, Papa?" she had asked last weekend and he had said, "Of course, of course. Where else would Papa be?" If there was no answer now she would wonder if he was lost somewhere in the city or if he was too sick to get to the telephone or if he had slipped in the bathroom again and knocked his skull on the sink like that time two summers ago. How she had panicked, that jewel of his. She had telephoned Mrs. Khan in the flat next to his who rang his doorbell and repeatedly called his name. A while later, the building-watchman began to pound his door. The police were summoned and soon a wailing ambulance arrived. They found him sitting naked on the bathroom floor, his head lowered, his bony hands crossed over his crotch, water from the shower above beating down his back, red rivulets coursing down his chest. Mrs. Khan had fetched an ear-splitting scream from the depths of her being and nearly lost her balance. Aman Lal remembered how residents in the building craned their necks out their balconies like vultures to watch him being whisked away on a stretcher. He felt vulnerable and small, a wounded prey. Down the pathway of the compound he was rushed and then out the building's gates. The sky had been a deep blue. A cawing crow had darted by. Aman Lal now felt a coldness trickle down his spine. He would have to be assertive. The phone service must return, he told himself. No two ways about it.

The lift doors yawned open suddenly and a sea of restless people burst out, flooding the room in seconds and disrupting the line that had formed neatly outside. At the same time, a crowd struggled to squeeze into the lift from the sides amid protests and scrimmages, with some people, having just arrived on the scene, taking full advantage of the fracas. When the doors snapped shut and the pandemonium ceased, the line began to reestablish itself. To his confusion, Aman Lal found he was now not closer to the lift but farther from it.

He tore away from the queue with a curse on his lips. He thought of jumping the line and barging somehow into the lift the next round. He'd shout out his age perhaps for an excuse. Suddenly his face felt hot with shame. He used to be a schoolteacher. Respected in most sections of Khar and even in some of the neighboring suburbs of the city. Retired or not, he had to set the example. In any case, didn't it seem as though the stairs would be quicker today? It would spare his white starched *kurta* a journey in a crammed lift. He should have headed for the stairs from the start. He glared hatefully at the lift doors and the people gathering there. In his mind he saw the lift plummeting down the shaft with everyone clawing at each other's clothes and shrieking inside. Aman Lal shook his head, hoping to flick the image away. Such nonsense his mind could conjure at times. He seized the iron banister of the marble stairs and braced himself. He took a deep breath and began a slow and tedious climb.

A line greeted him outside Room 36 on Floor 3 as well. Aman Lal was relieved to see it was moving faster than any he'd seen at the exchange. No sooner had he recovered his breath than it was his turn to enter the room. Room 36 was noisy, bright, and spacious with huge windows flung open along the far wall. People stood leaning against the sills now, smoking cigarettes, watching pigeons that twittered on the green dome of a mosque some distance away. Aman Lal's eyes shifted to the low ceiling of the room. Suspended from it were row after row of dirty tube lights, several blinking, others out of commission. Four ceiling fans whirred over desks arranged end to end in long rows. Officials were ensconced behind these desks; all faced the door. Many were shouting or chuckling into their telephones. Some were sipping tea from saucers, others were discoursing pointedly with customers nodding before them.

Aman Lal noted the desks were littered with thick, dog-eared books. Piles of paper stood here and there, several of which leaned precariously or lay in total disarray. He began to read the nameplates propped on the desks. To his relief, one in the very first row said "D. Varma."

Mr. Varma was a gaunt man wearing a shirt that might once have been bright blue. His arms were pressed stiffly to his sides, his dark eyes were locked on the entrance.

"Aha, come in," he said. "This way, sir. Mind the cables on the floor."

Aman Lal proceeded cautiously toward the man's desk and introduced himself. "Dinesh Varma," the man announced without rising and said he would be glad to be of assistance. Mr. Varma was in his mid-thirties. He wore a tidy pencil-line mustache; thick black hair flopped over his brow. The hair over his ears was scraggly. He extended his hand. Aman Lal shook it firmly.

"That nasty woman at the desk downstairs," Aman Lal said as he settled into his seat. Mr. Varma waved to someone leaving the room. Aman Lal wiped his neck with his kerchief.

"So what can I do for you?" Mr. Varma said, clasping his hands together.

Aman Lal shifted uneasily in his seat. Mr. Varma was looking hard and point-blank at him. He seemed preoccupied with other matters. Aman Lal scraped his chair forward. "My telephone is out of order," he said. "Yesterday morning it worked perfectly fine, first class, but then God knows what happened to it. It went dead. Just like that."

"Aha," Mr. Varma said with a deep nod as though Aman Lal had responded wisely to a query on a test. "Now, where do you reside?"

"57 Naidu Road. Ground floor," Aman Lal said.

"Naidu Road. I see. Is everyone's phone out of order in your building?"

"I don't know. My neighbor Mrs. Khan is away. Nobody else in my building has a phone."

Mr. Varma seemed lost in thought, as though some tortuous mathematical problem had just engaged his mind. His telephone rang three times and stopped. "Naidu Road," he said moments later, talking, apparently, to himself. He drew open a drawer on his left. He lifted a thick blue binder from it with both hands. He dropped it on the desk—there was a resounding thud—and swung it open. "So you live on Naidu Road," he said. He let a hand race down page after page, licking his finger before turning the sheets. "Naidu Road. N-A-I . . . Naidu . . . let's see . . . Naidu Road . . ."

About a minute and a half passed. Mr. Varma then scratched his forehead, rose from his swivel seat and headed toward a monstrous file cabinet in the rear of the room. He pulled open several drawers one by one, let his fingers walk over the tops of many files. Finally he drew a folder out, cracked it open, and rubbed his jaw. A man approached him. They exchanged a few words. Mr. Varma then replaced the folder and, after stopping briefly at someone's desk, returned to occupy his seat.

"So have you lodged a complaint, Mr. Lal?" he said.

"That is why I am here, Mr. Varma," Aman Lal said and smiled. "I called the exchange oh! many, many times from a restaurant earlier today but the telephone here was constantly engaged." He cupped his hand to the side of his mouth and whispered, "Maybe the exchange's phone, too, is out of order? Ha ha ha."

Mr. Varma was not amused. He sifted through a pile of sheets on the desk and eased out a page. He signed his name on it. "You must fill out this form. It will be processed and someone will be sent to your home in two to three weeks."

Aman Lal's smile disappeared. His gray brows gathered. "Two to three weeks?" he said. "No, no, no. I must have it working immediately. All it needs is your man to climb the telephone pole. It's only some loose wire somewhere. There's a child's kite tangled up there; that must be it. I live all by myself, Mr. Varma. Mrs. Khan, my neighbor, is in Khandala. I need that telephone. Someone my age must have one."

Mr. Varma nodded gravely and tapped the form with his finger. "Please fill this out," he said, "and bring it back here."

Aman Lal's fingers clamped the edge of the desk. He thought of Deepa pacing up and down her living room, cradling the telephone now and again to call Bombay. He imagined her dialing the long-distance operator every few minutes, her long nails drumming her chin. "No answer, Operator?" he could hear her delicate voice saying. "Really? Are you sure?"

Aman Lal swept his hand over his brow as if to erase the worries clouding his mind. "Mr. Varma," he said softly. "You see, I have only one daughter. She lives all the way in Darjeeling. She and her husband will be calling me this—"

"Mr. Lal, everybody who enters this room has some daughter or son living a thousand kilometers away and everyone lives alone in Khar and everyone expects to receive important calls from London and Paris in a day or two. Fill the form out in ink and bring it back to me. Black ink preferably."

Aman Lal turned red in the face. His left hand trembled faster. He shifted his attention to the form lying before him. There were instructions crammed in three languages. There was hardly any space for writing. He flipped the form over. The back page was mercifully blank. Mr. Varma was adamant, he thought. The form, whatever it was, would have to be completed and returned. Only God knew when he'd see a repairman actually scale the telephone pole on Naidu Road. This Saturday the phone would not ring. No one would sing Happy Birthday to him. Perhaps Mr. Varma ought to be told about the birthday. "Mr. Lal, everyone who comes to Room 36 has a birthday in one or two days," he would quip.

Aman Lal tried to arrange the thoughts heaping fast in his mind. He gathered himself and prepared to leave. "I have two children myself," Mr. Varma was saying, his voice subdued unexpectedly to a whisper. Aman Lal nodded without thinking. Mr. Varma glanced left and right and leaned forward. More words were leaving his mouth. Names were being mentioned. Manohar and somebody else. They were ten and seven years old. They both attended a fine English language school.

"St. Michael's," Mr. Varma said, and Aman Lal turned swiftly to face him again. "Do you know that school, Mr. Lal?"

"Why, yes. As a matter of fact, I—"

"Excellent! St. Michael's is now a very good school. My sons like it there. I'll share with you something else, if I may. Come closer. My younger boy Kiran likes mangoes. Manohar does too. It's their favorite fruit, Mr. Lal. Of course, they haven't touched a mango in years. But what can one do in these days of high inflation? Nothing, I tell my wife. Absolutely nothing."

Aman Lal rose at once from his seat and rolled the form in his hand. Mr. Varma presented him with his business card. Aman Lal turned it over for no reason a few times. "Fill out the form, Mr. Lal, return it to me, and I will have someone over at Naidu Road in two or at most three weeks. It is difficult for me to send someone sooner. One wishes it were simple. Naturally, things can always be speeded up but that takes some work, some give and take." He snapped shut the binder and sat back in his chair. "This *is* the mango season, isn't it?"

Aman Lal nodded absently. He found he was grinding his jaws. The card in his hand had razor-sharp edges. The corners pricked like needles. At first, nothing on it seemed legible but then he recognized Mr. Varma's name embossed in the center. "Assistant Senior Clerk, KTE" it said directly below. The lettering was crude, in ugly parrot green. At the lower left were office and home addresses. On the lower right was the office phone number. Aman Lal nodded solemnly in Mr. Varma's direction, curled his fingers to strangle the card and, without another word, proceeded to leave the room.

• • •

He was blinded momentarily when he stepped outside the exchange. The buildings facing him were drenched in sunlight; their yellow walls shone like gold. The coconut tree leaves, Aman Lal thought, were greener than before. The fluffy clouds were whiter than ever. Honking motorcars moved in spurts on the dusty street outside. A taxi driver, leaning out his window, shouted at someone to prod at a cow blocking the road. A hawker maneuvered his way between the cars, small garlands of white *mogras* dangling over his fingers. Aman Lal trudged down three steps that brought him to the building's concrete compound. Huddled in groups were men engaged in fiery debates. One man was shaking his fist at the exchange; another was shouting obscenities. Aman Lal excused himself and threaded through the crowds. When he emerged seconds later, a chorus of beeping horns assailed his ears. Autorickshaw-taxis parked by the curb were soliciting people emerging from the exchange. Aman Lal ignored them. He was going to walk the mile and a quarter home, a decision he had made once he was outside Room 36 and waiting for the lift to transport him down to the ground floor. He needed the walk. He needed to sort his thoughts. He straightened his *kurta*. He noted with dismay that a faint red stain (betel-juice?) had appeared on his left sleeve. He scraped at it furiously with his nails. It didn't go away. He glared at the exchange, at the windows on the third floor in particular, and shook his head.

How things had changed in Bombay. There was a time when one could get almost anything one desired if one asked for it politely. But now, the Varmas of the world had descended on the city, besieged it, pressed the Aman Lals into tight corners. Of late, he needed to make elbowroom nearly everywhere he went, had to pay extra for almost everything he sought. Some months ago, for instance, he wanted cauliflower from Khar Fruit & Vegetable Market and it had taken him about ten minutes to worm through the flock of buyers and get to Daulat Ram's cart. Once there, he discovered that cauliflower, tomatoes, and onions had been sold out, that cucumbers and brinjals had brand-new rates. Young people in Bombay were more hard-bitten, more aggressive than any generation he'd known. Things had never curdled like this, where the market had become like a corrupt stock exchange, where cabbages and bananas went to the highest bidder. "Salim! Three rupees for you whenever you buy my groceries," he had offered the building-watchman's young son that night. "Our big secret," he'd added with a stagy wink. To his relief (and disappointment at not having quoted less), Salim had agreed wordlessly and gone his way.

More schools like St. Michael's were needed to combat the Varmas of the world. Aman Lal had filled his journals on this issue, had even mailed long letters to newspapers in the city. None made it into print. Venal minds ran the newspapers, he supposed, as they did the shops and markets, pharmacies and temples, and, of course, the telephone exchange. It occurred to Aman Lal now, as he walked on the treeless crowded pavement, that they had won, he was facing defeat, it was necessary for him to succumb. "You're too righteous for Bombay," Deepa had told him once and maybe she was right. It was no use pining for bygone days, no point dwelling on the past. Times were different now, the city was a wilderness. Was anything straightforward anymore? Didn't everything have an unmarked price? Perhaps he would do what Mr. Varma suggested. Do it just this once. One's seventieth birthday is an important one. Who could tell if there'd be another? He wanted to hear Deepa's voice on Saturday, he loved the way she sang. When the service was restored, he'd forget the Varma incident, he'd erase the man's face, the man's voice, from his mind. Aman Lal placed his hand on his chest. His heart was thumping faster. He moved his hand to his belly. He felt knotted and entangled inside.

Deepa's offer to let him move in with her and her husband suddenly came to his mind. Her face now bloomed before his eyes. "But you love Darjeeling," she was saying. "The best hill-station in India, you've said hundreds of times." Aman Lal always cited the Naidu Road flat as his excuse. "Holds all memories," he would say. Her mother, he'd remind Deepa, joined him when he was twenty-one and she only eighteen. They had remained at each other's side for forty-three years. "I see her in the balcony at times. In the old wicker chair, Deepa." Together, they had chosen each item for their flat, argued and embraced in every room. They'd raised a lovely daughter there. Aman Lal felt a surge of longing for his wife. He looked for a place to sit but found none. If only she were here today, if only she were beside him now. When she died in his arms, he stroked her forehead tenderly, wondering what it was he held in his lap when from the kitchen there still came her joyful singing, when her soft footfall still reached his ears. "I hear her calling my name some mornings. Deepa, I've felt her take my hand." How could one sell what is now a monument? How could strangers take her place? That would be inviting death itself, he told Deepa each time. In any case, should a man not die where he was born? "Life should be a round-trip, child. Come full circle around." "Enough, Papa," Deepa cried in his mind, her face fading away. "Don't come. Stay there. Rot away in your rotten Bombay." Aman Lal shook his head as he crossed the street at the traffic lights. Years from now she would know what he meant. One day she would understand. He scratched at the stain on his sleeve again. Moving to Darjeeling was out of the question for him.

"Excuse me, what o'clock is it?"

Aman Lal looked down into big black eyes. A boy in a St. Michael's uniform stood at attention before him. "I think you mean, 'What time is it?'," Aman Lal said. He showed the boy his wristwatch. "I see, I see," the boy said, wagging his head. "Come here," Aman Lal said. "What time is it?" "Seven minutes to quarter to four," the boy answered and skipped away, his schoolbag bobbing on his back, his water bottle swinging from his arm. Aman Lal was seized with the urge to run after the boy, yank him by the elbow, shake him by the shoulders, and demand to know what he was doing outside school before five. "Go to Principal DeMello's office at once!" he'd roar, his finger pointing up the road. Seven minutes to quarter to four indeed. What kind of time was that?

An autorickshaw beeped three times on the street. Aman Lal grunted and motioned for it to halt. He scurried toward it with a frown. "Naidu Road," he barked, startling the driver, and climbed quickly inside.

• • •

That evening, while the sun was still up in the sky but concealed behind looming gray clouds, Aman Lal emerged from an old taxi on D.V. Street, a small straw basket cradled in his arms. The basket was stuffed with hay; four sweet-smelling mangoes lay buried inside. "Enjoy these, Varma!" Aman Lal said while paying the driver. "Eat them and die!" As the taxi rumbled away, Aman Lal scrutinized the business card in his hand. He grimaced as he crushed it hard and flung it on the ground. "Scoundrels," he said and ground the card into the gravel with his shoe. He looked to his left, then to his right. He'd been on D.V. Street many times before. What for but to bribe some crook or the other, he supposed. With a scowl, he approached a shabby four-story building in need of a coat of paint. Colorful saris, bedsheets, and white full-sleeved shirts were billowing outside balconies. Some people were peering down at him, their elbows poking out, their conversations dying as he neared. Screaming children ran barefoot through the compound in hot pursuit of a tennis ball. A tube light flickered on on the second floor. The silhouette of a woman flitted by.

"You!" Aman Lal snapped at a girl squatting on the ground, her dress pulled snugly over her knees, her arms wrapped firmly around her shins. "Where does Dinesh Varma live?" She stared at him in curiosity and fright. She breathed hard, exhausted apparently from an evening of playing. She pointed to a flat on the second floor and, as Aman Lal stepped forward, she sprang to her feet and scampered away.

Aman Lal proceeded toward the flat. More people craned their necks to take a closer look at him. One man in an undershirt spotted with holes yawned, scratched his armpit, and retreated indoors. A television blared in an apartment. Not far away a baby cried. The hiss of frying came from somewhere else.

Aman Lal began to ascend the stairs to the second floor. A dim bulb, swaddled in cobwebs, illuminated the steps. The walls, blue or some peculiar shade of green, had all kinds of scribblings. He was reminded suddenly of a similar building he had visited many years ago. It had been in better condition than this one. The staircase was narrower, he recalled. Bits of trash lay heaped on the sides then as now. Perhaps a friend of his wife had lived there. It was someone like that. He and his wife had visited soon after their marriage. A birthday celebration perhaps. Aman Lal paused on the ground floor landing and rearranged the mango basket against his chest. Lately, so much from the past ambushed his thinking. People he was sure he'd never met greeted him cordially on streets. They knew his name. They knew where he lived. They referred to conversations they'd had. Aman Lal resumed climbing, resting occasionally on each step. It was nice of that brat Salim to purchase the mangoes at such short notice. He'd protested, of course, saying it was Thursday, the day he washed motorcars in the neighborhood, but Aman Lal had held on to the boy's shirt and refused to let go.

"My telephone is dead, Salim. Dead! Don't you understand? I have to bring it back to life. Now go to the market. Fetch me four of the cheapest mangoes there."

Salim had returned, however, with four expensive ones and Aman Lal had held his brow and sighed. He wondered now if Salim, too, was swindling him, was in collusion with the Varmas of the world. When all of Bombay had ganged up against him, why wouldn't Salim? Perhaps he should reconsider Deepa's invitation after all. Maybe it was best he set out for Darjeeling. He was tired of bearing the weight of so many memories, fed up with living by himself. When had anyone visited him last? How long was it since he'd held or embraced someone? Yes, it was time to ask Salim to bring the suitcases down from the loft. Get them dusted and cleaned for the long trip north. He would visit tea estates up in Darjeeling, sit in Deepa's cool garden every morning, take a hearty view of the terraced hills around. He'd stroll along the Mall each evening, a kashmiri shawl flung over his shoulders for warmth. He'd spend hours with the orchids in Lloyd's Botanic Gardens, go to Tiger Hill one more time for the sunrise view. Perhaps when the phone service returned, he would tell Deepa she was right, that he was being obdurate, that his Bombay had indeed gone to the dogs. He'd say he would start shipping boxes to her one by one, that in three months—promise!—he would lock up the house. He would have all his memories in his head, he'd tell her. What else did he want anyway? He didn't need the house anymore. "Sentimental rubbish," he would say and they'd have a good long laugh.

He reached the second floor and approached a brown door. The nameplate said "D. Varma." He pressed the buzzer and waited. The sharp smell of spices hung in the air. He could hear movements in the house: the rustle of a sari, the jingling of bangles, the pulling back of a chair. A refrigerator door closed. Someone spoke. In his mind Aman Lal saw the door opening inch by inch. He pictured a boy looking up at him with sad drooping eyes. The basket nearly fell from his hands when the door did indeed open to reveal not one but two thin boys. Their faces, too, were narrow, their hair long and unkempt. One of them chewed something noisily. Both wore T-shirts stained with food and much too large for them. Their shorts had run out of color. Their quizzical expressions dissolved when they spotted the basket in his arms and before Aman Lal could say a word, the boys lit up their eyes, flung open the door, and threw up their hands.

"Mangoes! Mangoes!" they sang, color rising to their cheeks, their arms now flung around each other's shoulders. "Ma, they're here. Papa, the mangoes have come." They stopped jumping suddenly and tore away from each other. They slapped their hands over their mouths; their narrow shoulders shook with laughter. They stood this way for a while, too embarrassed to speak.

Aman Lal stood transfixed, open-mouthed, his tongue shrunk and dry. In all his life, he had seen nothing like this. Not once had Deepa jumped before a fruit this way. Never had anyone squealed with such delight to see him arrive. As Aman Lal watched the boys tittering behind their hands, he felt his heart tighten. His arms went stiff. He held his breath. This was an image he would never forget. This was yet another memory he'd cart with him to Darjeeling. "Cheapest mangoes," he recalled telling Salim and his face felt hot and pinched with shame.

"Is your father home?" he said, the words adhering to his tongue, refusing to leave his lips. He coughed and repeated himself.

Mr. Varma emerged from the shadows and brushed his sons aside. "Manohar. Kiran," he said. "Go down and play." As they stepped into rubber slippers, the boys glanced gleefully at Aman Lal and his gift. In moments, they bounded out happily, their hands slung around each other's waists, a series of giggles trailing them down the stairs.

"Thank you, Mr. Lal," Mr. Varma said. "Please come in." The ends of his sleeves were fastened with cuff links. Talcum powder was visible on his hands. The sound of bangles soon filled the room and a young woman in a green sari appeared. "My wife, Mr. Lal."

The woman joined her hands in greeting. Aman Lal did the same. The basket lay crushed against his chest, causing a mango to stir. The woman was small and delicate. Her feet peeped from below her sari. Silver rings adorned her toes.

"Will you take tea?" Aman Lal heard her ask. Her voice was as shy and gentle as he'd imagined. Out of respect for his age her eyes were cast on the floor.

"No, thank you," Aman Lal said, handing her the straw basket. Words were resisting his lips. He could barely recognize his voice. He felt ill suddenly and wished he were back on Naidu Road, curled on the wicker chair. Salim could have attended to this task. He needn't have come himself. "Cheapest mangoes," hammered unceasingly in his mind. He wished he could cover his face. "I must go," he said, straightening himself. "It is quite late."

It was then, as he reached clumsily for the door, he saw the dining table tucked in a corner. He gave no thought to it at first but then found himself drawn to it. It was a circular wooden table, a jar with plastic flowers marking the center. A scar joined two points on the circumference along a straight line. Aman Lal advanced toward the table. He moved his palm in circles over the top. He ran his thumbnail along the scar. He gripped the table with both hands. It had once belonged to him, he thought. He remembered sitting before the scar. "This straight line joining these two points on the table's circumference is called a 'chord.'" He'd said those words many a time. He flicked his eyes at the small ceiling, at the framed photographs adorning the walls, at the refrigerator in the corner, the floor fan next to it, at the windows barred by a simple grill, and then at Mr. Varma who was watching him with folded hands. Aman Lal moved away from the table. He had come to this house before, he thought, and stopped in the center of it. Several years ago. Many times, in fact. When, in his younger days, he went house to house to tutor algebra and geometry.

"I failed class nine," Mr. Varma said, breaking the silence now. He signaled his wife to leave the room and stepped forward. "When you came to the telephone exchange today, you reopened my wounds. My having repeated the class actually cost me a lot. It delayed everything by a year. My job. My marriage. Everything. I lost a whole year's salary because I failed class nine."

"Of course," Aman Lal said. "I mean, I see." Coldness rolled up his back, spread over his shoulders and raced down his arms. "I see. What—what time might it be now?"

"I failed class nine, Mr. Lal. We didn't have enough to eat but my father hired you nonetheless." Mr. Varma approached the table, studying his fingernails. "I hoped to be a doctor one day as my father wished. But then I failed because of school politics and my confidence vanished. My self-esteem suffered. I hold you and my ninth standard teacher responsible. The arrogance with which you spoke to my parents is still fresh in my mind. I still can't sleep sometimes because of this memory. Because of you. But maybe now I will."

Aman Lal felt dizzy. The room rocked back and forth and came to a halt. There was a throbbing in his ears, a pricking between his eyes. He feared he would run a fever. He staggered toward the door, coughing and mumbling that he should go. He made it. He scuttled out of the flat, clutching his left hand in his right. His heart knocked against his chest, a biliousness rose inside. He could hear Mrs. Varma asking what happened. Mr. Varma was telling her it was nothing. Aman Lal thumped his chest as if to stop the ache inside. He fanned open his fingers against the wall to steady himself and, like an invalid attempting to walk after months in bed, began to descend the stairs.

"Your service will be back tomorrow," he heard Mr. Varma call out. He didn't want to listen. Right now, he didn't care. He heard their door click shut. He heard Mr. Varma's voice again. On the ground floor landing, Aman Lal paused to catch his breath. The nape of his neck felt cold. His left hand was quivering. He clamped it hard under his right arm and clenched his fists. The incident, long repressed, was unfurling in his mind. He remembered the morning the couple had approached him, the father dragging the boy by the ear. Final grades had been released a day earlier. The mother and the boy were weeping. The boy had weals on his arms, a redness persisted on a cheek. The boy had failed geometry by two points. He'd had to be detained in class nine. "But you tutored him thrice a week all year long," the man yelled, his steely stare challenging Aman Lal's own. "You told me he was doing well. So how did this boy fail?" For years afterward, Aman Lal tried to forget how he harangued the man on behaving with propriety, how he priggishly went on and on about values, how he impressed upon them the standards of St. Michael's. He tried to forget, too, how he didn't say that just weeks earlier he and the ninth standard teacher in question had had a feud. "Take him elsewhere if you like," he had offered Mr. Varma's father instead, his chin held high, his eyes barely open, his balled hands shaking furiously behind him. "Hire some other tutor if you want. My requesting his class teacher for a retest is out of the question. St. Michael's believes in nothing of the sort. Kindly leave my office now. The boy has failed and that's that." The father glared at the mother. She shook her head and drew away. The man then lunged for the boy and struck him on the mouth. The woman screamed. She reached for the boy. The boy let out a cry and covered his face. "You gave birth to an idiot like yourself," the man said. Mother and son held each other closer. "He should have died when he was born."

He had forgotten the incident and now it returned to torture him, to haunt him for the remainder of his days. Four mangoes were what he had brought now but Aman Lal knew he would return with more mangoes or some such fruit to compensate for the one lost year for the rest of his life. He could not go to Deepa's now.

Now he understood this was why he could never leave Bombay. The guilt which he had painstakingly entombed had sprung alive like a demon to stab his heart. His conscience had not let him leave all along. It wasn't the memories of happier days but compunction that had ensured that he stayed.

Aman Lal emerged from the staircase of the building and stepped into the compound. His chest felt heavy, his feet like blocks of wood.

"Thank you," a young voice sang somewhere. He ignored it and walked on. "I said, 'Thank you'!" the voice said again. He stopped. He steered himself around. The younger of Mr. Varma's sons was advancing toward him, his wide smile revealing crooked teeth.

For a moment, Aman Lal didn't know what to say, what exactly the boy had meant. The boy stopped close to him. Several seconds passed. "Manohar?" Aman Lal managed to say. He hadn't meant to ask. He really didn't care.

The boy shook his head. "No," he said and giggled. "Kiran is my name." The other children were running helter-skelter behind him, screaming and calling one another's names. Some yelled for the boy to rejoin the game. He motioned for them to carry on and shouted something back.

Aman Lal was tempted to take the boy's slender hands in his own. He considered the boy's weight. Suddenly he found himself stooping to grab the boy under the arms. With a strength that surprised him now, he scooped him off the ground and held him high in the air. He sensed the children in the compound were slowing down their game. He knew the boy he held was eyeing the window of his house. Beyond him, the sky had turned a purplish-pink, the rolling clouds were grayer, a heavy downpour seemed imminent.

"Kiran," Aman Lal said. "That is a beautiful name. Do you know what it means?" The boy shook his head. Aman Lal found himself surrendering to the boy's bright eyes. "Kiran means a ray of light," he heard himself say. He sensed the hair on his arms was standing on end, that his left hand was steadier than ever. A gradual warmth filled his chest. He felt his throat constrict. A quiet communication was growing between him and the boy. An envelope of serenity was encasing them now.

"So you like mangoes, my good friend?" Aman Lal said.

"Yes," the boy said.

Aman Lal laughed. "Then I will bring you more mangoes next time," he said.

He heard Mr. Varma shout the boy's name from somewhere in the building. His wife then called the boy. The boy waved to them. He gestured that he was fine. Suddenly Kiran threw back his head and broke into a peal of laughter. "You're tickling me!" he cried and clamped his mouth with his hands. He managed to steady himself. Moments later, however, he was wriggling, seized with laughter again.

Aman Lal recorded every sound and image in his mind. His eyes were pooling with tears. He sensed a painful stirring in his heart. He tried to laugh along with the boy but instead began to cry. Here was a picture, a moment of joy, a new image of the city that would prevent his leaving. This was an emotion he had never experienced, one he'd cherish for the rest of his life. How, he wondered, would he express it in his journal at night? How would he describe it to Deepa on Saturday? Aman Lal closed his eyes and wrapped his arms around Kiran. How, he wondered, would he explain to her that meeting this child was fated, that now he'd never be free to leave for the hills?

# House of Cards

KHALIDA NOW KNOWS where her husband goes in the evenings. She knows why he won't make love to her anymore, why he is always tired at night. She knows why he's angry most of the time, not only with her but with everything in their small, two-bedroom house in Santa Ana, California. She thinks she even knows why he married her—a plain, unquestioning woman in her thirties—in a hasty arrangement last year, so late in his life, having flown all the way from America to Karachi, Pakistan. Yes, she knows where he disappears, what he does, and with whom. Today she knows why in the cinema, mall, and grocery store he glances at young men from the corners of his eyes.

It all came together for her this morning. Perhaps it was the guilty look on his face at breakfast that finally made sense to her, gave him away. She finds it no longer strange that he, a senior architect in Santa Ana, never looks into her eyes when she speaks to him but trains his gaze on the floor or on the wall behind her instead. His hunted animal look, so incongruous on a man aged forty-four, now makes more sense to her. And then there was last night's TV program that by chance she'd caught while waiting for him to come home. Boldly it discussed the issue, helping her make the connection. When she switched the set off, she understood why he'd wanted nothing from her family when he married her, why he'd refused all their gifts. Now she knows why he was impatient to flee Pakistan soon after the wedding and return to his double life in America. It's the unspeakable thing, Khalida thinks, the most immoral of deeds, one of the great sins in Islam. She shudders. She had better not think about his deeds, or his misdeeds, anymore. She has thrown up once today already.

She has been pacing the house all day. She knows almost no one in Santa Ana. Of course, there is Juanita Martinez two houses away. Rotund, gossipy Juanita, who likes to talk of the neighbors, their extended families, and her own large clan. After a few minutes, Khalida is bored with her. Other than gender, what have they in common? She had sought Juanita's friendship from loneliness, nothing more. Most of the time, she simply nods at whatever Juanita says. In any case, she finds it hard to understand her, Juanita's English being so heavily peppered with Spanish and some odd lingo Khalida has yet to identify. But even if Juanita were easy to talk to, could she tell her what she thinks Asif is up to? Could she bring herself to say such a thing to somebody she hardly knows? How do you say, "My husband goes to places where men . . . where they . . ." Khalida covers her face with her hands and shakes her head. Filthy, she thinks. Shameless. "Coward. Liar," she says aloud.

Now she understands why Asif was preoccupied on their wedding day. He had spoken no more than a dozen words to her that night, shown no interest in touching her. "In less than two days we'll be in California and free from this dungeon," he'd said, switching off the lights. "You'll like America. You can do whatever you want there." She hadn't expected him to turn on his side, show his back to her, and fall asleep so soon. Everything the older women in the family had prepared her for had not happened. She didn't sleep that night, her ears picking up laughter still coming from the other rooms in Asif's family home, her mind ablaze with the festivities that had brightened the week. Each time she closed her eyes, she saw the faces of guests who'd wished her well, their smiles doing little to conceal their envy of her moving to America, the land of rich possibilities and realizable dreams.

Khalida mulls over her options: she could stay on in the land of abundance and opportunity and live out this marriage, or she could leave and go someplace far away. She considers going back to Pakistan. She could pack her things one morning and ask Juanita to drive her to LAX. She doesn't even like Santa Ana. She had no idea this is what America would be like. No one talks to her. People look at her on the streets and won't even smile. She knows they mumble to one another in Spanish when they see her in her *salwaar-kameez*, but she has no idea what they are saying. "Look at her, that brown-skinned, almond-eyed foreigner who has come to our Santa Ana," they might be saying. "What is that loose outfit she wears? And what's with that long scarf over her head? Isn't she the one whose husband frequents those bars with men less than half his age?"

Khalida enters the kitchen. She is reminded of the spacious kitchen in her family home in Karachi, teeming with cooks and noisy servants. Her Santa Ana kitchen on the other hand is so small she feels suffocated. She looks at the potatoes, onions, and tomatoes lined neatly on the countertop. She ought to prepare dinner but she is in no mood for cooking, certainly not for eating. In any case, Asif will say he is going out with his friends for dinner. Then he'll disappear until midnight or so. Why bother with cooking? She suspects he returns home to her only because she has lent him respect by playing the role of his wife. And because he needs to get his rest so he can design buildings and houses the next day, if that is indeed what he does. She knows nothing about him now, she decides. She could just as well be sharing her bed with a stranger at night.

Khalida leaves the kitchen and heads for the living room. She straightens a picture frame on the wall. She considers moving the couch to a new place; perhaps she'll move all the furniture around. She catches sight of her slippers and decides she needs to get away from the house. She rushes into the bedroom to fetch her purse and house keys. Today she'll show Asif what she, too, can do. She'll leave the house and come back whenever she decides to. If he can disappear, well, so can she. This is not Pakistan, he should know. This is America, she'll tell him if he says anything to her. Women have freedom and rights here.

She decides to ask Juanita if she'd like to come along. If Khalida could drive, she'd go somewhere by herself. Where should she and Juanita go, she wonders as she walks up to the Martinez house, where toy parts are strewn all over an unkempt lawn. On green plastic chairs lie shirts and trousers drying in the setting sun. From the house comes the sound of Juanita's two-year-old son Miguel crying. Juanita's scolding punctuates his screams. Khalida presses the doorbell. Both Miguel and Juanita fall silent.

"¡Hola, Corlita!" says a beaming Juanita as soon as she opens the door. Juanita, in red rubber sandals and a parrot-green dress speckled with sunflowers, is sweating. Strands of her dark hair are plastered to her cheeks. "Come in, por favor."

"Ah, no," Khalida says. "I just want to go somewhere. Away from here. Will you come with me?"

"¿Qué?" Juanita says, puzzled. "You are feeling good, ¿sí?" She leans toward Khalida for a closer look. She asks what the matter might be.

"Everything is fine," Khalida says. "I want to go somewhere. That's all. We could take the bus to Laguna Beach. I thought I'd see if you want to come. Miguel would like it there."

Juanita shakes her head. Miguel cries again. Juanita turns to him in the house and says something harsh. She has many chores to do, she tells Khalida with a sigh. Her sister Maria is coming over for dinner. Also Maria's husband José and their three spoiled kids. There is a lot of food to prepare. "¡Deberías de ver cuánto comen sus hijos!" Juanita says, rolling her eyes. Khalida nods, pretending to understand, and turns to leave. "Why not you coming in, Corlita?" Juanita asks. "Or join for dinner. Una extra person no problem."

She should tell her, Khalida thinks. Here is a woman, a mother, who may empathize with her. Khalida's heart beats faster. Yes, she could tell her, but would that be wise? Perhaps it would be best to hold her tongue for now, be a coward like Asif. Then again she could pretend she is soliciting Juanita's advice on a matter involving a close friend in Pakistan. She has got to wrench this out of herself, get it all out somehow. It's bad to keep secrets locked inside you, Khalida's mother would often say. They can fester and rot and eat at your insides. Wasn't that what happened to Umar Chacha, their unmarried neighbor in Karachi? Wasn't that what drove him to kill himself one day?

"My husband," Khalida says. "He—"

"¡Dios mío! He beating you. I knew it!"

Khalida shakes her head. Nothing like that, she wants to say; it's far, far worse. But the words don't come to her lips. She can't tell her. You don't share such confidences with your neighbors. "No, I was saying that he will be coming late from work today, so I thought I would go somewhere and enjoy the evening. That's all."

Juanita moves to close the door. She says, "Now you tell me if anything going wrong, okay? Por favor, you just come over and tell Juanita."

Khalida manages a smile. She says she will tell her if something is the matter. Of course, she will, she adds. Who else can she tell? Juanita is the only person who talks to her in Santa Ana, in all of America for that matter. Khalida walks back to her house. She enters the living room, throws the keys and purse on the carpet, and collapses on the couch. A weight seems to press down on her. Part of her wants to get out of the house; part of her wants never to leave the couch. Her world is collapsing like a house of cards, turning to dusty debris all around her, and there is no one she can talk to.

She stretches out on the couch and stares at the ceiling. She plays with her earring. He'll slap her if she tells him she knows about him. He may storm out of the house if she says she knows why shiftiness marks his face. He may yell at her if she says she knows why he has had problems in bed for so long. Yes, he may do all that, but at least this dark secret will be out of her and lodged in the space that's growing between her and this man. There would be three entities in the house then. He, she, and the admission of this thing he does on the side.

She thinks he may tell her to get out of the house and go back to Karachi. But then he may fear she'll tell everyone there and bring shame on his family. No, he'll let her stay. The coward that he is. He'll tell her she is absolutely mistaken. The liar that he is. Who has been filling your ears with all this trash, he'll demand to know. I am innocent, he'll protest. How dare you speak such things about me! It occurs to Khalida he might cry. She doesn't know what she'd do if he does. She has felt nothing for him in the past few months. If anything, she feels disgusted by him now, by the image of him coupling wordlessly in dark places with unknown young men. He'd probably expect her to rush to him, gather him in her arms, and plead with him not to cry. Let's start again, he'd want her to say. Perhaps he'd expect her to cry, too, the unmanly man that he is, the deceitful husband he has become.

She rises from the couch and considers packing a suitcase. If not Pakistan, she could go somewhere else in America, this vast and joyless country, to some city unlike Santa Ana, to a place where people greet you, embrace you, ask about you, are concerned about your well-being. Where you are not treated like an unwanted outsider. Yes, she should leave. There is no place for her in this house or in this city. As for Asif's heart, there never was a place for her there. He had succumbed to pressure from Karachi to marry and had used her in the process. This hurts and disturbs her more than anything else. She had done him no harm. Why did he cheat her? Why trap her into a marriage he knew was a sham from the start?

This is the plan then: She'll pack a suitcase now and go to Juanita's tomorrow morning, soon after Asif leaves for work or wherever it is he goes. She'll spend some time with Juanita, hold her hands, and tell her she is grateful she made a friend in Santa Ana. Then she'll return home and call for a taxi to LAX. There she'll wait for a flight to Pakistan. She has the credit card Asif gave her, she still has some money from the weekly allowance he gives her. She'll be OK. She'll purchase a one-way ticket home. She'll tell them all in Karachi she missed them so intensely she had to fly back for a visit. She knows she will never return to Santa Ana. Asif will telephone, insist she come back. He may even come to Karachi to fetch her to keep up the pretense. She hopes he will. She imagines meeting him in his family home where she hopes he'll make a big scene. *That's* where she'll confront him, she thinks. In front of all his family members, all the servants, she will speak the truth about him. This is how she'll get back at him for the injustice he's done her. It will be the price he'll pay for having strayed in the vilest of ways.

She enters the bedroom. She drops to her knees and pulls out a suitcase from under the bed. It's the blue one she brought with her from Pakistan. She unzips it; it yawns open before her. She looks around the room. She gazes at a recent photograph of herself taken one evening in Karachi. In it, she stands before the curved arch of the Mazar-e-Quaid, the mausoleum's white marble, appearing sunset-red, providing a serene backdrop. She'd had the picture framed in her first week in America. She remembers the morning she hung it on the wall. "It's nice," was all Asif said when she showed it to him that night.

Khalida looks away. She feels too tired to even think anymore. She sighs. She pulls the empty suitcase closer to her. What to take? What to leave behind? She kneels by the suitcase for a long time, wondering how to start.

Photo by Michael Capriotti

**IQBAL PITTALWALA** was born in Bombay, India, and came to the United States in 1985 to pursue a Ph.D. in atmospheric science at the State University of New York at Stony Brook. While writing his dissertation, he experienced writer's block and signed up for a writers' workshop, not knowing it was strictly a fiction-writing class. This serendipitous turn of events helped him discover his passion for writing stories. After completing his dissertation, he attended the University of Iowa and received his M.F.A. in creative writing from the Iowa Writers' Workshop in 1995. His stories have appeared in many venues including *Seattle Review*, *Blue Mesa Review*, and *Confrontation*. He lives in Southern California, where he is a science writer at the University of California, Riverside.